PRAISE FOR THE NOVELS OF KATIE MacALISTER

Memoirs of a Dragon Hunter

"Bursting with the author's trademark zany humor and spicy romance . . . this quick tale will delight paranormal romance fans."—*Publishers Weekly*

Sparks Fly

"Balanced by a well-organized plot and MacAlister's trademark humor."—*Publishers Weekly*

It's All Greek to Me

"A fun and sexy read."—The Season for Romance

"A wonderful lighthearted romantic romp as a kick-butt American Amazon and a hunky Greek find love. Filled with humor, fans will laugh with the zaniness of Harry meets Yacky."—*Midwest Book Review*

Much Ado About Vampires

"A humorous take on the dark and demonic."—*USA Today*

"Once again this author has done a wonderful job. I was sucked into the world of Dark Ones right from the start and was taken on a fantastic ride. This book is full of witty dialogue and great romance, making it one that should not be missed."—Fresh Fiction

The Unbearable Lightness of Dragons

"Had me laughing out loud. . . . This book is full of humor and romance, keeping the reader entertained all the way through . . . a wondrous story full of magic. . . . I cannot wait to see what happens next in the lives of the dragons."—Fresh Fiction

Also By Katie MacAlister

Dark Ones Series
A Girl's Guide to Vampires
Sex and the Single Vampire
Sex, Lies, and Vampires
Even Vampires Get the Blues
Bring Out Your Dead (Novella)
The Last of the Red-Hot Vampires
Crouching Vampire, Hidden Fang
Unleashed (Novella)
In the Company of Vampires
Confessions of a Vampire's Girlfriend
Much Ado About Vampires
A Tale of Two Vampires
The Undead in My Bed (Novella)
The Vampire Always Rises
Enthralled

Dragon Sept Series
You Slay Me
Fire Me Up
Light My Fire
Holy Smokes
Death's Excellent Vacation (short story)
Playing WIth Fire
Up In Smoke
Me and My Shadow
Love in the Time of Dragons
The Unbearable Lightness of Dragons
Sparks Fly
Dragon Fall
Dragon Storm
Dragon Soul
Dragon Unbound
Dragonblight

Dragon Hunter Series
Memoirs of a Dragon Huner
Day of the Dragon

Born Prophecy Series
Fireborn
Starborn
Shadowborn

Time Thief Series
Time Thief
Time Crossed (short story)
The Art of Stealing Time

Matchmaker in Wonderland Series
The Importance of Being Alice
A Midsummer Night's Romp
Daring in a Blue Dress
Perils of Paulie

Papaioannou Series
It's All Greek to Me
Ever Fallen in Love
A Tale of Two Cousins

Contemporary Single Titles
Improper English
Bird of Paradise (Novella)
Men in Kilts
The Corset Diaries
A Hard Day's Knight
Blow Me Down
You Auto-Complete Me

Noble Historical Series
Noble Intentions
Noble Destiny
The Trouble With Harry
The Truth About Leo

Paranormal Single Titles
Ain't Myth-Behaving

Mysteries
Ghost of a Chance

Steampunk Romance
Steamed

ENTHRALLED

A DARK ONES NOVEL

KATIE MACALISTER

FAT CAT BOOKS

This is a work of fiction. Names, characters, places, and incidents either are the product of the author's imagination or are used fictitiously, and any resemblance to actual persons, living or dead, business establishments, events, or locales is entirely coincidental.

Cover by Croco Designs
Formatting by Racing Pigeon Productions
katiemacalister.com

This book is dedicated to my dear friend (and fellow WOW junky) Marian Goepfert, because she's wickedly funny, has an inner strength that amazes me, genuinely cares about other people, and loves her kitties. And she dies more than I do in WOW. Smooches, my darling!

12 JUNE 1889

Madame:

I return herewith the novel with which you attempted to beat me soundly about the head and shoulders earlier this afternoon in Green Park. As I stated at the time, I in no way intended to accost your person, and was simply attempting to rescue my coat from where you had sat upon it in mistaken belief that the City of London provides gentlemen's coats as covering for benches in their metropolitan parks.

The coat is a favorite of mine, and while I understand that you took umbrage with me wishing to reclaim it, I remain blameless in the assault you insisted I was conducting. I do not know the HR person to whom you threatened to report me, but I regret the incident nonetheless.

Yours sincerely,
Keeley Moore

ONE

"Hey, Beast, how they hangin' today?"

A spate of raucous male laughter followed the inquiry. Keeley Moore heaved a mental sigh, and sent up a prayer to whatever deity would deign to hear it.

Please, just kill me. Right now. Kill me this very second, and I swear by all I hold dear that I will convert to whatever religion you lead, and serve you to the end of my days. Which would be forever, since I would be dead. That's a hell of a deal. You'd be getting a devoted servant all for the cost of the time it took to smite me dead on the spot.

"This here's the Beast, Taylor. Don't go beyond the yellow line on the floor of his cell. Last man who did that was a mindless slave in less time than it can take you to say 'Mississippi.' The director was extremely annoyed."

Right now, Keeley pleaded with the unknown deity. *Do it now. If you do, not only will you earn yourself my undying—ha!—gratitude and promise of servitude; you'll also save countless mortals from being turned into brainless playthings of monsters. Surely you must want to protect mortals from them. Killing me right here, right now, will save untold lives.*

"I thought the director wanted slaves made. Isn't that why we're all here?" a second male voice asked.

Maybe the deities weren't paying attention to him. Maybe they were all busy with other things. Fear gripped Keeley's gut, causing his breath to hitch before he got control again. He reached out again with his awareness, every iota of his being trying to reach a benevolent god who could end this torment. *Hello? Perhaps you don't understand the gravity of the situation. I'm a Thrall. Yes, a Thrall. I used to be a Dark One, but then I was made a Thrall when a madman discovered a dormant Thrall, and used his blood to—but that's a lot of backstory you probably don't want to hear. Suffice it to say that now I'm a Thrall, and being used by monstrous men who won't be happy until the mortal world is in their grasp. So you see that ending my life now will be a benefit to everyone, not just me.*

"Not us," the first male voice said quickly. "Them, but not us."

"Them who?" asked the second.

"The people. The ones who don't have family to notice when they go missing. They're the ones we feed to the Beast. Not members of the Collective."

No smiting occurred. In fact, nothing happened other than a sudden and intense desire to scratch an itch on his nose. Keeley held his breath, hoping against hope that the guards would think him dead. *Thanks for nothing,* he mentally snapped at the universe in general. *If the whole world is enslaved because you couldn't be arsed to smite me, don't come crying to me!*

"He's … er … he's not breathing, is he?" That was the second man speaking. Keeley tried to smooth his expression out to one of vacancy, and mentally crossed his fingers. "Is he dead? He looks dead. I've never seen a dead person before, but he looks very, very dead."

"He's not dead. That's just the Beast up to his old tricks. He likes to try to lure us in close to him, then whammo! He's on you in a second and your will is gone. He used to be a vampire, you know. Vicious, they are. Bloodthirsty. Literally."

"A vampire?" he heard the other man say on a gasp.

"Well, they use another name for it. Dark Dudes or something like that, but it's the same thing. Brutal night-walkers. And everyone knows the only way you can kill those is a stake through the heart, and since the Beast here isn't staked, he's alive."

"Are you sure about that? He's not breathing at all," the second man repeated.

"Absolutely. No way he could die in here on his own."

"Maybe someone did something to him?"

If only someone would, Keeley thought.

"Not possible. See those runes on the walls? Those are spells the director had drawn to contain the Beast. That's what keeps the bad people out. Or in, if that's what the director wants. All those runes mean there's no magical crap going on here, including someone offing our prize possession. Get up, Beast. Your dinner's on the way."

Keeley, with one last mental glare at what he imagined was a vast panoply of deities who refused to help him, cracked open one eye and stopped holding his breath. "Go away, Tennyson. I'm not hungry."

"Ha ha ha ha," laughed the guard named Tennyson in a manner that irritated Keeley like nothing else. Well, that wasn't strictly true. Life irritated him more. "Ha ha ha. Not hungry. You haven't eaten in seven weeks. Another two weeks and you'd go into a coma. They go into comas, Thralls do, if they don't eat for a couple of months." The last was addressed to a new man whom Keeley had not seen before.

Hope flared to life in him as he eyed the new recruit. Like all the other members of the Collective, he was dressed in a black suit and tie, white shirt, and black sunglasses—what was colloquially known as standard garb of the Men in Black. Unlike the urban legends, however, these men were all too real.

"You stay here—no, don't go beyond that yellow line—and open the door as soon as I fetch his meal. And don't talk to him. He's a master manipulator. He almost got the director himself when they first brought him in here."

The new man who had been addressed as Taylor turned to look at Keeley. Although his eyes were hidden behind the shades, Keeley was adept enough in the reading of expressions to note the man was apprehensive. Good. He might be able to use that. But he'd have to hurry. "So, you're new. I'm Keeley. I'm not really a monster, no matter what Tennyson says. I am, however, a danger to everyone and, without putting too fine a point on it, need to be put out of my misery. Let's talk about what you want out of life. I have no doubt that whatever you seek, I can help you obtain … assuming you destroy me."

It was baldly put, and Keeley wished he had more time to be properly persuasive, but there simply was no time for finesse.

"Er …" The man looked a bit startled. "What?"

"The wish for my own death seems odd to you, doesn't it? But if you were repeatedly forced to conduct acts of destruction that were morally repugnant to you, how would you feel? I'm willing to bet that you're a decent sort of chap, and you wouldn't want to continue to be a tool of torment any more than I want to."

Taylor shook his head. "No, I understand you wanting to die. I mean, you're the Beast. You don't have much of a life, right? But what did you mean by what I seek? You mean enlightenment?"

"If that's what would give you pleasure, then by all means." Keeley sat up, straining his ears for the sounds of Tennyson returning. The clink of the shackles binding his wrists and ankles sounded loudly in the mostly soundless room, and had the new recruit backing up a couple of paces.

"Er … ," he said again, glancing toward the door.

"I can't reach you, if that's what you're worried about," Keeley said, standing up. "This is as far as I can move away from the wall. But even if I could, I wouldn't hurt you. I can see you're different from the others. Smarter. More sensitive. *Empathetic.*" That was a long shot, but it behooved him to be as flattering as possible.

"I … my wife says that I am too sensitive about things, but I always thought of it as just being caring."

Keeley nodded, still straining to hear any sounds of the approaching Tennyson. Dread formed in his belly, dread and self-loathing and a bone-deep sense of sorrow that he knew would take weeks before it faded.

Please, he begged again. *Please don't let them do this. Not again. Think of those who have been lost. And those who can yet be saved. Let me die now in order that they might live.*

"I'm not absolutely certain that I understand exactly what you do," Taylor admitted, gesturing toward Keeley. "The lieutenant said that you chew people up and spit out the remains. But that can't be right, because I've seen the enthralled, and they don't have bits missing from them. So … what is it you do?"

"I don't do anything willingly. Your friends—Tennyson and the group of mad scientists behind him—starve me until I'm barely alive; then they throw an innocent person in here, pump me full of a drug cocktail that drives me into a bloodlust, which in turn forces me to attack the victim, and then drag away the remains to be part of their mindless, soulless army." In a moment of insight, Keeley knew that it was useless to continue. There was no way this man would help him escape. He was trapped there, alone, at the mercy of men who didn't understand the concept of the word, and would be used to create an army of mindless drones until they used up all of his life force, bringing on the inevitable end.

"Mad scient—"

The words stopped as there came a knock at the door, warning that it was about to be opened. The guards had taken to doing so since the time Keeley had slipped his chains and had almost escaped before he was Tasered to insensibility.

Despair and regret and guilt gripped Keeley. He wanted to howl that he was not a monster, that it was others who controlled him, controlled the outcome. … His throat ached as he swallowed back the guilt, and said hurriedly, "They think I enjoy this. They don't understand that with every enthrallment, they risk releasing an unstoppable fate. They refuse to believe that each person they force me to enthrall drives me closer to madness, and with that madness comes destruction."

"Of who?" Taylor asked, his voice a whisper.

Keeley closed his eyes against the knowledge that he was close, so close to the edge of control. "Everyone," he answered.

The door opened. Keeley watched with black despair as the slight form of a young man was pushed into the room. The young man stumbled and fell, lying without a sound on the ground, either drugged by the Collective or perhaps overdosed on substances of his own choice. It didn't matter which—the young man was now doomed to an eternity of hell.

And Keeley was one step closer to being made the monster he'd fought against since he'd been captured.

Tennyson smiled, a large syringe in one of his hands, while the other held a Taser. "You want to fight, don't you? He always fights, Taylor, even though he knows he can't beat us. Just don't get too close while I bring him into submission. He came close to breaking the neck of a guard two months ago. You just let me remind the Beast that he's here to serve us, and then I'll let you watch while he turns this junkie into a servant of the Collective."

Keeley didn't wait. He leaped forward, kicking out at Tennyson, catching him under the chin and sending the man staggering backward. In vain did he struggle against the chains binding him to the wall, hoping against hope that this time, he'd free himself.

Tennyson snarled profanely, and shot him with the Taser. Keeley swore against the rush of pain, willing his muscles to resist the electrical charge, but it was no use, and he knew it. Even as he dropped to his knees, he struggled for control, managing to say, "One … day …"

"That's right, you make yourself sound as tough as you like, but just you remember that you're the one crawling on the ground," Tennyson said, approaching him to kick him viciously in the ribs several times. Keeley felt the bones give way, knowing that at least a few were broken, driving deep into his organs. He did no more than grunt with the agony of the assault, his muscles locked and refusing to heed his brain's command. "And I'm the one who has the power of life and death. Don't you ever forget that."

Anything. I will do anything you ask of me. Please take me now so that I am no longer the instrument of inhuman madmen, Keeley begged one last time, but even as Tennyson jabbed the horrible cocktail of drugs into his neck, he knew that his pleas had fallen on deaf ears.

There was no salvation for him. No hope. Nothing but a future of endless nightmares.

And blood.

So much blood.

TWO

OTHERBOOK
Social Media for the Otherworld

To: Ellis

You there?

To: Ellis

Ellis? Your little light is green, which says you're connected to Face … er … Otherbook. Hello?

To: Ellis

Golden, glorious grape juice! There are days when I really dislike modern technology. What am I doing wrong with this Messenger app? Why isn't it reaching you? Now I have to ask Merrick, and he's busy with the whole doom doom doom thing.

To: Ellis

Wait, you haven't fallen overboard and drowned, have you? Ack! Please tell me you're not dead!

To: Tempest

Lovey! We just got into port (don't I sound nautical?) and I see that you've been trying to message me for the last week. I told you that the interwebs would be spotty while we were at sea, and that I might not get any e-mails or messages you sent, so your grape juice panic is all for naught. We had a wonderful cruise from Dubai to Singapore. Our version of

Drag Dracula was beyond fabulous, with everyone on board the ship truly enjoying it. We even got the captain up onstage one night! It's been such a nice break from the club to do a season with the cruise lines, but alas, all good things have to come to an end, and we're flying home to Monaco after a brief stop in Australia. What is a doom doom doom thing, and do I want to know what the ever-dishy Merrick is doing to it? Of course I do! Spill all.

To: Ellis

Thank the moon, stars, and zippy, zippy comets that you didn't fall overboard! I was worried that someone might throw you overboard, since tolerance of Dark Ones in that region of the world is slim to none, or so Merrick says. I think it must be the sunshiny climate, because who in their right mind wouldn't love a vamp? But that's neither here nor there.

The doom thing is rather sketchy, to be honest. It took me a while to pry the info out of Merrick, because you know how vampires are—über-protection mode when it comes to anything that concerns their loved ones. But eventually I did get out of him ... wait, let me do this properly. I signed up for a life-journaling class so that I can write down all the adventures Merrick and I get into. Running to the laptop so I can type rather than voice-to-text.

To: Ellis, Tempest

Darlings, are we chatting? I forgot that you got me on this vampy social media thing. What's going on? And hello, Ellis. I'm glad to hear you and your troupe of vamp dancers are doing well.

To: Roxy, Ellis

Auntie! I forgot you were on here, but I'm delighted to hear from you. Let me just switch to my laptop and I'll catch you up to speed with everything that's going on. Ellis, you remember my aunt Roxy, don't you?

To: Tempest, Roxy

Hullo, Roxy! Long time no chitchat. Yes, the boys and I are having a blast, although I'm looking forward to having a home that isn't prone to rocking. I hope all is well with you and your hub.

To: Ellis, Tempest

All is peachy keen, but now I've read back all the chat and I'm dying to know what's going on.

To: Roxy, Ellis

This is much better. Everyone settled? Do we all have snacks and beverages? It's going to be a long one. The scene: the official Moravian Council headquarters in Vienna. The cast of characters: Merrick and yours truly, Han, and Ciaran (so three of the official Four Horsemen). Also present is the famous author Christian Dante (Ellis, Christian is married to Allie, who is Aunt Roxy's friend), and a very intense man named Andreas.

"Are you sure you wish to do this?" Merrick asked as soon as Andreas entered the room. "You have been told about the risk of becoming a Horseman?"

Andreas, who was German, kind of scoffed a little, which I knew would irritate Merrick. "Of course. I am not afraid of anyone, the Revelation included."

"You should be afraid," Han said, giving him a long look.

"They have stepped up their game," Ciaran added, also giving Andreas a good, hard stare. "Five Dark Ones have disappeared in the last three months. The Revelation know we are hunting for them."

To: Ellis, Tempest

Er … who or what is this Revelation?

To: Roxy, Ellis

Oh, sorry, Aunt Roxy. The Revelation—also known as the Collective, and evidently in the past as the Triumvirate—is a group of baddies who have targeted people in the Otherworld who they can corrupt. Evidently, they are led by a man named Alphonse de Marco, as well as my cousin Carlo.

To: Ellis, Tempest

Cousin Carlo? I don't have a … oh, is that your dad's side of the family?

To: Roxy, Ellis

Yup. Cousin Carlo is a bit … well, let's just say crazy and leave it at that. Anyway, Carlo is working for or with Alphonse, although we don't know exactly who all the top guys are because whenever one of the vamps gets close to the leadership, they disappear.

The vamps, not the baddies.

Merrick says the Revelation used to go after anyone with power like mages and diviners, but for the last fifteen or so years, they've picked on Dark Ones exclusively.

To: Ellis, Tempest

So they are anti-vamp? Why?

To: Roxy, Ellis

Not so much anti-vamp as wanting to experiment on them in order to make them … well, kind of slaves, I guess. This is what everyone thought, mind you, but then … well, let me get back to the good stuff so it's laid out properly.

"They know we won't stop until we've finished them off," Han said (he's a little more bloodthirsty than I like, but given the doom doom doom situation, I don't blame him).

"They targeted us through Nico, and they will try again." Ciaran narrowed his eyes at Andreas, who looked very much like he wanted to pull a rude face, but he managed to get a grip on himself, and instead just looked mildly bored.

"They may try, but I am not Nico," Andreas said, and the others nodded.

This was purely a formality, since Andreas had been interviewed by Merrick and the others several times, but I gathered this was the official recognition of making him the new fourth Horseman, so everyone was being a bit more formal and using their respective "this is all very serious business" manners.

"Then we are of one mind," Christian said, glancing at the others with an equally serious expression. "There is one issue I wish to mention before you leave."

"The rumor," Merrick said, his jaw tight.

"What rumor?" I asked, giving him a meaningful look.

He avoided my gaze, which means he's been keeping something from me. I pinched his leg, since he knows I hate being left out in the cold. He covered my hand with his, his fingers stroking mine in a way that made me go boneless with pleasure, until I just wanted to …

Er … moving on.

To: Ellis, Tempest

snicker

To: Roxy, Ellis

Ahem, Auntie.

"What rumor?" I asked again, this time spreading the look to the other vamps there. They all suddenly became busy with their phones.

Glorious pink poodles, Merrick! What's going on?

He sighed into my head, something that sounds weird, but is oddly reassuring. "A rumor has been going around the Otherworld that something … untoward … has happened."

"Untoward as in a vampire getting the ever-living crap-ola pinched out of his manly thigh because he won't tell his Beloved the latest gossip?" I asked, tapping his leg.

"No." He was silent for a moment, his attention focused inward. I could feel him sorting through various thoughts, trying to make a pattern from a jumbled mess. "The rumor is regarding an impossibility. It is said that the Revelation have a being who can't exist."

"What sort of being?" I asked, starting to get worried. Merrick tended to be a bit focused on the goals of the Four Horsemen—and for good reason, seeing as he was saving fellow vamps' lives—but all five of the men present looked particularly grim.

"There are many words for him," Merrick said slowly.

"Werreir," Ciaran said.

"Guerroieor," Han said. "Chivaler."

"Overmaistren," Andreas added. "Old One."

Silence filled the room, broken when Merrick said, "Thrall."

I looked first at his expression, then to the others. "That's a lot of names, but what exactly is this overmas … overmeis … er … Thrall?"

"The progenitor of Dark Ones," Christian said, his fingers tapping softly on the table. "It is Thralls who we are descended from."

"And that's bad?" I asked, confused.

"Very," Merrick said, his hand once again warm on mine. "They are not like us. We carry the stains of their sins—the loss of souls for unredeemed Dark Ones—but they were not like us. They were savage, brutal, killing for the joy of it."

"Turning those who they did not destroy," Ciaran said, nodding. "Making slaves of their victims."

"And each time they did so, they came closer to *le Reniement*." Han frowned at nothing.

"The betrayal?" I asked, digging around in memories of previous French classes.

"The Breaking," Han corrected. "At least in this case, that is the translation."

"They were destroyed, all of them, more than a millennium and a half in the past, but their offspring became Dark Ones," Christian said. "We carry their blood, but not their savagery."

A little chill skittered down my spine. "I almost don't want to ask this, but I feel like I have to know. This Breaking thing—who or what gets broken?"

"Everyone," Merrick said, his fingers tightening on mine until I had to wiggle them to let him know he was hurting me. "If the Thrall reaches his Breaking point, no one around him will survive. That is why we must investigate this rumor. If it's true that the Revelation has located a Thrall, we will not be safe. Not Dark Ones, not mortals, not even the Otherworld itself. The Thrall *must* be found."

I glanced around the room, my heart sinking at the stark expressions on the faces of the men. "And when you find him?" I asked, wanting nothing more than to drag Merrick off to safety, where he would be protected from any threat. "What will happen to him?"

No one spoke for a good minute before Christian, with a little sigh, said, "He must be destroyed. For the future of everyone, the Thrall cannot be allowed to exist."

To: Tempest, Roxy

Holy shitsnacks! There's some big bad vamp chomper going around? I'll tell the boys. Maybe we should stay in Australia. Maybe we should close down the club in Monaco. Holy, holy hellballs, Tempest! Doom doom doom is right. What are we going to do?

To: Ellis, Tempest

Good lord! I had no idea there was a big bad behind the vamps. I assumed it was something to do with demon lords. But I'm still a bit confused about these Thralls. What does this group of baddies want with them if they are some sort of vampire ticking time bomb?

To: Roxy, Ellis

I'm not sure. I asked Merrick, and he muttered something in Italian, which he knows is unfair, because despite living here for four years, I suck at the language. Honestly, I don't know why the Revelation would want a group of slave-making, violent, proto-vampires who may well explode on them at any time, but that's just me. They must have a reason, and I suspect that we're going to find out sooner rather than later.

To: Ellis, Tempest

Glorioski. Well, I hope your husband and the other Four Horsemen find this Thrall, and make him disappear.

To: Roxy, Ellis

I do, too. Otherwise … the alternative is just too horrible to contemplate.

JUNE 13, 1889

Dear Mr. Moore,

Thank you for returning my book, although how did you know it was mine? Oh, wait, was it the calling card inside that I was using as a bookmark? I assume it was, even though the card is now gone, which means I've lost my place and will have to figure out just where I left off in it. You didn't ... er ... glance through the book, did you? Because I'm not normally the type of person who reads erotica, but I have a history degree, and I know for a fact that this particular book is rare. Or it will be. And hence, will be really valuable in, oh, let's say a completely random time of about a hundred and thirty years.

As for the fondlage on my behind–that, sirrah, is another matter. You absolutely copped a grope when you were pulling your coat out from under me, not to mention the rudeness of a man who expects a woman to sit on a damp bench when his coat is lying right there waiting to keep said woman's bottom warm and dry. In fact, the word "cad" comes to mind.

Although it was nice of you to send me back my smutty book that I hope someday will do much for my retirement fund.

Yours in icy reserve,
Jenna James

THREE

"If you look over to the west side, you'll see the town of Tybo Flats proper. To the north of that is the mine, which is closed due to massive cave-ins a few decades ago. South is the dried riverbed where some paleontologists are hard at work excavating what is rumored to be a new type of dinosaur. And of course, to the north, where we are headed now, are the famed alkali flats where so many sightings have been made."

"Miss Jenna, just what sorts of aliens are we gonna be seein'?" The nasal drawl that accompanied a raised hand at the back of the bus made me think of the worst Southern stereotypes. "Are we gonna see them grays that the preacher on TV said lurk in the night just waitin' to grab you when you ain't lookin'? Or are we gonna see some of the ET kinds with the big lumpy haids and long spider fingers?"

I sighed to myself before pressing on the button of the PA system microphone, yelping when Mac hit a rut without slowing down, causing me to careen into the grab bar that ran from the bus roof to the floor. After a quick glare at Mac, I turned back to address the speaker. "I'm so sorry about the roads. Tybo Flats doesn't have a huge municipal budget, as you can imagine. As for your question Mrs. … er … Walsh, was it? I'm afraid the Outta This World Tours doesn't promise you actual aliens, as was covered in the Imaginarium introductory session."

"That dog and pony show?" The woman, who was seated dead center in the last seat in the bus, gave a snort audible to me all the way at the front, despite the white noise of the clip-on fans hanging from the seat backs that we used in lieu of air-conditioning. "I wasn't fooled by that! That was just those animal tronics that Disney uses. They weren't no real aliens. And what about them Midnight Walkers? I want to see those."

"That's right, you have them here, don't you?" one of two women sitting up front said rather breathlessly. "Beth, didn't you say they have those blue people here? The ones who sparkle at night like the vampires?"

"That's what they said on *Mysteries Abound*, and you know Jack Rayburn is never wrong," Beth's buddy Lolly answered, the two women nodding together in unison.

Mac uttered a rude word at the name of the eighties paranormal-show host, now deceased. I ignored her, and said with a quick glance out the window, "Actually, the Midnight Walkers don't sparkle at night, and they certainly aren't vampires."

"But they're blue, aren't they? I did some research on them—I'm premed, and I want to specialize in genetic disorders—and the articles I read all stated that the Midnight Walkers had a distinct blue cast to their skin due to some deficiency in their genetic structure from inbreeding, but *Mysteries Abound* said that it was known through the area that they were … *other*." Lolly, who wore a bright African-print turban, spoke the last word in almost a whisper.

The other four tourists on the bus murmured excitedly.

I could feel Mac looking at me. I gestured behind my back for her to keep her eyes on the road. "How very fascinating your research must be! Yes, it is said that the Midnight Walkers all had a blue-tinted skin, but nothing was ever proven."

"But what about them blue-skins being the result of impregnation by aliens," called Mrs. Walsh from the back, sniffing irritably. "That's what I heard they were. All that anal probing goin' on, you know."

"Unfortunately," I said, forestalling what I was sure was going to be more comments from Mrs. Walsh about the area's second biggest claim to fame, "there are no blue people to be found. That is, there are no members of the Walker family who show signs of the rare chromosomal issues that made them so famous a hundred and fifty years ago."

"It's a wonder your nose isn't growing," I heard muttered from the driver's seat.

I ignored her. "However, that doesn't mean that we are going to have a boring trip to the flats! Far from it. As you know, our driver today is MacKenzie Fitzwilliam. Mac has lots of experience working with such prestigious organizations as the Jet Propulsion Laboratory—"

"Fired after six days due to a trumped-up story about misuse of a proton collider," Mac murmured.

"Industrial Light & Magic—that's the Lucasfilm people—"

"Not so much *worked for* as claimed an office and joined a robotics project for eight months until I was caught and banned for life from the ILM campuses," Mac told the steering wheel.

I took a deep breath, glancing at the vlogger girls in the front seats, but they were too busy filming themselves to hear Mac's comments. "And of course, she spent copious amounts of time with her father, Sam, a famed pyrotechnical specialist who worked on many Hollywood movies."

"Convicted arsonist, died in prison, but had the best firework shows in the entire San Fernando Valley," said Mac.

I smiled at everyone again, thankful for the noise of the fans and bumpy road that made it hard to hear conversation. "Mac understands the excitement that comes with visiting Tybo Flats, and she's kindly set up some special effects for your enjoyment."

The tourists murmured excitedly as Mac pulled over on a wide dirt shoulder. I opened the door to the bus, and ushered everyone to a sign we'd placed earlier in the morning.

"Now, let's see," Mac said when I hurried back to the bus. She pulled out from under her seat an electronic firing-system board most commonly used by hard-core firework aficionados. "Shall we go safe or singeing their bangs?"

"Safe, Mac, safe!" I said quickly, rubbing a small fresh scar on the left side of my forehead. "You almost blew me to kingdom come last month, and I just know that woman from Vegas who was standing next to me when you set off the pyrotechnics is going to make me pay for her weave. You know how expensive those can be."

"She shouldn't have been wearing flammable synthetic hair," Mac said, watching through the windows as she cued a cardboard cutout of a 1930s sedan with two figures silhouetted in the back seat, followed by a trio of orbs that popped up and wobbled back and forth. "The tour-agreement fine print clearly states that any flammable clothing and accessories is the responsibility of the bearer. Besides, I ran out of the stuff I used for that explosion. Sure made a hell of a light, though, didn't it? I couldn't see out of my peripheral vision for almost a week. Wish I could find more of it ..."

"You do, and I'll fire you," I swore.

"You can't. I'm the only one who can do the light show you need for the *turistas*. Stop giving me that look—I'll do the safe version for this group. Although if you'd just give me three hundred and seventy bucks, I could get a very cool decommissioned laser. It would add some serious oomph to the tourist shows."

"You already have a decommissioned laser, as I well know," I said, absently rubbing a second scar, this one small and round, about the size of a pea, and located on my elbow.

"*Pfft*. You Midnight Walkers heal fast," she said, giving me a laughing look from the corner of her eye. "Must be all of your alien DNA."

"Oh, ha ha. Very funny." The tourists oohed and aahed as Mac's light show lit up the area around the orb trio, everyone taking pictures and videos. I looked at my watch again, then glanced out across the alkali flats to where a smudge of black rippled with heat waves rising from the ground. "We're going to have to pick up the pace if we want to get to the caves early."

"You're the one doing the talking. I just drive. And blow things up. Speaking of that—"

"No. I don't have three hundred and seventy dollars to give you for another laser."

"Not that." She tucked the board away as the tourists, now that the reenactment and light show was over, wandered back our way. "I made something for you. Something you can use at the Crabs. It'll take down even a full grown bull MIB."

The Crabs was what locals called the Krebbs Pharmaceutical Group, a global company that was swathed in mystery about exactly what it was they produced, and whom they produced it for. Rumor had it that they were for hire, making everything from plagues and viruses on down to plain old items of chemical warfare. It was their research and development division that stirred a veritable hornet's nest of conspiracy theories, though, including the inevitable group of men and women who were clad in black suits and standard-issue sunglasses. Given their ominous presence, the locals firmly believed everything they read or saw in popular media regarding Men in Black.

I glanced again across the flats at the black smudge, wondering once more why such a big and evidently prosperous company would plop down a bunch of scientists in the middle of Nowhere, Nevada.

"If it's another version of your homemade pepper spray—" I started to say.

"Naw, that blew up. It's a gun that—"

"No guns," I interrupted. "You know how I feel about firearms."

"I do, but I also know you're going to need all the help you can get if you think you can just crawl through a hole in the fence. If I've told you once, I've told you a hundred times—you have to have a backup plan. You just seem to jump into everything without considering what you will do if things go bad," she answered with a meaningful waggle of her eyebrows as the tourists reached the door.

I ignored the familiar refrain, having heard Mac harp on that particular shortcoming all too often. Besides, I told myself as I hopped down to help those who needed a hand up the steps, it wasn't that I didn't consider alternatives—I simply had confidence that my way was the right way. And everyone knew that self-confidence was vital to having a successful life.

A few minutes later we set off again, the standard spiel rolling off my tongue without much effort. The frequent stops—twelve in all—kept even Mrs. Walsh mostly silent as we crept around the twisty road that ran around the southern tip of the flats.

It wasn't until we passed a small campus of low one-story black buildings behind razor-wire-bedecked chain-link fences, marked every ten feet with dire warnings about trespassers, that I told my little group, "We have just one more spot to visit this morning—the Moon Cave, where, in 1974, three children were lost for eight days and emerged with tales of trips to various planets. We'll stop at the cave for two hours so that you may enjoy the sack lunches and explore the opened areas of the cave thoroughly. If you present the vouchers we gave you before we set off, you will receive a complimentary guided tour through a part of the cave not normally open to visitors."

We pulled over at a parking lot that held a couple of dusty cars, and got out the cooler filled with iced bottles of soft drinks, water, and a local brand of beer, handing out the lunches and beverages to our group.

It took ten minutes to hustle them all up to the entrance of the cave, where several picnic tables were set up, before Mac and I escaped back to the bus.

"Right," I said, taking my place in the front seat. "I'd say let's synchronize our watches, but you never wear one, so just be sure that you don't come back before two twenty. That should give me time to get in, locate Britt, and be back at the road by the time you are on your way."

"Gotcha. So, you going to do what you said you were going to do?" Mac nodded to the entrance of the Krebbs base as we slowly drove by. It had a definite military feel about it with a twelve-foot-tall fence and a large barred gate complete with two manned guardhouses on either side. During the day, the gate was open, but at least four uniformed people lounged around the entrance, all of whom bore firearms. "Your magic thing that you can't show me, but insist you can do even though it violates every law of physics?"

"It may violate every law, but that doesn't mean I can't do it. Sometimes. Well, twice before, and I see no reason to believe I can't make it happen again. Besides, physics is overrated. 'There is more in the heavens and earth, Horatio,' and all that."

"Dude, you did not just dis science, the very same science that puts food on your table, and allows me to build wondrous devices in your she-shed." The bus jerked to the side, bouncing painfully over a large rock before Mac came to a skidding halt on the dirt-covered shoulder. Around us, dust rose in a veritable cloud, obscuring our view outside for a few minutes. "Are you sure you weren't high or something when you thought you could move through walls?"

"No!" I said, outraged. "You know how I feel about recreational drugs. Besides, it wasn't so much moving through walls as just … well, kind of projecting myself about ten feet forward. At least, that's what happened last week, when I was recovering from you damn near blowing me up. Last night I tried it again, and the next thing I knew, I was outside the house, in the neighbor's yard."

"You should have called me to see it. I could have filmed you and submitted it to one of those places offering money for proof of ESP and ghosts and things. Just think of the equipment I could buy with the reward money." Her eyes glazed over for a moment.

"You have more equipment now than can be safely stored," I pointed out. "I won't even go into the dubious ethics of what you're doing with all that decommissioned equipment. If you keep getting more, you'll end up with enough for a full-fledged nuclear reactor."

"Don't be silly," she scoffed with a little snort. "Like I'd want one of those?"

"I should hope not," I said.

"I could have put together a reactor any time in the last three years. Now, a proton synchrotron, that's another matter." Her eyes narrowed in thought. "I'm going to have to contact Amir on the Dark Web and see when CERN is having their next garage sale."

I stared at her for a moment, not sure if she was joking. It was never easy to tell with Mac.

"But!" she said, unbuckling the seat belt. "First we have to take care of this."

Her gaze slid to the rearview mirror. I glanced back, and noticed that now that the dust from our sudden stop had cleared, the guards at the entrance to Krebbs had come out to the road to look at us.

"I got this." I answered her warning look before she even put it into words. "It'll work, Mac. Stop worrying."

"I just hope your magical thing isn't all due to you inadvertently imbibing some edibles, because the MIBs are not going to understand if you really aren't a magical marvel," she said with a little shake of her head.

"They won't notice anything," I said with much more confidence than I felt.

While it was true that the previous night I had managed to duplicate the experience I'd had the week before (when I was relaxing after the fireworks show that Mac had let get out of hand), I wasn't one hundred percent sure I could do it again. Not in the light of the day, and under pressure.

But what choice did I have? I nodded toward the gate behind us. "We're getting attention. Let's go out and eyeball the tire like it's giving us an issue."

We both got out and moved to the rear of the bus, bending over to look at the tire. I could feel the interest of the guards some sixty yards back, and knew that we were the focus of their attention.

"I heard a rumor that some physicists in Russia have mastered translocation," Mac said softly. She pulled a socket wrench out of her pocket and began tapping the tire with it. "But only on a subatomic level. For you to be able to blip yourself … well, I just really hope it works, because otherwise we're out of luck."

"Blip?" I tried the word out. It felt good. "I like that. Blipping. I blip. I have blipped. I will bloop. That's a good description of what it feels like."

"If it doesn't work, I'm fully on board with us going in with guns blazing," Mac said, her eyes alight with the same fanatical glow they got whenever she worked on what she called her little projects, but which most authorities would refer to as illegal, potentially radioactive devices. "I have these new neural disruptors that don't do any actual damage—they just make people very, very dizzy. And nauseous. And possibly have projectile diarrhea, but that's just a side effect, and not an actual feature I'd count on. I can go back to my lab and grab us each a disruptor, and—"

"No guns, not even the barfing kind. And *ew* on the side effect. Is that why you had me order so much anti-diarrhea medicine? I thought you said you had food poisoning?"

"You know I don't test on animals," Mac said with a pained expression. "We can drop off little packets of meds for the guys we shoot if it bothers you—"

"No guns of any kind," I repeated. "I will blip."

"They have laser sights. We won't miss."

I straightened up from pretending to look at the tire, and gave her a pat on the arm. "You have lasers on the brain, and no, I don't mean that literally."

She gave a one-shouldered shrug. "I have had. My part will never be the same. Or the synapses on that side of my head."

"I'll be fine without the barf guns. Just be at the rendezvous point at two twenty, because I have a feeling Britt isn't going to be happy, and waiting around for you may try her patience."

Mac and I stood glanced back.. She waved at the guards, all of whom were openly watching us, before we turned and entered the bus.

"Let me just get my phone. …" She pulled out a Frankenstein object that was the result of her merging several cell phones into one, aiming at me. "Right. Test subject is about to blip approximately … what would you call that? Thirty feet? Forty?"

I glanced at the back of one of the low squat buildings that was about forty feet beyond the fence next to us. "Fortyish. OK. Getting focused now." I stood with eyes closed, shutting out the sound of not just cars passing but the fans running lethargically in the early summer heat, and even the odd drone of machinery from the Krebbs facility, while adopting the calm mental state that I'd managed the night before. Once I had that, I reached out and pulled aside what I thought of as the strands of matter that wove together to create the world, and stepped through it, leaving Mac and the bus behind.

16 JUNE 1889

Miss James:

This is to acknowledge receipt of the copy of Any Port in a Storm, or A Young Man's Folly amongst the Sheep. *I am unsure of why you felt I needed a copy of this prurient sort of literature, but I will attribute your gesture to one of general goodwill rather than a comment about either the gender (not to mention species) I prefer for romantic endeavors.*

That said, the chapter regarding the acquisition of garments better suited to women rather than sheep was particularly eye-opening. Who knew they made stockings for ewes? I certainly didn't, and I'm not at all sure that I couldn't have gone through the course of my life without knowing that fact.

However, I have never been a fan of ignorance for ignorance's sake, and thus with the assumption that your gesture was intended to inform me about the possibilities available regarding sheep as potential romantic partners, I thank you for the book.

It cannot leave me but wondering if your family is aware of your interest in such a ... rare, I believe was the word you used? ... form of literature. Perhaps your husband is the connoisseur of all things ewes? Father? Older brother? I fervently hope they do not discuss such things with you. Or at least that they do not do so against your will.

Should you find yourself in a situation where points regarding ovine corsets and silk stockings are forcibly pressed home to you in a manner that leaves you uncomfortable, do not hesitate to contact me.

I am a physician, and have devoted myself to the betterment of the human condition. You might consider me a cad for the manner in which I retrieved my favorite coat, but I am not so far gone to polite dictates as to turn my back on a young woman forced to endure the dressing of a ewe for illicit congress.

I am, madam, your servant.

Keeley Moore

FOUR

"Ow," I whispered, and doubled over, clutching my shin that had jammed into a trash bin, and rubbing my leg while I simultaneously marveled at the fact that the magic mind thing I'd discovered the week before had indeed worked a third time. "That is seriously cool. I hope Mac got video of it."

I was in some sort of an office. In front of me was a desk littered with paper and two laptops. I ducked down so that the tan cubicle divider hid me from view as I quickly examined the surroundings. Cautiously, I lifted a shade enough to peer through a small window. Out on the road, Mac was just pulling away.

"Hey, Jesús, do you have—" A woman rounded the entrance to the cubicle, pausing when she saw me hunched over. "Er … who are you?"

For a moment, I was panicked at being caught, then remembered the detailed cover story Mac and I had worked up the night before. Confidence, I knew, was key. If I acted like I belonged there, no one would question me. I straightened up and gave the woman a cool glance. "Hmm? Oh, I'm Anna Walker."

She stared pointedly at my chest.

"Ugh, that," I said, giving her a little "don't you hate these things?" nod of my head as I pulled out of my pocket one of the replica name badges Mac and I had cobbled up. I clipped it to my shirt, making a show of getting it just right. "This is a silk shirt. I hate to get it so wrinkled with these horrible clampy bits."

"Ah. Yes. They do tend to chew fabric if you get it caught on something," she said in a neutral tone of voice. She scanned my identity badge, her eyes opening wide. "Oh! You're from—oh! I'm sorry, I didn't realize. Is … is something wrong with Jesús? I mean, with an Alpha Level here in his office, and all."

"I couldn't possibly tell you something so confidential," I said, silently blessing Mac and her high-powered camera lens. She'd been watching the people who had come and gone from the facility for the last two days, and said she'd picked out a particularly important-looking man's badge upon which she'd based mine. Evidently she'd picked correctly. I moved past the woman, pausing next to her to say softly, "You will tell no one you saw me here."

"Oh, no one," she said on a breath, looking slightly sick.

I gave her a nod and, with confidence I didn't quite own, strolled down the narrow corridor. Just as I reached one of the doors, a young man with dark hair and a goatee emerged from a restroom, obviously heading for the cubicle I'd just left.

"Jesús," I said pleasantly, nodding as I passed him.

He nodded back, pausing to look after me in confusion when I walked out the door.

I counted buildings, striding along the cement pathways that snaked between them, hoping that our guess about the biggest structure was correct, and that it housed the dormitories rumored to be used by the bulk of the employees.

At the sight of a pair of armed guards strolling in front of the entrance, I did an about-face. "Damn. Damn, damn, damn. Now how am I going to get in?" I slid on a pair of sunglasses, since everyone there wore them, and moved along the side of the long building trying not to look like I was lost. A few people glanced my way, but no one paid much attention when I strolled around to the back. I peered around, noting a couple of security cameras that appeared to be aimed toward the fence about twenty feet back.

With studied nonchalance, I moved close to the building until I judged myself out of view of the cameras, and, with another quick look to make sure no one was around, faced the back of the building. "Right. Clear mind. Think about space like it is a woven fabric, move aside a few strands, and blip!"

I blipped. Luckily, the room I found myself in was a bathroom. Unluckily, the space where I emerged was occupied by a stall door, which caused me to rebound painfully off it, resulting in me staggering to a halt in front of a very surprised woman in the act of brushing her teeth.

"Man, I have got to cut down on those three-martini lunches!" I told her with a weak smile before hurrying out of the bathroom and into a long room with more cubicle walls, these ones arranged around bunk beds, obviously giving the residents a modicum of privacy. I waited a moment to be sure that the woman from the bathroom wasn't going to raise an alarm, but no one called out for me to stop, so I hurried down the center aisle, consulting my phone and the latest text I had from Lucy.

From: Lucy

According to Never Home Alone, Britt's phone is located at the following building. Since she is never without her phone, I'm sure you'll find her at the same location. I'm equally sure she'll flip you shit about her being old enough to make her own decisions, but she is not. At least, not emotionally. And the man she's decided she's in love with is absolutely, one hundred percent at fault for luring a nineteen-year-old to join him in whatever horrible sex den he's set up at the Crabs. Save my deluded child, Jenna, before she makes a big mistake.

I looked at the map that Lucy's tracking software had provided, and counted the building blobs. According to the map, an hour ago, Britt's phone, at least, had been just a few feet away from me. I continued down the corridor, pausing when the cubicle walls ended, and a couple of closed doors indicated more private rooms.

I tapped at one of the doors.

"It's about time you came back. I'm getting tired of—oh." The young woman who answered the door was of middling height, with a round face, long, glossy black hair straight out of one of those ancient Japanese artworks, and a sulky expression that drove home the point that Britt might think she was in love, and old enough to run away with her boyfriend, but in reality, she lacked the maturity for such a situation. "What are *you* doing here?"

I ignored the accusation in her voice and pushed past her into the room, saying, "Hi, Britt! You don't mind if I come in, do you? Wow, this room is a lot nicer than the dorm setups. Is that a private bathroom?"

"Mom sent you, didn't she?" Britt asked, her hands on her hips, the door still half-open behind her. "I told her that I am an adult, and she can't make me go back home if I don't want to. And I don't."

"I get that, I totally do," I said, sitting on the end of a large bed, carefully selecting the bottom corner, where the blankets weren't rumpled. The bed was unmade, and the room, while infinitely nicer than the accommodations in the outer room, looked like a whirlwind had hit it. There were clothes, cosmetics, and random items near and dear to nineteen-year-old girls' hearts scattered on every surface. I nudged aside a couple of flip-flops with jeweled straps and smiled. "I know how important it is to feel in charge of your life, but here's the thing—your mom is worried that your … er … friend isn't everything he says he is."

Her expression turned dark with suspicion. "Mom's just jealous because Ramon is interested in me and not her. Not that he would be, since she's pregnant. And ten years older than him." She emphasized the age difference as if it were centuries. "There's nothing wrong with him. He's perfect in every way."

"Well, there's perfect, and then there's *perfect*," I said, calculating the likelihood of Britt coming willingly with me. With Lucy close to term, I'd promised to do everything in my power to get Britt away from the dubious Ramon, but I had a feeling it was going to be a more difficult project than I'd first imagined. "From what Mac found out via one of her contacts on the Dark Web, Ramon is actually heading up a program with a pretty heinous purpose—in a word, torture."

"Oh, that," she said with a snort, moving away from the still-open door to stand in front of me, her arms crossed, her expression still pugnacious. I glanced at the door, wanting badly to close it just in case someone strolled by, but didn't see how I could do that without her raising a fuss. "It's just the leeches he's doing that to."

"Leeches?" I asked, confused.

"Yeah, leeches. You know." She made a sharp, undefinable gesture. "The bloodsuckers. Vampires. Only Ramon says they're really not. He called them something else, but I forgot what. He says they're vampire ancestors, and they were all gone, but then his boss found one who was dead, and he took some DNA or something from him, and found a vamp, and made a new one. The not-vampire guys, that is. So, it's not like it's real torture, because the vampire is evil and shit like that."

My blood ran cold in my veins. Words came to mind, ones that seemed to be wrapped in a miasma of darkness. "Not vampires … Dark Ones."

"Yeah, that's the name of the vampire before he was turned into a … Thrall, I think, is what Ramon said was the name. Ramon works in the lab. Right now he's just doing whatever the chemist dudes tell him, but one day he's going to take over the lab," she said with lofty disregard of just how juvenile she sounded. "He's smart and sexy, and he told me I could live here with him so we can be together, and when he goes back to San Francisco, where his boss works, I get to go with him. So if that's the only thing you've got against him, you can just go back to Mom and tell her that she's way off base, as usual. Thralls are evil. Ramon is just trying to save us from them."

I was distracted by a sense of something in my head bumping around in the shadows of my awareness. I tried to pull it forward into the light, but the memory—assuming that was what it was—continued to rattle around just out of my mental reach. "That doesn't really make sense," I said slowly, letting go of the elusive memory.

"Did you hear me?" Britt was closer now, her hands on her hips. "I said you can go. Ramon and I are in love. He's going to marry me. We're going to have a house in California, and I will get an agent and become an actress. Or maybe a dancer. Ramon says I dance really good."

"That sounds like a fun plan, but your mom is worried about you, and I think you and she should talk about this before you go off to get married to this torturing dude." I stood up and took her by the arm.

A glance at the clock half-buried beneath a crop top told me that I wouldn't have time to convince her to go with me. I'd just have to risk blipping us out to the road, praying that I could take her with me.

Damn, I should have tried this with Mac ahead of time, but I didn't have that option now. I'd just have to trust I could do it. "I'm sure you two can work out an agreement. But right now, if you would just stand here next to me for a few seconds while I clear my mind—"

A few moments later I realized I had underestimated Britt. She jerked her arm out of my grip and ran to the door, yelling for guards. I hesitated for a moment, unsure of whether I should just grab her and try to get her all the way to the side of the road, or leave her and report to one of my oldest friends that her daughter was a lost cause, but before I could decide, two men and a woman ran into the room, weapons drawn. Britt stood behind them in the hallway, a smug smile curving her lips.

"Your mother is not going to be happy about this," I told her when the guards, after hearing Britt tell them I wasn't an employee of Krebbs, and was there to kidnap her, marched me past her and out the front door.

She rolled her eyes, but managed to refrain from saying anything.

The next half hour was painful, at least from a tedium standpoint. I was grilled repeatedly as to my identity and reason for infiltrating the Krebbs facility, both questions of which I answered truthfully.

They didn't believe me.

"Look, this is ridiculous," I said, glancing at the clock on a nearby wall. "We've been here for thirty-three minutes, and we're just going around in circles. I've told you my name and the reason I'm here—to rescue a friend's nineteen-year-old daughter. I do not work for any government. I am not an industrial spy. I operate a sightseeing tour, that's all."

"And your family?" the male Men in Black asked, leaning against the wall.

I shrugged. "I'm an only child, and my nearest relative lives in Alaska. Why do you want to know?"

"Just checking if there is someone we should notify as to your whereabouts." He glanced toward the woman MIB, who stood next to the table.

Feeling a best defense was an offense, I said, "Oh, I have friends who know I'm here."

"Local friends?" the man asked.

"Yes," I said slowly, wondering why they wanted to know. "Regardless of that, you can see that it was just a pure fluke that I happened to get through the gate without anyone seeing me."

"That is impossible," he said. "Our perimeter is monitored."

I shrugged, and smiled. "Not that well if I strolled in without anyone seeing me. What say we call it good and I go on my way, and you can fill in a report to the head mucky-mucks telling them that one of their employees is seducing nineteen-year-old girls."

I admit my attitude was flip almost to the point of being

rude, but I was riding high on a cloud of self-confidence. After all, I was the possessor of a magical ability that, while still mostly unknown to me, was pretty darned impressive.

If these goons thought they could confine me in this building, they were sorely mistaken.

All I had to do was focus my mind, and I'd blip away, leaving them scratching their heads at the amazing disappearing woman. Those and other such thoughts kept me relatively calm despite the situation, and I was able to look upon the MIB interviewing me with almost a clinical interest.

The man in question gave me a sour look and turned his back on me to consult with his partner, a tall woman with tribal tattoos peeking out of her shirt collar. She had an Australian accent, and although I couldn't see her eyes, she exuded a hair more warmth than her colleague.

I squirmed on the hard wooden chair that I'd been more or less forced onto, and wondered what the two MIBs—not to mention the ones who I had no doubt were watching through a large mirrored window located directly across from me—would do if I suddenly blipped out of the room.

"You will tell us the truth, and then possibly we will discuss letting you leave," the female MIB said, moving around to face me. She took a seat on the other side of the metal table that sat in front of me, bolted, I couldn't help but notice, to the floor. Suddenly, the woman took off her shades, and gave me a warm smile. "I know this seems like a frightful nuisance, but you have to understand our point of view—we have had a security breach, and it's in our best interests to find out how and why that breach was made. I'm sure you won't mind helping us figure all that out."

"Oh, you do good cop really well," I said, giving her a smile of my own. "That little throb of sincerity in your voice was particularly effective, but I'm afraid there's nothing more that I can tell you than what I already did."

I made a show of looking at the clock again before standing up. "And although I appreciate the fact that one day I can tell my grandchildren how I met actual Men in Black, I really have to be going."

"And just how do you expect to leave?" the female MIB asked, donning her shades again. "We have seen your identification and by now have run you through our databases. We have a list of your friends who live locally, and we know how to take care of them should they cause us trouble. In addition, we are perfectly within our rights to detain anyone we suspect of being a threat to the employees of Krebbs International, and I'm afraid your refusal to work with us deems you a potentially dangerous individual."

"You have no idea," I said with a little chuckle, then, with a mental apology to the confusion I was about to wreak, reached out to find the threads that let me move through space.

"She's casting a spell! Stop her!" the woman MIB instructed, lunging across the table to grab me at the same time her male buddy simply bent and swung me up and over his shoulder.

"Ooof—what the hell?" I shrieked as soon as breath returned to my lungs. It had taken a few seconds, during which time the man stalked out of the small interview room in which I'd been held, and started down a corridor, followed by his buddy. I tried to struggle, but the woman was fussing with something in her hands, something that glinted off the blue-white overhead lights that made the corridor positively glow with odd runic symbols etched on the walls. For a moment I caught a glimpse of the item in her hands, and began to struggle anew, reaching out with both my mind and hands to find the weft of space.

She jammed the needle of the syringe into my neck, making me see funny for a few seconds.

"Saint Winifred's shiny ten toes," I yelled, and tried to throw myself off the MIB's shoulder, but something odd happened—I seemed to be encased in a warm, sticky molasses, a pervasive sensation that had me slumping against the man, my brain only dimly aware of what was going on around me.

I surfaced for a few minutes to find myself half-propped against a wall in a room that was empty of everything but a toilet, sink, and metal cot, but immediately slumped down to the floor even as my fingers desperately sought to find the magic blipping place.

Time passed. How much, exactly, I wouldn't figure out until later, but all I knew was that I'd occasionally claw my way to consciousness, aware of a desperate need to find a way out of the situation, only to be pulled back into insensibility by whatever the MIB had shot into me.

A sting on my shoulder, along with the painful grip on both my arms, had me rousing again, this time to find myself being frog-marched down a hallway to a couple of elevator doors.

A young man in the standard MIB outfit looked up from a desk next to them.

"Yes?" he asked, his voice as impersonal as the rest of the stainless steel and white walls that made up the Krebbs interior.

"Dinner for the Beast," one of the men holding me said.

"Huh?" I fought to rally my wits, the haze that had wrapped around me slowly dissipating. "What? What dinner? I'm not hungry."

"Who, not what," the other man holding me said, and all three MIBs laughed just like someone had told an uproarious joke. I managed to straighten up from where I'd drooped forward, and, focusing my eyes on them, glared.

"What the hell do you think you're doing?" I asked when the man at the table tapped on his computer, and a hum came from the nearest elevator. Clearly, he'd called it to come up for us. I looked around wildly, seeing a window at the far end of the hallway. I didn't know where they were taking me, but I had a strong suspicion I didn't want to be wherever that destination was. "This is kidnapping, pure and simple, and I'm not going to stand for it."

"Trespassers get what they have coming to them," Right MIB said.

I didn't wait to debate the issue.

With a moan, I slumped down as if I'd fainted, jerked both my arms out of their hold, and, with my thumbs tucked outside my fingers, made fists my self-defense instructor had insisted would serve well, punching Lefty as hard as I could in the balls before swinging my foot up to catch Righty in the same spot.

I bolted toward the window even before the elevator dude got to his feet, slamming into someone who had emerged from a office. The woman tried to grab me, but fear gave me a speed I don't ever remember having, and I simply spun away and continued running for the window.

For one horrible moment right before I reached it, I thought I'd have to dive through it in the best action-movie manner, but luckily, I saw the catch on the window before I cut myself to ribbons crashing through the glass, and yanked it open, kicked out a screen, and hit the ground running.

That lasted all of ten yards before Right and Left MIBs caught up with me.

"You fucking bint!" Righty snarled, jerking me up from where he'd tackled me, driving me down into soft dirt. "You think you can escape? You're stupider than you look if you think you can get away from us."

"The Beast ... is not going to care if you're ... conscious or not," panted Lefty as he stopped before me.

I spat out dirt and a few oaths as the men yanked me back onto the concrete pathway. A small crowd had gathered at the window, which we passed when the two guards marched me back toward the entrance.

"This isn't over," I said, coughing with the dust that I'd inadvertently inhaled.

"It is for you," MIB on the left said, an unpleasant smirk on his now-sweaty face.

"But not before you suffer," Righty added.

"And you *will* suffer. The women always do. The Beast likes them to fight," Lefty said, giving my arm a particularly painful squeeze.

Panic hit me again, spiking through my guts with the sharpness of a razor. "You can't be serious." The panic triggered fear so palpable I could taste it on the back of my tongue. "You're going to feed me to a wild animal?"

"By the time he's finished, there won't be anything left of you but an empty shell," Right MIB said. "A pliable empty shell."

"When the Beast is done with you, you'll feel like a new person," Lefty said with another laugh. "Dibs—I get her first."

It was the way he said it that made me feel like vomiting.

"You had the last female first, and you know how I feel about sloppy seconds," Righty snapped. "It's my turn to get first crack at her."

"And this is where I nope the hell out of here," I said, my skin crawling. I had no clear idea of what I was going to do, but obviously, I was in dire peril. The last few minutes had shown that escape on my own two feet wasn't going to end well unless I had a head start. If there was any time to use a blipping superpower, now was that time.

I shoved aside all thoughts of the men, the soft noises of air-conditioning units outside the buildings, and the sensation of danger that raised the hairs on my arms, and focused my mind on one thing—escape. Without worrying about where my ability would take me, I jerked forward, momentarily freeing my hands, and, without a moment's hesitation, tore the fabric of being, diving through it with the shouts of my captors echoing in my ears.

JUNE 17, 1889

Dear Dr. Keeley Moore,

I don't have a husband, am an only child, and my dad died in a mining accident, so if you are worried that someone is showing me smut against my will—or trying to make me dress up a sheep—you can rest your obviously overworked mind.

Although I would like to put a cute outfit on a sheep. I love those little buggers, especially the fluffy white ones with black faces, and think they would look adorable all dressed up. Not that I have unsavory desires in that regard—for one, I'm female, and therefore lack the equipment to act upon any sheep-based lust, and for another, ew. I like sheep, and think it would be fun to have a wee baby lamb and dress it up, but I do not want to have sex with them, or any other animal.

You're welcome for the book. I thought you might enjoy it.

I may not be here for long—I was … er … accompanying someone to London at this particular time, and I don't know when she will be done doing her thing, so that I can accompany her back home. Regardless, thank you for the letter. It's kind of nice to chat with someone, since I'm not supposed to mess around with too many people. Just in case.

Slightly less frosty regards,
Jenna James

PS Keeley is an interesting name. I like it. What's the etymology of it, if you don't mind me asking?

FIVE

Time and space and the essence of life itself swirled around me in a miasma of chaos, but instead of finding myself twelve or more feet away from my previous position, I frowned at a slight depression in the red-brown dirt, barely visible in the faint glint of moonlight.

"What are you doing out here?"

I looked to the left of me, confused. I was outside my bedroom, in the small space that separated my house from my neighbor's. Slowly I got to my feet, feeling an almost overwhelming sense of déjà vu. "Mac?"

"Yup. Just got back from meeting with someone who has a connection for a positron collider." She strolled past me toward the back of the house, where she lived in the oversized shed that was filled ceiling to floor with machines of her own invention. "May have to tap into a couple of neighbors' meters in order to avoid The Man noticing the power consumption that will result from it, but it promises to be a sweet deal. A really sweet deal. Have fun doing whatever it is you're doing."

She drifted away, leaving me standing there staring after her, until I said softly, "This all happened last night. What am I doing here again? I already lived this—"

For a second time in the space of a few seconds, I was dumped into another inky abyss of confusion, one that spun me around a few times before I found myself falling out of nothing onto a black-and-white marble floor.

"Oomph," I grunted, the fall knocking me temporarily senseless.

"I see our last meeting has failed to impress you," a woman's voice said, high and lilting in tone, but filled with a steely edge nonetheless. "This saddens me, sister."

Sister? "Huh?" I pushed myself off the cold marble floor and looked up.

Three women sat in a row at a long table covered by an embroidered white cloth, the table set with a delicately painted china tea service. The woman in the middle poured a cup of tea and passed it to the woman on her left.

"I feel like I'm Alice visiting the Mad Hatter in Wonderland," I said without thinking, wondering if I'd gone insane.

Was it the magic blip? Maybe it did something to me. Maybe it was killing off my brain cells every time I used it.

Another spurt of panic drove me onto my feet, I looked around wildly, rubbing my forehead just as if that would help clear up my mental confusion.

Silence fell on the pleasant room. While the silence was filled with awkwardness and (on my part) worry and distraction, the room itself was a joy to behold. It could have been found in one of those glossy British magazines that featured country homes of the landed gentry, all gleaming polished wooden surfaces, big vases filled with glorious fresh cut bouquets, and floor-to-ceiling windows and French doors that opened onto an idyllic, lush garden.

It was definitely not a small town in the armpit of Nevada.

"That is interesting, but I am not sure how it is pertinent. Your name is Jenna, not Alice, and although I do have a fondness for Lewis Carroll, I am not the Mad Hatter, or even the March Hare." The woman who was obviously presiding over the table poured another cup of tea, which she passed to the woman on her right.

"Do I ..." I rubbed my head again, feeling completely adrift. "Do I know you? You know my name, but I don't remember meeting you. Or being here. Or, for that matter, where exactly here is."

"That is grammatically confused," the woman said, dropping one cube of sugar into a third cup. She eyed me silently for a moment before pouring more tea. "You do not know us?"

I shook my head, gesturing toward the open door, beyond which the beautiful green garden almost shimmered in the sunlight. "No. I've never been here. I'd remember a pretty garden like that."

All three ladies stared at me, their respective cups held motionless for a few seconds.

The middle woman set hers down with a sharp noise of china upon china, while the other two glanced at her before sipping their tea. "I find myself somewhat puzzled, Jenna Walker Boyle."

"Yeah? I'm seriously in the land of addlepated, myself," I said without thinking, looking around for a way to escape. I wasn't absolutely certain that these three women meant me harm, but after the experiences of the last few hours, I wasn't going to discount the possibility.

"Despite your statement, you *have* been here. Several times, in fact." The woman made a wry little smile. "Far too often."

"Look, I don't want to call you a liar or anything—" The two women next to Main Woman gasped. I ignored them, trying to keep my wits together in case I had to blip the hell out of there. "But I'm not an idiot. I would know if I've been here—wait, where exactly are we?"

"You are in the house of the Sisterhood of Weavers," the woman answered. "I am Abbott, the head of the order. To your right is Lemmas, and on the left is Marley. Brought together as we are, we make up the Council. We guide the Sisterhood."

"Weavers?" I shook my head, glancing at the wall where

a large tapestry hung depicting a medieval scene with a few dragons and a bunch of men on horseback. "I'm sorry, but this just doesn't make sense. I can't even knit, let alone weave."

"We are not that sort of weavers." She poured another cup of tea, gave me an assessing look, and dropped a couple of cubes of sugar in it before rising and moving around the table to bring me the cup. "Drink this."

"And we're back to *Alice in Wonderland*," I said, reluctantly taking the cup. "This is so weird. I mean, one minute those evil men were talking about doing the most heinous things to me, and the next I was déjà vu–ing harder than I ever have before, and now I'm here."

"Drink the tea," Abbott counseled, returning to the table, and gesturing toward a comfortable-looking armchair.

I glanced out of the window, hesitating.

"Yes, you would be able to leave if you knew the way out, but I believe I would like to have this situation cleared up before you depart us," she said, just as if she read my mind.

I stared at her for a few seconds before deciding that I'd just about had enough. My brain couldn't cope with much more strangeness. Instead of fighting it, I was just going to assume that everything would make sense sooner or later, and sat down, sipping at the fragrant tea.

"Now," Abbott said, folding her hands together as she leaned forward slightly. "Let us be clear on all the facts. You state that you have no knowledge of the Council, this location, or the Sisterhood of Weavers?"

I shook my head, taking another sip. The tea really was very good, strong but with a lemony hint that gave me an odd sense of comfort. I might possibly be out of my mind, but at least insanity had good Earl Grey tea.

"I see." She turned to the woman named Lemmas. "Do you have an accounting of the last time Jenna was brought before us?"

Lemmas tapped on a tablet computer. "I have accounts of all seventeen times."

"Seventeen?" I stared at her. "You're kidding, right?"

The look Lemmas gave me said much about her not having a sense of humor.

"As I said, I have accounts of all seventeen times Jenna Walker Boyle was brought before the court on charges varying from minor infractions, such as the twelve times she was caught taking mortals through the portals she created to times inappropriate to them, the four instances of taking payments from immortal beings in exchange for portal generation, and finally the last incident before today, during which she used her powers to Travel while under an interdict placed upon her explicitly forbidding the use of her Weaving abilities. Upon her summoning before the Council, she pleaded guilty with extenuating circumstances—visiting a romantic male partner—after which she suffered exsanguination."

"Exsanguination?" I grasped at the last word, none of the accounting making any sense to me. Horror crawled over me like so many spiders, my voice rising with each word. "Is that something to do with blood? You de-blooded me?"

"In a manner of speaking. In this instance, exsanguination is a term the Sisterhood uses for the removal of its lifeblood: your memory," Abbott said with cool indifference. "It is a form of punishment for those members who use their abilities for their own gain, rather than for the service of others, as is our purpose."

"You wiped my memory?" I was on my feet now, the urge to flee strong, but at the same time, I felt the need to confront these monsters. "What the hell? What the actual hell?"

"As Sister Abbott says, it is punishment for those who go against the tenets the Sisterhood holds dear," the woman named Marley said with a quick glance at the others. "It is forbidden for Weavers to Travel for their own purposes."

"Traveling meaning … ?" I asked.

Marley made an annoyed gesture. "Traveling is better described colloquially as joyriding through time for one's own pursuits. Since such acts usually have a specific purpose, the punishment is to remove the Weaver's memories of the visit, thereby negating the results of their misdeeds."

"You people are nuts," I said after a few seconds during which I was speechless. "Even if I was this Weaver person that you say I am, all I can do is small blips. Nothing more than twenty or so feet."

"And yet, you just took it upon yourself to Travel back approximately fifteen hours."

"I did? You mean the déjà vu thing a few minutes ago? That was actual time travel?" To say my skin crawled was an understatement, but while part of my mind was shrieking to get away from the obviously crazy people, the other part was whooping with joy. I could time travel! "Wow. I had no idea. I mean—that's seriously badass. But that's not really joyriding. It certainly doesn't give you the right to wipe my brain!"

"On the contrary, it gives us every right." Abbott plucked a grape from a plate, chewed it, and gently dusted her fingertips on a snowy-white linen napkin before continuing. "If we did not have the harshest of repercussions for misuse of a powerful ability, one that is highly desired and which leaves the Weavers at risk of abuse, either by themselves or by others, then the mortal and immortal worlds would be rife with chaos."

My brain continued screaming that none of this made any sense, and I needed to get out of there immediately. But at Abbott's words, something caught my panicked mind's attention and resonated in a way that I couldn't ignore. It was as if a jigsaw puzzle piece snapped into place with a satisfying click.

A series of images flashed in my head like a film on fast-forward: a woman standing in front of me in what I thought of as medieval garb, gesturing toward a garden, while behind her, a curved stone tower rose.

A group of small, dirty children, bare legged and armed, chasing a leather ball as they ran down a cobbled street, running smack-dab into a couple of men wearing Elizabethan doublets and ruffs.

A dark-haired, beautiful man with pale gray eyes lying on a bed, lifting a hand—my hand—to his lips in a poignant kiss.

"Holy cats," I said on a breath I hadn't realized I'd been holding. "I'm a time traveler. An actual bona fide time traveler. This is so much cooler than just blipping a few feet! Holy everlasting cats and dogs!"

The last few words were shouted, echoing in the refined room.

"It would appear," Abbott said after a moment's uncomfortable silence, "that the exsanguination that was conducted upon you during your latest transgress was performed … improperly."

"Well … yeah. It's completely wrong to take someone's memory, no matter what they've done," I said, still grappling with the realization that I was filled with a strange ability that opened up literal worlds to me. Mac was going to have a fit when I told her! No doubt she'd demand I take her all sorts of places to see important scientific discoveries. "She is so going to crap her pants," I said aloud.

Abbott cocked an eyebrow. My cheeks warmed at the inadvertent comment.

"You might consider the punishment for misuse of your Weaver abilities as wrong, Jenna, but I assure you that they are wholly in line with the rules that govern our house, rules which, I need not add, you yourself agreed to when you became a Weaver."

"I did? Oh. Well … I must not have known better," I said rather lamely.

"The exsanguination is intended to remove only those memories acquired during the Travel through time and space, not your memory of anything to do with the Sisterhood," Abbott continued, ignoring my comment. "For you to be unaware of who and what you are for—" She paused and glanced at Lemmas.

"Er … the original interdict was put into place one hundred thirty-one years ago," Lemmas said after tapping around on her table.

My jaw dropped a little until I realized that it was leaving me staring like an idiot. "What the hell? I'm not a hundred and thirty-one! I just had a birthday and I'm only thirty-six."

"No, you are not. You were born—" Another tap at the tablet. "In 1922."

"But—I remember my life. Remember having birthdays for at least the last ten years."

"Yes, well." Lemmas slid a glance toward Abbott. "That would be the improperly applied exsanguination. It was rendered when the interdict was renewed in 2011."

I looked down at myself. I was ninety-nine years old? But how could that be when I looked and felt and remembered being thirty-six? "Wait, that doesn't fit. If I was born in 1922, how could I get in trouble a hundred and thirty-one years ago?"

"I admit that your personal timeline is a bit odd, and I would not mind having my memory about it refreshed," Abbott said with a slight nod to the left. "Marley?"

"Yes, of course," that woman said, pulling out her own tablet and consulting it. "The original interdiction was placed upon the subject in 1889, which date she had Traveled to in the course of her business with the Weavers' Guild. Later, she admitted to Traveling there three more times on her own, and without express permission of the guild, in order to visit a romantic partner. On the last occasion, she was summoned before the Council, and the interdict was placed upon her, whereupon she was restored to her current time, which was then 2002."

"So I was born in 1922, and when I was … what, like eighty years old, I went back in time and hooked up with someone, and got in trouble for it?" I asked, wondering if I should take notes.

It all seemed so very confusing.

"Yes. An exsanguination was conducted at that time, as per our rules," Abbott said, her gaze serene. "It appears that did not disturb the balance of your mind. Unfortunately, the interdiction appeared to wear off nine years later, and it was the exsanguination performed at the interdiction renewal in 2011 that, for lack of a better phrase, went awry."

"I don't understand this," I said a little plaintively.

"That's what happens to those who Travel," Lemmas said primly, and picked up her teacup again. "Their chronology becomes skewed and twisted back upon itself."

"I guess I'm just confused about what exactly a Weaver is. You said we time travel, so why did I get in trouble for doing that?" I asked.

"It is our job to aid those who have received approval to Travel to times past," Abbott said, her voice soft yet with a thread of steel in it that had me sitting up a little straighter. "We do not Travel on whims, or because we met someone interesting in the course of our duties. Such events would bring havoc and chaos to the world. The guild is very strict about the circumstances that must be met in order for an individual to engage our services."

My thoughts were so tangled it was a wonder my brain could even function. I was a super-old, blipping Weaver person? I thought of passing out in sheer, unadulterated shock. I thought of tearing out my hair and screaming that none of this was possible. I thought of just walking out of the room and finding my way back to my safe, if not quite sane, life.

Instead I sat back down, crossed my legs, and strove for an attitude of nonchalance. "OK. I'm old. And I can time travel. I had a Victorian boyfriend. That's all kind of weird, but I'm going with the flow. Why am I here now, though?"

Abbott looked a bit pained. "Under normal circumstances, use of your Weaver abilities while you are under interdict would result in an expurgation."

I stared at her in blatant incomprehension.

She sighed to herself. "Expurgation is the permanent removal of your abilities, and banishment to a place of punishment where you will remain for the rest of your time."

A cold, clammy fear grasped me at that. I'd only just discovered I was a time traveler, and now they wanted to put me in jail? "And interdict?" I asked.

"It is a prohibition bound unto you. The interdict itself should stop you from using your Weaving skills until such time as it is lifted, but somehow, you have done what should be impossible and destroyed the interdict. I find that very interesting." The look in her eye was speculative, and not entirely friendly. "That you are still alive tells me you were involved in an event of extraordinary power. Would you tell us what that was? For our records, you understand."

"Event of extraordinary power?" I repeated, rubbing my forehead again. It was a self-soothing habit that I had long tried to break, but now seemed not the time to work on that. "I don't have—wait, you mean the fireworks that Mac exploded? Those knocked me back, and burned the fake hair of one of the tourists, but it wasn't really powerful. I mean, no one was hurt. Well, I was half-blind for a bit because of the dazzling light, but my vision came back within fifteen minutes or so."

Abbott looked thoughtful. "Describe this firework explosion, please."

"There wasn't much to it, to be honest. Mac said she got the fireworks from some guy on the Dark Web—she loves that place—and that the seller promised that it was something special that would knock everyone's socks off. I think she said the name on them was Arcane something. Arcane Wrath? It wasn't a very pretty firework, really, just a big explosion of blue-and-white light."

"Arcane Wrath," Abbott said on a half sigh, giving her buddies a portentous look. Lemmas tapped on her tablet, no doubt adding that information. "I should have known it would have to be mage-based in order to destroy the interdict."

"OK, I understand some of those words, but not all, and that's kind of annoying. Did you say mage like the magic guys in video games?"

"I said mage, yes, but I mean the immortal beings who are masters of arcane magic. What this Mac person purchased was, I suspect, an illegal spell. You are lucky that any mortals with you were not harmed, since the spell had enough power to damage the interdict. It was that which allowed you to Travel."

"So this interdict thing that got blown off by the fireworks ... magic ... *whatever* ... is basically a type of ankle bracelet that keeps me from using my time travel stuff?" I shook my head. "Do I even want to know how that works?"

"It would serve no purpose," Abbott answered. "The fact remains that you were forbidden to use your Weaving abilities, and yet you did so. Such a blatant disregard of the punishment bound to you cannot be disregarded."

Frustration and anger fought each other for control inside of me. "But I didn't know any of that," I protested, shoving down the notion that I might not have cared even if I had been aware of it all. Just thinking about those two evil MIBs made me sick to my stomach.

Abbott inclined her head. "It is for that reason—the incorrect application of the exsanguination that removed all of your memory rather than those pertaining to your prohibited Travel, and the fact that you did not deliberately remove the interdict—that I am willing to allow you another chance."

I had gotten to my feet while she was speaking, and now sagged with so much relief that I had to grab the back of the nearest chair. "Oh, thank you—"

"However," she interrupted, pinning me back with a look that I felt stripped a few years from my life span, "be warned that this is an extraordinary circumstance, and not one which will be repeated. A new interdict will be placed upon you, after which you will be prohibited from Weaving. Hear me, Jenna Walker Boyle—if you remove the newest interdiction and Travel, or use any of your related abilities, we will have no choice but to exsanguinate you and send you to the Akashic Plain, where you will remain in punishment."

"Akash-what, now?"

I swear she was about to roll her eyes, but evidently she had a steely control over such things, for she simply tightened her lips for a few minutes before answering, "It is what mortals think of as limbo. It is a place of banishment. Take heed of my warning, and do not force us to send you there."

I opened my mouth to say something—just what, I didn't know—but before I could so much as squeak an answer, I was once again thrown into a swirling miasma of chaos.

"This is the one," I heard Abbott say. I had fallen to my knees, and looked up, getting somewhat drunkenly to my feet.

Before her, a tall man with cold, pale blue eyes stood considering me. Judging by the slight curl of his lips, he didn't like what he saw. "She destroyed the previous interdiction? I will wish details of the removal."

"I will naturally send them," Abbott said, inclining her head.

"Hey, now," I said, staggering to the side, my head still spinning. "What—"

"This interdiction I place upon you," Cold Eyes said, sketching a symbol in the air before my face. For a second, a sharp pain dug into my brain, leaving me breathless and momentarily stunned.

I pitched forward into an inky abyss that seemed to open up at my feet, Abbott's voice coming from a distance. "I sincerely hope she does not remove this one. It is her last chance. . . ."

Sound roared in my ears, while the ground lurched and heaved beneath my stumbling feet.

"Who, not what," came a man's voice, cutting through the confusion and blackness that temporarily obscured my view.

Hard fingers bit into both my arms. I realized with horror that whatever the man with the cold eyes had done had returned me to the moment before I escaped the building in the Krebbs compound. Once again, I was being marched in to be torn to shreds by some horrible beast.

I stared with rummy confusion at the man who sat next to an elevator tapping on a computer. He looked up and frowned just as the doors slid open.

"Wait—this isn't right. Don't I escape?" I asked him as the men hustled me into the elevator.

"Escape? There's no escape here," the MIB on my left said, a cruel glint in his eye.

Slowly, the last of the confusion ebbed in my brain, and I realized I'd just missed my opportunity to run as I'd done before.

And this time, I couldn't blip my way out. Not with the interdict that Cold Eyes had slapped on me.

I slumped as the men hauled me down the hallway. What the hell was I going to do now?

SIX

To: Roxy, Ellis

Guys, exciting things are happening! We're in the US because … wait. Going to do this literarily. Is that a word? It should be.

OK. Here we go.

"Can you be ready to leave in two hours?" Merrick asked yesterday afternoon.

Kelso and I (Kelso is my white shepherd who I found abandoned in Italy, Aunt Roxy) were lounging around the pool, which Merrick doesn't normally like to do with us unless the sun is not quite so bright, but once he appeared, Kelso and I sat up.

"Sure," I said, pulling off my sunglasses so I could see Merrick's face better. He looked worried, which in turn made me worried. "Where are we going?"

"The US." He started to go back into the house, but by then Kelso and I were up and following him, Kelso in hopes that Merrick would take him for a walk around the neighborhood (something that Merrick actually likes, although he refuses to admit it) and me because vampires may be sexy as the day is long, but man, do they have issues with dishing the important info.

Sorry, Ellis. No offense intended.

To: Tempest, Roxy

None taken, darling. Go on with your story. And please tell me I get to read your book when you're done writing it, especially the parts where you pant and sigh over Merrick.

To: Roxy, Ellis

That's just because you want to pant and sigh over him, too.

To: Tempest, Roxy

Of course I do. The man was made for pantage and sighage.

To: Roxy, Ellis

You'll get no argument from me. You should see his bare chest. Hoo!

To: Ellis, Tempest

Once again, I am forced to say *snicker*.

But I second the literary lauds, Tempest. Please do go on.

To: Roxy, Ellis

And his thighs. I mean, thighs on a man shouldn't make your mouth water, should they? And yet, Merrick's thighs … er … sorry. Got a bit distracted by a thought. Where was I? Oh, the trip. Right.

"Why? Did you guys find this Thrall dude?" I asked, going into the bedroom to start pulling out some clothes and stacking them on the bed. "What part of the US? I don't know if I should pack for warm weather or cold."

"Nevada. California. Possibly Utah," he answered, tapping on his phone, no doubt setting up our travel arrangements.

"So warmish weather. Did you find the Thrall?"

"No. Possibly. Han found a record that indicates the Revelation is running a research facility in some small town in Nevada, using a dummy corporation to hide it. There's a rumor that they are doing something very secret there. Han thinks it has to do with the Thrall. We're going to check it out."

"Awesome. I don't suppose you'll let me in on the actual

action this time?" I put on my best puppy dog eyes, but Merrick is impervious to them.

"It's too dangerous. If the Revelation took you—" He stopped speaking and turned away, but I felt the anguish in him. It had me dropping the suitcase I'd just dug out of the closet and moving over to wrap my arms around him, my face pressed against him.

"They won't ever take me away from you," I promised.

I won't cover the next half hour because I couldn't possibly discuss something like bare naked frolics with Merrick in front of my aunt and bestie, but you can take it as read that I reassured Merrick that nothing would part us, even if it meant I had to let him handle the dangerous stuff.

Two hours later we dropped off Kelso at his favorite doggy-daycare place (the woman has two little girls who love him, and always beg for him to spend time with them), and flew to the US. We got here this morning, met with Han and Ciaran and Andreas.

"We will see what is going on at this laboratory," Merrick told me once we found a hotel in a very small town. "Would you do a little research for us?"

"Of course," I said, saluting and pulling out my laptop.

Despite what Ellis may tell you about me being a stranger to technology because of my upbringing, I have much Google-fu. "What do you want looked up?"

"Helots," Merrick told me.

"Huh?" I asked, and waited for him to spell it for me.

"It's the Revelation's word for the slaves Han's informant told him they were making." Merrick gave the back of my neck a little tickle before donning the long duster coat and fedora that all the vamps wore when they went out into sunny weather.

"Via the Old One," Han said with a curled lip as he also slipped on a hat. "All the more reason to take care of him."

"Slaves?" I entered the word, but looked up, confused. "Why would they want slaves? Slaves like the Vikings had, or enslaved black people that were brought to the US?"

"A slave is a slave is a slave," Ciaran said, and went out to get into one of the two cars they had rented.

"I suppose so, but I still don't understand why the Revelation would want them."

Han and Andreas left, leaving me with Merrick.

He pulled his brow together, clearly thinking hard. *Are they making slaves from you vamps?* I asked.

No. I don't think so. According to Han's informant, it sounds like the slaves originate from the Thrall, which would fit in with the lore.

"That worries you, doesn't it?" I said, leaning into the hand caressing my cheek.

"Yes."

"Why?"

The hum of the air conditioner was the only sound for a full minute. Then Merrick sighed and said, "Because if that's true, then it increases the likelihood of the rest of the lore being true. If the Revelation has been using this Thrall to make slaves—helots—then he could well be close to Breaking."

I made a face, standing in order to kiss Merrick. "You remember our deal: I let you do the dangerous stuff, and you make extra sure you are careful and don't get hurt."

He smiled, and my soul lit up with happiness. "Trust me, the last thing I want is to leave you alone in the world. There's far too many Dark Ones who would be on you in a second if I wasn't around to keep them away."

That's not true, by the way. But he likes to pretend that I'm some sort of femme fatale. So I sent him on his way with only three more reminders to be careful, and then I dove into the world of helots.

I found squat. Sigh.

To: Ellis, Tempest

Sigh indeed. I just love a good romance. Keep at it, kiddo. I'm sure you'll dig out something for that vamp of yours!

19 JUNE 1889

Miss Jenna James:

My overworked mind is relieved to know you have not been forced to act as an ovine procuress, and I do agree with your statement regarding Scottish Blackface sheep—they are charming when dotted about the hillside. I do not, however, share your desire to dress them up. I suspect that is something unique to you. Or you and the author of the book which you pressed upon me.

I appreciate the interest in my name, but I assure that it is not in the least bit uncommon or worthy of calling out. Further, I have no information as to why my parents named me Keeley. My mother was from Madras, India, and unfortunately died while giving birth to me, and my father did not long survive her, so I am unable to ask them.

Since you have been so kind as to offer me a book you thought I would enjoy, I would like to return the favor, and am enclosing Carmilla. *It is an unusual book, but as you are an equally unusual woman, I suspect you will enjoy it. Regardless, I look forward to hearing your thoughts on it.*

Respectfully,
Keeley Moore

SEVEN

Keeley had almost convinced himself that he could achieve a coma state by willpower alone, but just as he had slowed down his breathing and heart rate to an almost undetectable level, a bang on the door jerked his awareness back to reality.

"Dinner, Beast. You'll like this one," Tennyson said, throwing a body at him. He barely had a moment to glimpse a woman in a taupe linen tunic and jeans before she slammed into him, knocking the infinitesimally small amount of air remaining in his lungs out, and banging her head on his in a manner that had him seeing stars for a few seconds. "Go ahead and chew her up well. We have plans for her afterwards."

"What the hell—" the woman on top of him moaned, and partially sat up, one of her knees digging painfully into his groin. "Ow, my head!"

For a second, Keeley thought he might be able to reach Tennyson before the latter injected him with the dread concoction, but while he was trying to extricate himself from beneath the woman, pain bit into his shoulder, spreading across his chest in a burning heat that was all too familiar.

"Run," he managed to say, his voice more a croak than anything else.

"Huh?"

The woman slid off him, spinning around to face the door just as Tennyson and his bastard friend slammed it shut. "Run where?"

Keeley's soul wept with the futility of it all. The cocktail of drugs that the madmen used to trigger the bloodlust now roared through his body, forcing a response that was impossible to refuse, and yet, he struggled to do so every time. "Nowhere. It's too late now. If you believe in a god, I'd advise you to pray now, because I'm told that later you don't have the mental wherewithal to do so."

The woman turned toward him then, and for a moment, he felt as if time had come to a screeching halt. He knew that heart-shaped face with freckles scattered across light brown skin. He knew the silky hair that seemed brown, but was instead filled with so many different shades, varying from dark blond to cocoa, that it seemed to shimmer and change color with each movement of her body. And he knew her eyes, the very same eyes that had once stirred the dark shadows of his soul, and promised salvation. They were also brown but, like her hair, carried flecks of gold and red that seemed to glint even in the dull light of his cell.

It was Jenna. *His* Jenna. The woman who had torn out his heart a hundred and thirty years before, stomped all over it, and left him a bitter, angry, soulless shell of a man.

Until a hundred years later when the madmen found him, and turned him into a monster.

"You're … you're not an animal," Jenna said, studying him with an oddly clinical gaze. "They said they were feeding me to a beast—"

"Animal? *You* call me an animal?" he snarled, the pain of her betrayal cutting deep into his being. "It is you who have treated me with inhuman callousness—"

"Me?" she squeaked, looking stunned.

He didn't have time to process the mantle of perfidy she had dared to don, for just then the bloodlust fully hit him, slamming into his gut, forcing him to double over on the bed, fighting the need that drove him into fulfilling his birthright. "Stay … back … ," he managed to get out between panting breaths, wanting to save her at the same time he wanted to make her suffer for her cruelty. "Door."

She glanced around her, backing up until she was pressed against the metal door, watching him with mingled amazement and horror as the bloodlust drove him to his feet, fighting the chains that bound him to the wall. Agony ripped him apart from the inside, rending from him both his will and his civility, leaving him with one purpose—to consume.

"Oh my god, you're in pain, aren't you? What did they shoot into you? The stuff they gave me just made me sleepy." She started toward him, one hand held out just as if she was going to comfort him.

He wanted to yell at her to get away, to stay back where he couldn't reach her, at the same time he wished desperately to tell her he saw through her deception. As if the pain of the bloodlust weren't enough, his heart and soul, those poor beleaguered objects, cried in anguish at the thought of Jenna returning to finish the job she'd started so long ago.

The bloodlust overrode those emotions, however, claiming every ounce of his attention. He knew that even if he could save her damned traitorous hide, Tennyson and the other guards would simply shove her within his sphere of reach, and then all would be lost.

He wanted to explain that to her, but it was impossible. He couldn't speak. He could only hope she had enough self-preservation to remain out of his reach against the door. Perhaps there was some way she could escape when Tennyson returned …

"You're bleeding. Those bastards have you chained up. Hang on. I have some tissues—" She moved forward while reaching into a pocket, pulling out a blob of white that fluttered to the ground when he lunged, the bloodlust firmly holding him in its grip.

She squawked, fear flaring to life in her eyes as she started to struggle.

Dammit, he hated that fear as much as he hated what she'd done to him. A sense of protectiveness that he had thought long dead sputtered briefly to life despite the bloodlust, allowing words to be uttered in a strange, guttural voice. "Sorry. Don't want—"

The smell of her drove him beyond bearing. It was both familiar and strange to him, but it sank deep into his bones, driving the bloodlust into an even greater frenzy.

With a noise that he knew was all too similar to a savage growl, he breathed on a spot where her neck met her shoulder, the scent and feel of her flesh too much for him.

He bit, aware of her gasp of pain, fighting the drive to take her, possess her in the most fundamental way a man could take a woman. Sexual lust fought with the bloodlust, while memories of the love she had spurned danced in and out of jumbled images in his mind.

Jenna looking up at him with laughing eyes.

Jenna promising that she would never leave his side.

Jenna not bothering to even bid him good-bye when she walked out of his life.

He was taking too much of her blood. He wanted, almost as desperately as he wished for his own life to end, for her to be punished for what she'd done to him, but he had always been an honorable man, and even though circumstances had spelled disaster for her, he could not bring himself to punish her.

"Dear goddess, that was … hoo!"

He bent over, struggling to regain control, praying that would be enough to satisfy the bloodlust.

It wasn't. It never was.

With another savage growl, the unbearable urge that possessed him drove him to bite his own wrist.

"What are you doing?"

Her eyes, which had been smoky with what he realized was passion, widened with horror when he stood and wrapped one arm around her, holding her against him in a grotesque parody of a lover's embrace even as he grasped her neck with his bleeding arm, the blood from his wrist mingling with that from her shoulder.

"Holy crack on rye!" she screamed into his collarbone, trying simultaneously to shove him back and get her knee up to unman him. "What are you doing? You bit me! Hard! Oh my god, are you bleeding on me?"

The bloodlust ebbed, finally satisfied that he had fulfilled his purpose of being, and with that, reason and control slowly returned to him.

For a moment, he was grateful that this hadn't been the moment of Breaking. He knew he was close, so very close, but at least he had been spared that for another day.

"I'm sorry," he said, releasing his hold on her neck, and loosening his grip on her. "I would like to say that you deserve this, but I would not wish this damnation on even my worst enemy."

"*Deserve* this?" She backed up and held a hand to her shoulder. "Why would I deserve you to bite me so hard you drew blood? What have I ever done to you?"

He collapsed back down onto the cot, his body drained. The struggle to control the bloodlust, to refuse its demand, always left him shaking with exhaustion. "You can drop the attempted deception, Jenna. I am in no state to put up with your lies."

"Lies!" She looked first outraged, then furious. "I don't lie! Which, let me tell you, is a right pain in the ass when a friend shaves her head and asks you if she looks like Uncle Fester, and she does, but you can't lie outright and say she doesn't, so you have to find something else to focus on."

He stared at her in mingled disbelief and anger. "What are you talking about? You don't have an uncle."

"No, I don't!" she almost yelled at him, then gave him a long look. "Hey, you know my name. How do you know who I am and that I don't have an uncle?"

"I told you not to bother trying to deceive me," he said, gathering about himself the sense of injured, righteous pride that he'd worn for over a century. "You may wish to pretend the past did not happen, but that won't make it go away."

"The past?" She froze for a few seconds, her eyes wide. "Oh no. Do I know you? Or rather, did I know you at some point?"

His lips thinned. He wanted badly to rail at her, but to what end? In a minute or less, she'd be a mindless drone used by the madmen for their own purposes, and he'd be returned to his state of living hell. Of the two of them, he didn't know who would be more miserable. "You could say that."

"Oh man. I'm so sorry. You see, it turns out that I have a … well, kind of a special talent."

"You are a Weaver," he said despite his intention to simply ignore her until the change took hold of her mind.

"That's right!" She gave him a bright smile that somehow seemed to bathe him in a sense of warmth. "I'm so glad you know about that, because trying to dance around it was going to be difficult. Anyway, this woman named Abbott wiped my memory after I did something—or seventeen somethings, I'm not quite sure what other than a comment referring to me as joyriding through time—and I've basically been a poster child for amnesia since then. So I'm sorry if we knew each other before the brain wipe, but I'm not lying to you about anything; I just don't remember you."

What was this? His first urge was to immediately scorn such a ridiculous idea, but a memory of Jenna telling him about how she'd been in trouble with the head of her Weaver organization in the past made her outrageous statement a little more believable. "Why would they wipe your memory?" he asked, not even trying to keep the suspicion from his voice.

Her shoulders twitched. "I gather they were supposed to remove the memory of whatever it was I was doing in the past, but instead, they did a full hard drive wipe. Which, let me tell you, is way out of line, because it means I've spent forever without the coolest ability ever, and I want it back. How … er … how well did we know each other?"

"Does it matter?" Keeley closed his eyes and leaned back against the wall, mentally adding up all the innocents he had enthralled. How many more would he be forced to damn before the Breaking? And would the sin of turning Jenna, the woman he had loved beyond all reason, end up finally driving him insane?

"It does to me," Jenna said with an irritated sniff. "I get that you're bent out of shape because I don't remember you, but you don't have to be rude. Why did you bite me? And what's your name?"

"Keeley," he answered before he realized he had done so. He opened his eyes and looked at her, puzzled.

"Keeley?"

"Keeley Moore." He narrowed his eyes. "How do you feel?"

"Me?" She dabbed at the bite on her shoulder, but all that remained was a faint smear of his blood. "My head hurts where it hit yours. And my shoulder is a bit pinchy where you bit me. Which, by the way, was totally uncalled for, but I assume that had something to do with why the Men in Black called you the Beast. Oh man, you didn't just give me rabies or something? Because I have a needle phobia, and if I have to do a bunch of shots, I'm going to be seriously pissed."

She looked it, too. She appeared at the same time irate, annoyed, and wholly, utterly delectable.

No! he mentally shouted to himself, even as a detached part of his mind was more than a little surprised that she wasn't at that moment on her knees, screaming in agony as his blood changed her into a mindless slave. No, he would not notice how delectable she was. He had given in to her lure once, been swayed by her promises of eternal devotion, and ended up betrayed, tormented, and alone.

But it wasn't her fault, that annoying sane voice in his head pointed out. *Not if the Weavers removed her memory.*

He shoved that thought down, telling himself that what could happen once could well happen again. He'd never give her that power over him again. "Why are you talking?"

She looked simultaneously appalled and furious. "Dude! That's the rudest thing I've heard in a long time. I guess the reason they call you the Beast is because you have no manners!"

"You misunderstand," he said, making a gesture that did little to express his confusion. "Not why are you speaking to me. I like you doing that." He closed his eyes for a few seconds, annoyed that the last sentence had slipped past his guard. "What I meant was, why are you speaking when you should be rolling on the ground in torment as your will and autonomy are burned out of you?"

She touched a spot on her breastbone, her eyes as big as those of a startled doe. "My autonomy? I don't want to be rolling on the ground in agony for anything, let alone losing my autonomy. What exactly did you do to me when you bit me? And who the hell are you?"

"*Who* I am relates to our past, and is unimportant," he said, firmly ignoring the desire to take her in his arms and kiss her the way that used to leave her breathless. "*What* I am now is far more important to you. You don't feel the slightest bit unwell?"

She was silent a moment, obviously taking stock, then shook her head. "No, as I said, my forehead hurts a little, but that's all."

"Hmm."

The analytic side of his mind thought about that. Perhaps it was because she was meant to be his Beloved, the one woman in the world who could salvage his soul?

Or it might be that her Weaver genetic makeup disturbed the transition. He made a mental note to investigate the subject of her genetics at the earliest possible opportunity, since it might open up a path to a cure for the slaves, but then remembered that he had no future. There would be no opportunity to do anything but suffer and cause suffering. If only he could end his existence, then, at last, he might have some peace.

And what about Jenna? the dark side of his mind whispered. *Are you such a monster that you could leave her to the madmen?*

He pushed those thoughts away, telling himself she had been the one to abandon him.

"Just out of curiosity, why do you want to take my autonomy from me? Does it have something to do with our past? I'm getting a bad vibe from you, like you're pissed at me about something, but as I've said, I don't remember you, so if you are mad at something I did in the past, would you please accept my apology, and move on?"

"No," he said succinctly, and, to change the subject, announced, "I am a Thrall."

"Oh, you're the guy that Britt mentioned." She looked thoughtful for a moment, then to Keeley's utter surprise sat down next to him on his cot, and patted him on the leg in what he was sure she thought was a comforting manner. "You're supposed to be some sort of a not-vampire, aren't you? Wow. This is kind of amazing, don't you think? I mean, if you'd asked me yesterday if I believed in time travelers and vampires and vampire-light guys like you, then I'd have said you had spent too much time consuming funny mushrooms, but here I am, taking it all in my stride."

"You are an odd woman," he said, completely taken aback by the fact that even without her memory, she didn't appear to be afraid of him. "You weren't this way when I knew you. Then you were … quirky, yes, but not odd. You are now odd."

"If you had your memory wiped, I bet you'd be a bit off-kilter, too," she told him, and gave his thigh another pat.

"What are you doing?" he asked, looking down at his leg. It felt warm and slightly tingly where she'd touched it.

"Explaining to you that I don't remember you. What's a Thrall when he's at home?"

He opened his mouth to tell her she must be insane, closed it when he realized he couldn't say that, and said instead, "It's me, isn't it? I'm the one who's insane. One of the deities I was entreating decided to answer my pleas, but instead of killing me outright, they made me insane, instead. Bastards."

"You wanted to kill yourself?" Jenna was silent for a moment; then to his surprise (and secret pleasure), she wrapped her arms around his torso, and pulled his head to her chest. "I'm so sorry that you feel that way. I don't have any training in counseling people who feel like you do, but I want you to know that I'm here, and that you are wanted and needed, and have importance in people's lives."

He blinked a few times, his face pressed into her cleavage. For a moment, memories swamped him, and he gave in to the pleasure of her touch, of the feeling of her soft breasts caressing him, of her scent, which always reminded him of a clear summer morning. But then reality pressed in, and he pushed himself out of her hold.

"If you do that again," he said sternly, intending on warning her against touching him, but what came out of his mouth was something wholly unexpected. "I will lay you down on this cot, strip your clothing off, and make love to you in a manner that you used to tell me left you walking funny."

Her eyes widened again even as he damned his lack of control—or the insanity with which the unnamed deity had evidently smote him—but her pupils dilated in a manner that indicated she was as aroused as he was. "You … that is … dude! Hoo! I mean, really? Right here? Not that I'm saying I would, but man alive, I have to say, it's kind of an interesting idea. Although not one appropriate to say to someone you just met."

"I met you more than one hundred and thirty years ago," he corrected. "And shortly after that, you swore eternal love and devotion, promised to redeem my soul, and then promptly abandoned me, leaving me near death."

"I did not!" she said, standing up and looking outraged. "I couldn't have done something so heinous."

"And yet, you did." He eyed her. "That, however, isn't what concerns me. I am most curious as to why you aren't changing."

"Into what?"

"A helot." He made an awkward gesture. "The madmen call them slaves, but that's just another name for a slave, one who has been enthralled."

"And that's what you tried to do to me?" Jenna looked horrified.

"Yes," he said simply, waiting for her to scream at him for the injustice of it all. He felt it was penance to watch those he was forced to harm suffer, their agony tearing away bits of his life force just as surely as the bloodlust destroyed his sanity.

"Why would you—oh." She stopped suddenly and eyed his chains, then sat down next to him again, and gave his leg yet another pat. Once again, she surprised him, her gentleness touching parts of his being that he had thought long dead. He fought the need to kiss her, reminding his long-dormant libido that she may have been the one person who could have saved him—back when that was an option—but now it was a moot point. "I'm sorry. It's obvious you don't want to be here. What did they shoot you up with?"

"A drug that I very much would like to get hold of," he said, shifting slightly to the side in an attempt to move away from the warmth of her presence. He had to put some distance between them in order to focus, to keep the painful memories of the past and the futility of the present uppermost in his mind. "What, if you don't mind me asking, are you doing here? How did you come across the madmen?"

"The Men in Black, you mean?" Her shoulders slumped. "I was trying to save a friend's daughter who has been lured away by one of the employees. Do you think I'm not a hel-op—"

"Helot," he corrected.

"Helot because I'm a Weaver?" She thought for a moment. "And what did you mean I abandoned you rather than redeeming your soul? You don't have a soul?"

Just her nearness was making it difficult for him to remain focused on his rage. Unable to keep from doing so, he wrapped an arm around her, and pulled her up to his side, the heat and softness of her body pressed against him acting like a balm to his savaged being. "I do not. As the former you knew, I was born an unredeemed Dark One, without a soul. You were my Beloved. You swore to remain by my side until the end of our days, but then you left me. At the altar, as a matter of fact, since you insisted we be married."

She stared at him with open-mouthed amazement, and if he'd had any suspicion that she had lied before, he knew now that she'd been speaking the truth. The shock and distress shone too brightly in her eyes to be manufactured. "Keeley, I'm sorry. I'm so, so sorry that my brain was wiped just when you needed me. But wait, Dark One. I've heard that term before. It's a...?"

"Dark Ones are what mortals like to call vampires, although we are not at all like the modern conception of such beings."

"So that's why you were all bitey," she said, her expression changing from delighted to annoyed. "Boy, that really toasts my cheese. I love vampire books! And to think I had one of my own to enjoy, but the Weavers made me screw the whole thing up. I'll lodge a complaint with Abbott and the others, although I'm not sure what good that will do. Long story short, I got in trouble for time traveling without permission to see you. They yeeted me back to my then-present, which was 2002, after which they wiped my brain. They did another brain wipe and some weird anti-magic thing around 2011 when the previous interdiction wore off, but the new one went bad and took out all my memories, not just the ones of you. What about you? I assume your life went on after they yanked me from your time?"

"Yes," he said, refusing to remember just how much pain he suffered after she had abandoned him. "It went on."

Without any hope.

Or light.

Or reason to live.

"I'm sorry," she told him, her eyes dark with emotion.

"It's not like I can change the past. Although, I suppose if I really *can* time travel …"

"I would caution against thinking that way," he said, touched by her obvious distress despite the sane part of his mind warning him from falling victim again to her bright, shining self. Just because she appeared at the darkest time of his life didn't mean anything. She was as doomed as he was. "It's likely to cause even more problems."

"I suppose so," she said, slumping into him, one hand absently stroking his thigh. "It's really a shame that you had to suffer for something that wasn't of your own doing. However, I've never been a crying-over-spilt milk sort of person, so what we have to do is figure out how I can help you now. Obviously, you need to get out of here."

"I do. However, if you keep touching my cock like that, I really will make love to you right here and now."

She stared at him for a few seconds, her pupils once again dilated. "I'm not touching your penis," she said, glancing down at where her hand was resting on his thigh. The tips of her fingers were resting against his now straining fly. "Oh. I … uh … I appear to be wrong about that. I didn't mean to, though. I mean, I don't often touch men I've just met, let alone grab onto their noogies. Wow. You are really packed in there, aren't you? It looks painful."

He closed his eyes for a moment, well aware that, despite his statement, she hadn't moved her hand, which just made him even more aroused. His libido, awoken after more than a century, now raged through him just as the bloodlust had done earlier, forcing him to struggle to keep from stripping the once love of his life naked, and reacquainting himself with all her delights. "The word painful doesn't begin to describe it. Jenna."

"Keeley," she answered, swaying into him, her breath warm on his cheek.

"If you do not remove your hand from my cock—"

"You'll make love to me right here, right now?" she asked, leaning a little farther into him until her lips brushed his.

He fought the urge to grab her and kiss her as she deserved, to strip the breath from her lungs with the force of his passion. He had to fist his fingers in order to keep from touching her, stroking her silken skin, to renew his memories of just how well her body fit against his. "Yes."

"How about I just kiss you, instead?" she asked in between light little kisses that fluttered across his mouth.

He closed his eyes again, drawing every ounce of strength he possessed to keep from claiming her as his body desired. She was his Beloved, the one woman in all of time meant for him, the one whose life was irrevocably joined with his.

Except she wasn't. That Jenna lay in the past, and this one … this one had no future. Not with him.

Why not? the troublesome part of his brain asked, and a dawning realization struck him that although he might prefer death to the life he was forced to live, Jenna probably felt differently. And if he was not there, who would protect her from the madmen?

It's not my problem, he told himself. *I'm too dangerous. The Breaking could happen at any time.*

He rejected that idea before it finished forming.

Even as he reluctantly acknowledged the fact that he could not leave Jenna to suffer if it was within his power to help, there was no future to be had with her. He was simply too great of a risk to remain in her presence.

He'd have to find someone else to take up the role of protector. Someone he trusted, someone who could guard her where he could not.

"No," he answered, leaning into a snap decision. "No kisses. No leaning your soft, enticing breasts against me. No stroking my thigh, and for the love of any god of your choice, stop touching my cock!" If there was the slightest chance that he could get Jenna out of there before the madmen found that she hadn't been changed, he had to take it.

He might not be able to make love to her as his body, mind, and heart demanded, but he would move the stars and planets themselves to find someone who could keep her safe.

He ignored the painful fullness in his trousers and got to his feet before gesturing to her. "Up."

"Why?" she asked, slowly rising from the cot, disappointment rife in her eyes.

"What do you have in your pockets? Anything we can use to pick a lock?"

She patted her pockets, shaking her head. "They took away my house keys."

"Peste," he swore, eyeing her hair. It had been pulled back into a ponytail, no doubt with an elastic band. That would do him no good.

"Wait, I have this." She reached up and extracted from the top of her head a hairpin. Immediately, a cascade of hair fell down over her forehead. She pulled out a second hairpin, then blew upward, adding, "I'm trying to grow out my bangs. Will a couple of bobby pins work?"

He could have whooped with joy, but a man as tormented and tortured as he was never whooped, let alone with joy. "Yes," he said, taking the two objects from her, immediately bending one into an L shape.

Before he could bend the tip of the other pin, the ground seemed to tremble slightly, followed immediately by a dull roaring noise that was audible through the ventilation hatch near the ceiling of his cell.

"What the hell was that?" Jenna asked, staring up at the grille covering the hatch. "An earthquake?"

Keeley closed his eyes for a moment, listening intently, his nostrils catching the faintest whiff of a scent that spiked fear deep into his gut.

"Smoke," he said, jamming the bobby pins into the lock holding the chains to a bolt on the wall. "That's smoke. There must have been an explosion."

"Er …" An odd expression passed over Jenna's face, one he couldn't pinpoint beyond wariness. "Explosion? Are you sure?"

"No, but it would account for the tremor." He met her gaze for a few seconds before returning his attention to the lock. "I don't want to frighten you, but you should know the truth. The complex is likely to be on fire, and we're trapped in here."

"Oh goddess. I didn't think she would set the place on fire. I mean, I wasn't absolutely sure she'd do anything, although I did tell her to meet me at a specific time, which has to have been hours ago, so she'd have to know that I'd been caught when I didn't show up. But to blow up the place?" Jenna paced the length of his cell, her hands gesturing as she spoke. "That's a bit extreme, even for Mac."

"I assume Mac is your lover?" The words were out even before he realized it, and he made a mental note to have a long talk with himself about speaking without first thinking. It must be a result of being caged alone, with no one to talk to, for so many years.

"No!" she said, still pacing and waving her hands around. "I don't happen to swing that way. I mean, I would if I wanted to, but I haven't met a woman who rings my chimes. Or a man, for that matter." She stopped pacing and slid a glance toward him. "Although it sounds like I did at some point."

"You did." Keeley spoke with a grim finality that was all too probable if he didn't get them out of the cell that had suddenly become a death trap. To his relief, the last pin clicked into place, and the lock sagged open. He pulled the chain free from the wall bolt, and set to work on the smaller locks holding the shackles closed.

Jenna stopped pacing to loom over him, watching as he manipulated the shackle locks. "Mac is my friend. She's … kind of unique. Eccentric. Maybe a little bit mad scientist, but in a good way. She never tests her equipment on anything living that's not herself, first. Even if you get free, how are we going to get out? The door is locked. Can you pick it, too?"

"Possibly. Hopefully."

"And then?"

"If there's been an explosion and fire, assumedly we will be able to escape in the resulting pandemonium."

"Oh. That makes sense. Especially if Mac is looking for me." She watched him closely as the first shackle fell from his wrist, saying, "I've never seen anyone pick a lock. I'm amazed you can do that with just two bobby pins."

"You have seen it. You've done it," he said, frowning as he worked through the pins on the second lock. "I taught you myself."

"You did? Dammit, that Abbott has a lot to answer for, wiping all my cool memories. Was I any good at it?"

"No."

It took four minutes, but at least he was free, but not without the sense of urgency increasing until Jenna was pacing the floor again, alternately asking him if he couldn't hurry up, and demanding to know how they would escape.

It took him another six minutes to get the door lock opened, but at last they emerged into the hallway.

Right into a group of the madmen's guards.

JUNE 20, 1889

Dear Keeley,

Oh my god! You like vampire books, too? How cool is that?

I have to admit that this wasn't like the ones I normally read, but still, I had no idea that they had gay vampire books in Victorian at this time.

Thank you so much for the book. Maybe you'd like to have a coffee sometime and talk about the book?

Man, why isn't it 1897 yet?

Also, have you ever heard of Weavers?

Excitedly,

Jenna

EIGHT

I will say one thing for Keeley: he may have been chained up in a cell for an indeterminate amount of time, but that incarceration didn't seem to cause any loss in muscle tone, let alone reflexes.

"Ack!" I screeched when we escaped his cell only to run into a herd of five MIBs who were in the act of tearing down the hallway. I had a brief moment's hope that Mac's explosion—and I was dead certain that she was responsible for whatever had happened to set everyone in a panic, since that was her modus operandi—I hoped that the MIBs would be so deranged by the explosion that they would ignore us emerging from a cell, but that thought died a cruel death when three of the five immediately tackled Keeley.

The two others headed for me. I didn't hesitate even a second to consider whether it was smart to go against what Abbott had said; it seemed second nature to reach out and find strands of space and slip through them a few yards until I was behind the two men. I kicked at the back of the knee of the nearest, sending him pitching forward into the wall, which he collided with before rebounding into his friend, who had started to turn around toward me. I caught him in the chest with another kick (mentally thanking my self-defense teacher for going above and beyond by teaching women extra ways to protect themselves), which knocked him into the first MIB, resulting in the pair crashing to the floor. One grabbed the other, using him to get to his knees, but I simply punched him in the windpipe before repeating the action on the second one. They collapsed back, stunned.

I spun around to help Keeley, but he was down to just one MIB, the other two lying on the floor, both unconscious and bleeding from their noses and mouths. The remaining MIB, however, snarled something in a language I didn't know, a wickedly long dagger flashing before he stabbed it into Keeley's shoulder.

A red haze of fury seemed to wash over me, and I mentally swore an oath at the Weavers for stripping me of most of my abilities.

"No!" I screamed, and again reached for the fabric of space, appearing on the MIB's other side, trying to remember where the vagus nerve was located, but before I could do so, Keeley—with a grimace of pain—yanked the dagger from his shoulder and slammed the hilt upside the head of the MIB.

"Oh my goddess, you're hurt!" I rushed to Keeley even as the MIB hit the floor to join the others.

"It doesn't matter," he said, glancing first in one direction, then the other. We were in the middle of a long, antiseptic hallway, now quickly filling with smoke. Alarms sounded in the distance, as well as voices shouting and a couple of gunshots. "Quickly, we must leave before more of the madmen find us."

He turned and ran to the right.

"It's this way," I yelled, dashing off to the left, in the direction I remembered from earlier. I spun around a corner, saw three men in long black coats, all wearing fedoras that shaded their faces, menace rolling off them as they stalked down the corridor, and immediately did an about-face, racing back the way I'd come. "More Men in Black on the way!" I shouted as I leaped over the bodies lying on the floor, catching sight of Keeley just turning a corner at the far end of the hallway. I stumbled for a moment when I glanced back at the bodies, wondering at the fact that I was able to blip when Abbott and the tall man had said they were interdicting me, but I shoved that thought down. It wasn't important at that moment—what mattered was to get Keeley to safety.

I caught up to him as he hesitated at an intersection. Blood soaked the side of his shirt, leaving a dark red trail on the slick white floors. "Keeley, I know you don't think it's a big deal that you've been stabbed, but you're losing a lot of blood."

"I'll survive," he said, pushing me to the left, down another hallway. "I think the lab is this way."

"The lab? What lab? If you want a doctor, we need to go upstairs, where there are probably fire trucks and aid units."

"I'm not leaving until I find the lab. This is the only chance I'll have to get a sample of that drug they use on me to trigger the bloodlust, not to mention whatever they did to make me a Thrall," he answered, his voice a growl. Smoke was rolling down the hallway now, leaving me coughing, with burning eyes and an almost unbearable urge to drag Keeley up the flight of stairs we passed as he ran down the hallway.

We found a couple more MIBs as we hunted for the lab, but they were too focused on getting out to worry about us. One stopped to stare as we approached, reaching in his jacket for a weapon, but Keeley's fist punched out as we ran past, snapping the man's head back, sending him into the wall with a nasty crunching sound.

"Man, I wish I had the upper-arm strength to do that," I panted behind Keeley as he yanked open a door, dashing inside without a look back at me.

"Hey, who are—ack!"

The voice that spoke from inside the room sounded familiar. I peered inside, then shouted as Keeley lifted by the neck a woman standing at a small refrigerator. "No! Keeley, that's Mac!"

"Jenna?" Mac, who flailed one arm, sounded like she'd swallowed gravel. He set her down, hard enough that it rattled a small rack of glass tubes held in one of her hands. Her gaze flickered from Keeley to me, even as she coughed a couple of times and said hoarsely, "I knew it! I knew they must be holding you prisoner here. Who's Chokey McChokerson?"

"His name is Keeley, and he says he's a Thrall, although I'm not one hundred percent sure I understand what that means."

"A Thrall? You're a Thrall? An actual Thrall? The progenitors-of-vampires kind of Thrall? The guys who explode when they make too many Thrall Babies?" Her eyes widened as she stared at him.

Keeley looked momentarily offended. "We don't explode. We simply go berserk, and become a threat to the mortal and immortal worlds, causing endless death and untold savagery until we are ritually destroyed by means of a triumvirate of a demigod, a demon lord, and an archimage. And do not call the slaves we make *Thrall Babies*."

"Why?" she asked, tipping her head to the side, a familiar gesture, since Mac has an almost endless well of curiosity. "Is it demeaning? Non–politically correct? Kind of rude?"

"No. I simply don't like the term." His eyes narrowed on her. "You are mortal. How do you know so much about Thralls?"

"Hoo," I heard Mac say under her breath. "And you're bleeding. That means your blood could … hoo."

"Hoo what?" I asked, moving around the counter so that I was in front of Keeley. "I second Keeley's question. How is it that you know what a Thrall is and I don't?"

"You don't hang out on the Dark Web like I do," she said absently. I couldn't help but notice the speculative look she gave first Keeley, then his bloody arm, but I didn't have the time or energy to ask her what she was thinking.

Keeley made a disgusted noise and turned away to begin searching the lab.

"That's what a Thrall is? An explodey, vampire guy?" I couldn't help but ask. I hated feeling like I was the last one to find out things. "Why didn't you tell me?" I asked Keeley.

"You didn't ask," he answered without looking up from the drawers of a chem table he was yanking open and examining.

"Well … that's because I had no idea what to ask. Wait, Mac, if you and your creepy buddies know about Thralls, do you know what a Weaver is, too?"

"Of course I do. Weavers time travel and can summon portals." She pursed her lips. "Although my friend Tito—he's a moderator in a white hat hackers group I'm part of—he said that there aren't a lot of Weavers around anymore, because they muck up the space-time continuum. Not sure I believe him, because he also said that Thralls all went dormant about six hundred years ago, and Bitey Boy here is proof that's wrong."

"'Bitey Boy' is almost, but not quite, as offensive as 'Thrall Babies,'" Keeley said in a near growl.

"You and your Dark Web buddies," I murmured, shaking my head. "What in the name of the good, green earth are you doing here? That *was* your explosion, wasn't it?"

"Of course it was," she said, a smugly pleased expression fading when she watched Keeley rip open the door to the fridge and start extracting the vials inside. "Did you think I was going to let those Men in Black get my bestie? Hey, Mr. Thrall, I don't know what you're looking for, but the creeps who were in here when I arrived cleared out everything that looked important."

Keeley spun around to look at her, his eyes narrowing. "You saw them?"

"Yeah, two women stuffing things in a frozen gel pack case. A couple of men left just as I hit the hallway, but you know how men are." She made a face. "The women didn't say much, just told me to get out while the getting was good."

"Peste," Keeley swore, then asked her, "What are you doing?"

"Saving Jenna, of course," she answered.

"I told you about Mac." I looked out of the door, coughing. There was no one to be seen in the hallway now, but the smoke was getting thicker, and visibility was dropping. "She's my friend. That's beside the point—we really need to get out of here."

"What are you doing here in the lab?" Keeley asked again. His eyes were dark with suspicion. "Do you have anything to do with the madmen?"

"Not that I know of, although some of the guys in the Illuminati underground crew are a few carrots shy of a stew," she answered, her tone conversational despite roughness from being nearly throttled. "I'm here because this is where the Men in Black keep their bioterrorism weapons. You don't think I'd let the opportunity to get in here pass me by, do you?"

"*I* certainly don't," I said, knowing my friend all too well. "But we have to get out. Keeley's been stabbed and … oh man, you're bleeding all over the floor. We have to get you to some medical aid."

He looked down at the floor, frowning at the splashes of blood that followed his path around the lab. "It's not important."

"Like hell it isn't," I said, sighing to myself and reaching underneath my tunic to unhook my bra. It took a moment of struggling before I pulled it free, and headed toward Keeley with it.

"What do you think you're doing?" he asked, backing up a step as I approached.

"I'm going to bind your wound so you don't leave a blood trail for the MIBs to follow us. Dammit, stand still and let me wrap my bra around you!"

"You do realize that I'm a physician, yes?" he said in a haughty tone. "And, as such, am quite able to evaluate the wound."

I paused for a second. "No, I didn't realize that. Have you always been a doctor? That is, were you one when we first met?"

"Yes."

"Really? Why? You're a vampire—you're immortal, aren't you?" I shook away the questions even as I asked them. "Never mind, it's not important."

"Perhaps not to you, but it was to the many mortals who I helped," he said in that same half-distracted, half-annoyed tone.

"Regardless of your medical knowledge and immortal status, your shoulder has to be bound or you'll end up leaving a clear trail." I approached him again with my bra.

The expression he bore said many things, most of which gave me a bizarre urge to laugh, but he did stop trying to avoid me and allowed me to peel back his shirt. It was sodden with blood, so I tossed it on the counter. A long, jagged gash sluggishly oozed blood, running down his arm and dripping from his fingertips. I folded the bra cups into a pad and bound it to him, then snatched up a discarded lab coat and helped him slide it on over his bad arm. "The bra straps are stretchy and will hold it tight to you until we can get you seen to. Boy, your aftershave is really nice. Kind of spicy, like frankincense."

"I'm not wearing any aftershave, and as I've told you repeatedly, I'm fine," Keeley said, irritation evident in his voice. "Mortal medical treatments are unnecessary, which you would know if you'd remember me."

"Well, I don't, so you're just going to have to tolerate wearing my bra on your arm." I let myself sniff the air a couple more times, the scent of Keeley's soap or whatever it was that he used that left him smelling so good, tiny molecules of it sinking into my pores and filling me with a strange sense of need. I shook that away, and tried to focus on what was important. "Mac, stop pocketing things. You don't know what the MIBs have been doing in here."

"Something heinous, no doubt," she said, poking around on the table. Out of the corner of my eye, I saw her cut off the blood-soaked arm from Keeley's shirt, stuff it into a large stoppered beaker, and add some sort of pale liquid, but before I could ask her what she was doing, Keeley snarled a profanity.

"I should have known that the deities wouldn't leave me so much as a drop of the drug," he all but spat, slamming shut doors to two other fridges after examining the lack of contents. "They've cleaned out everything useful."

"Well—" Mac started to say, but Keeley stormed out of the lab without waiting for her to finish.

I looked at Mac. She looked back at me, saying, "He's an odd one. What did he mean about you not remembering him?"

"It's a long story, and yes, he is," I answered, then ran out after him. I had a fear that he was deranged due to profound blood loss, and wanted—for some reason that I couldn't fathom beyond normal human kindness—to get him the help he needed. Mac was on my heels as we caught up to Keeley, who was peering down an intersection. Smoke billowed down it toward us.

"It'll be no good looking for the second lab now. Hold on to me," Keeley commanded, one hand on the wall, no doubt so he wouldn't get lost in the smoke.

I grabbed the back of his lab coat with one hand, and Mac with the other, my eyes and nose streaming, my lungs now burning as smoke choked me. Grayish-black splotches started to form in front of me as I desperately tried to get untainted air into my body. Just as I felt like I was about to pitch forward into the same black abyss that had swallowed me when the MIBs shot me up, a steel band curled itself around my waist and, with a pained grunt, hauled me up several flights of stairs.

By the time we reached the main floor of the building, I was alternating coughing while gasping for air, fighting the same red wave of emotion that had hit me earlier and an almost desperate need to tend to Keeley's hurt, all while holding a stitch in my side.

Mac, damn her svelte hide, was barely breathing hard, while Keeley, wounded as he was, looked as if he'd just had a lovely stroll instead of half-carrying me up six flights of stairs. We burst out into a small lobby that was empty of people. Keeley deposited me on a hard wooden chair, squatting down next to me to peer into my face.

"Can you breathe now?" he asked. I was too out of it to read his expression, but I thought I heard a thread of concern in his voice. I nodded, still gasping in great lungsful of mostly untainted air. The air system must have been piping the smoke into the lower levels, while the aboveground one was spared. Need, desire, and an intense sexual awareness wrapped around me, blurring my vision for a few seconds.

"Jenna?" he asked, his hand warm on my arm.

I turned my head and, before I could stop myself, bit his thumb.

He jerked his hand back, an expression of astonishment making his eyes wide, all while his pupils dilated.

"Oh, goddess," I said hoarsely, clearing my throat against the smoky rasp. "I'm so sorry. I don't know why I did that. Did I hurt your thumb? It must be the drugs they gave me earlier, because I just want to do things to you that I shouldn't be thinking about, since I just met you a short time ago."

He made an annoyed sound and got to his feet, moving over to a black desk that had been pushed askew. "I've told you a number of times that I'm fine, my thumb included."

"There's fine, and then there's bleeding all over the place and thinking you're fine, but really, you're delusional because there's not enough blood to get oxygen to your brain," I said roughly, coughing a few more times before I managed to get to my feet. Thankfully, the strange red tint to my vision seemed to fade. I was surprised when I rounded the desk to find two men lying crumpled on the floor, moaning and twitching as if they were dreaming dogs. "What the ... ?"

"Sorry, my bad. Had to take them out in order to find out where the lab was," Mac said, stepping over them.

Keeley yanked a laptop on the desk around to face him, typing furiously with one hand.

I glared first at the way he held his hurt arm close to his chest, then at the trail of blood that still followed him. "Fine, my shiny pink behind. Right, let's get you some help."

"I don't need medical aid," he murmured, his attention on the laptop.

I tottered to the door and opened it to peer outside at the rest of the Krebbs compound. Although black smoke was visible billowing upward, the buildings nearest us didn't appear to be on fire.

Distant shouts and calls drifted over to me, along with the muffled but persistent sound of an alarm going off somewhere nearby. "I don't suppose you've seen Britt, have you, Mac?"

"No, but there were three helicopters that took off right as I was placing the explosives, not to mention a veritable caravan of black vans peeling out of here, so I have no doubt she was with them."

"Dammit! I can't believe the little rat called the guards on me. Well, I'll have to deal with her later. Right now it looks like it's all clear—"

Just as the words were leaving my mouth, a small group of people rounded the corner at a trot. I stared at them in surprise, then turned back to Mac. "You brought the tourists with you?"

"Didn't have time to take them back to town," she said, obviously distracted as she stood next to the two unconscious men, frowning down at them, fingering something in her jacket pocket.

"Mac! Tourists!"

"Huh?" She looked up. "What about them?"

I pointed to the group of five women when they came to a halt at the door. "You brought our customers to a bombing. A *bombing*, Mac."

"So?" She leaned to the side to look around me. "You guys had fun, didn't you?"

"It was awesome," one of the two vloggers—I think she was Madison—said, spinning around so she could film herself standing in front of me. "We got it all, everything from Mac placing the devices, to the building walls collapsing in on themselves."

"That video is guaranteed to go viral," the other young woman added, holding up her selfie stick to film us. I had a vague memory of Mac telling me her name was Tucson, but that seemed rather unlikely. I made a mental note to ask her later.

"I thought it was overdone," Mrs. Walsh said with a sour look and a sniff. "All those electronics and fussy things. All you need is a couple of quarter sticks of dynamite. My brother used to go fishin' with quarter sticks of dynamite. That'll take care of any problem, that will."

I watched them for a moment, then looked back to Mac. She was kneeling down by the two unconscious men, her back to me. "I'm holding you to blame when these people send us bills for therapy."

"You're fussing too much," Mac answered, poking at one of the MIBs, and to my surprise pulled out a syringe.

"What do you think you're doing?" I asked her in a whisper.

"Just a little experiment I saw talked about on a forum devoted to whistleblowers. One of the guys claims to have worked for some group that was doing weird-ass things to vampires, and I just bet you I know what he's talking about. Don't worry, I'll make sure these guys are on board with it first," she whispered back.

"With what? Wait, I don't have time, but you do know that you're way too deep in all the questionable stuff you find online, yes?" I said, adding with obvious warning in my voice, "Just don't do anything to get us into trouble."

"Pfft," she said, and pulled out a sealed beaker from her pocket. "As if."

I looked back at the tourists, and sighed to myself. Far from looking traumatized, they looked happy and excited. I decided that if they were willing to go along with the adventure, then I should just embrace it, and turned back to deal with my biggest concern. "Keeley, we really should get you out to the paramedics. Assuming there are some, and I can't imagine why there wouldn't be any."

I moved over to him as I spoke, my gaze on his face, trying to assess just how close he was to passing out. *And why are you so worried about him?* a little voice in my head asked, but I told it to go talk to the voice that was asking why I was able to blip if I had an interdict on me, and instead put my hand on his good arm. "Keeley? What is it you're searching for? If I promise to help, will you let a doctor look at you?"

"I'm in premed," Lolly called from where she'd joined Mac, who had turned around so that she was facing the wall, her hands moving busily. I assumed she had yet another of her weird devices, but figured the MIBs deserved anything she dished out to them. "Do you need help?"

"No," Keeley answered, forestalling me as I was about to ask her to eyeball his wound. He frowned at the laptop for a moment, then turned and looked at the door, holding out his uninjured hand for me. "It should be the next building over. Come."

"What's the next building over? The paramedics?" I asked with another assessing glance at his face. His color was a little pale, but he didn't look the deathly white I was expecting. For one, like me, he appeared to be of an ethnicity that leaned toward a darker skin tone, and for another, there were two spots of faint color high on his cheekbones. I took the hand he offered, one side of my mind happily squealing to itself about the way his fingers twined through mine. "That would surprise me if they were. I'd imagine that all the emergency services are set up by the front gate."

"We aren't going to the gate. At least, not yet. Not until I've had a look at the director's office," he answered, pulling me out the door past the group of tourists.

"Mac?" I called, glancing over my shoulder as Keeley turned to the left.

"Be right there. Just taking care of a little problem," she answered without glancing up.

The tourists fell into place behind us. "Who's that?" I heard Tucson ask her friend.

"Dunno, but he's going to have every woman over the age of sixteen thirsty as hell," Madison replied.

"Not to mention a lot of guys," Tucson agreed.

"This is Keeley," I said, half-turning even as the man himself tugged at my arm. "He was a prisoner of the Men in Black that run this place. As you can tell by the blood trail he's leaving everywhere, he was injured when we had to fight some of the MIBs in order to escape. Also, I'd like to point out that as a rule, Outta This World Tours does not condone violence in any way, shape, or form."

Two MIBs dashed out of the building we were passing, immediately swerving toward us upon sighting Keeley.

He dropped my hand, did a spinning kick that sent the first one slamming back into the glass door through which he'd just come, punching the second in the face before the first one even hit the ground.

"Unless, of course, the people in question are inhuman monsters, in which case, all bets are off," I amended, gesturing at the group as they paused to take pictures of the fallen MIBs, and a few more of Keeley. I wondered if it would be bad form to ask for copies of the latter.

"This is the best tour I've ever been on," Lolly told Beth. "It beats the underground-sewer clown-coven tour by miles."

"And considering how good their taco bar was, that's saying a lot," Beth agreed.

I wanted to ask them just how the taco bar was set up, but at that moment Keeley tried the door of another of the innocuous low buildings, finding it locked.

With a martyred sigh that I could hear a few yards away, he simply kicked the door in the lock a couple of times until the metal crumpled.

Mrs. Walsh, who was stopped next to me, eyed first the door—which Keeley yanked more or less off its hinges—then the man himself before turning to me. "I'm gonna give you four stars. You lost one for that crappy lunch and leaving us with your insane driver for three hours, but the rest of this tour is rock solid."

"Thank you," I murmured, following Keeley into the building, avoiding shards of glass from the destroyed door, and bits of twisted metal on the doorframe itself. I donned my tour leader voice to add, "Mind your step here, people! The footing is a bit unstable. It would appear that Keeley is taking us into an administrative building, although I have many doubts that we'll be able to find the medical aid he needs here. However, this does offer us the opportunity to see just exactly how the Men in Black run this company."

Keeley, who was proceeding down a narrow corridor between two rows of cubicle walls, paused to look back at me. "Are you giving these people a tour of the madmen's lair?" Disbelief was rife in his voice.

I made a vague gesture toward them, half-apologetic, half-self-righteous. "Mac has a good point. They are enjoying themselves, and it would be stupid to ignore things that might interest them just because we happen to have been held captive and are in the process of escaping. That would be bad business."

"We're social media influencers," Madison said, filming Keeley with her phone. "We have a combined total of over one million peeps on TikTok. We can make or break a business."

I eyed her, wanting to dispute that fact, but decided now was not the time to burst her particular bubble. Besides, I had an uncomfortable feeling that she might well be right.

I swear Keeley was about to roll his eyes, but instead he sent a glance heavenward and muttered something about some deity having a lot of fun at his expense, before he stalked down the rest of the aisle, heading straight to the only office with proper walls and a door.

Like the other building, this one was empty of personnel, although as I hurried after Keeley, I was braced and ready to find someone in the office. Instead, I found him at the desk, ripping open the drawers, snarling to himself in what sounded like Latin. A computer power cord lay coiled on the top of the desk, clearly having once been plugged into a laptop.

"What exactly are you looking for?" I asked, stopping at the door to watch him yank out drawers and dump the contents on the table.

"Data," he said abruptly.

"What kind of data? That is, data in what form? A hard drive? Laptop? Tablet? Cell phone? Hang on, do you know what those are? How long have you been imprisoned?"

"I was captured in 2001, and yes, I know what a mobile phone and laptop are. I also know what a flash drive is, any of which I'm looking for," he answered, flinging various papers and office accoutrements from the desk in order to upend the next drawer.

"Oh. I guess that stuff was around then," I said, prodding the dark spots in my memory. Why had it never occurred to me that I couldn't remember before 2011?

"Some of it. But the madmen allowed me to have those devices on a limited version of intranet. I couldn't explore the Internet, but I am fairly conversant with modern technology."

"Gotcha." I watched him for a moment, noting the blood that was still running off his fingertips. Mentally, I warred with the desire to tell him he could kill himself by being stubborn if he so desired, and the need to save him from himself.

The desperate need in me to help him won out. I turned around to face my group of tourists, clapping my hands for attention. "All right, ladies, we're looking for a flash drive, or any piece of technology that can hold data. Let's search the cubicles."

Obligingly, they scattered, Beth telling Lolly, "This is so exciting!"

"It is, although I don't know what we're looking for. Wouldn't it help if we knew what we were supposed to be finding?" she answered from a cubicle.

"Information on a company called Revelation," Keeley called from the office. "Or mentions of a man named Alphonse de Marco. Alternately, anything to do with Thralls."

"The who, now?" I turned around, my hands gesturing with vague motions as I tried to find something to do to help Keeley.

"Revelation. It's the name of the organization the madmen belong to. De Marco is their head, or so one of the more talkative guards said."

"This is like an escape room meets Agatha Christie," Beth said excitedly, emerging from one cubicle and dashing into another.

I went to the nearest desk and started searching for anything informative, but evidently all the employees here had time to remove their respective computers, for I found nothing but the usual detritus one would expect in desk drawers.

"Hmm."

I stood up, a box of assorted sticky notes in my hand, to peer over the wall into the office. "What sort of a *hmm* was that? A good *hmm*?" I asked Keeley.

He stood with a small silver metallic box in his hands, turning it over as he examined it. "It's a *hmm* of possibilities. This is apparently some sort of a lockbox. If you were the director of an organization bent on enslaving mortal and immortal beings, what would you put in a small, portable lockbox that evidently bounced under a chair during what I can only imagine was a hurried evacuation?"

I thought for a moment, then smiled. "Details of my nefarious plans?"

"Let's hope that is so." He glanced around the room but didn't seem to see anything else he liked. "I believe this is all we will get. I must find a car. Do you have one?"

"I have my tour bus—but I can't leave without Mac." I followed after Keeley as he started down the aisle toward the front doors. "Ladies, I believe we're leaving. This way, please. Mind the glass and razor-sharp stabby bits of metal."

The group assembled and trotted after us. Mrs. Walsh had a big brown paper bag in her arms.

"What do you have there?" Beth asked her, trying to peer in the bag.

"Saltwater taffy. Someone here had a sweet tooth, and finders keepers," Mrs. Walsh said with a righteous sniff.

We emerged into the smoky sunshine. A few buildings down I could see a small knot of people, none of whom bore signs of being anything but emergency personnel.

I scanned them, looking for Britt, but didn't see anyone who resembled her. Mac must be correct in that she'd gotten away earlier.

"Where is your bus?" Keeley asked just as Mac ran around a corner, two men on her heels.

"Mac! Behind you!" I yelled, trying to get around the clump of tourists in order to help her, but Keeley was faster. He took one look in her direction, narrowed his eyes on the men behind her, and started toward them.

"No, no, go the other way! These guys aren't bad—they're mine!" she yelled, gesturing us on. "But there's a couple of badass MIBs on our tail!"

"What do you mean, these men are yours?" I asked, confused. The two men behind her looked like MIBs, although they'd lost their shades, suit jackets, and ties, and the expressions on their faces were identical ones of besotted affability.

"They're my drones. My Thrall Babies. My whatever-Keeley-calls-them," she answered as she raced past us. "I made them!"

I looked at Keeley. "Did she just say she made Thrall Babies?"

He did roll his eyes then, but, gesturing at the tourists to proceed, took me by the arm and ran after the others. "Yes, and I'd like to know how she managed that, but at this moment, we must get away before the director returns."

"What makes you think he'll—" I glanced over my shoulder as a shout sounded behind us. The same three men I'd seen before in fedoras rounded the corner and ran after us. "Ack! Never mind, we can talk about it later. Run, ladies, run! Baddies after us!"

The two vloggers whooped with what I thought of as inappropriate joy as we bolted through the crowd of fire units and other first responders. "This is so cool!" Tucson yelled to Madison.

"I think we should make a found-footage film out of this," she answered. "We'll make millions!"

"What's a Thrall Baby when it's at home?" Mrs. Walsh asked no one in particular, puffing loudly as she ran ahead of us. "Is it alien? Or spooky? I like spooky. I wouldn't mind a spooky Thrall Baby all my own."

"You run a very odd tour," Keeley said as we ignored inquiries from the medics, heading through the gate and following Mac when she turned to the right, running parallel to the outer fence.

"You know how immoral it is to make slaves," I lectured Mac when I caught up to her, puffing loudly and making yet another mental note that I really would have to renew my gym membership. "The very name tells you how wrong it is, not that I understand how you knew how to do so. How did you make them? Keeley has to do the bitey thing on them to make them go mindless."

"I told you that I read about it on the Dark Web. I learned a lot of things from the guy who said he worked with a group—probably related to these guys—who did all sorts of weird experiments on vampires. He said a simple solution of saline and infected blood was enough to half turn people. They aren't the same as what a Thrall makes, evidently. These guys are just kind of ... persuaded ... rather than forced into the role," she answered, flashing me a grin before turning to look over her shoulder. "Guys, you don't mind being my devoted squad, and doing whatever I want you to do, right?"

"That's right," one of them said in a Russian accent, never taking his gaze from her.

"We live to serve you," the other said at the same time, his mouth moving in an odd manner that I realized was him making kissy-lips at her.

"Do I want to know what you intend on doing with—" I started to ask.

She waved away the question. "Later. Those three dudes

with the hats are some sort of super-level MIBs. You should have seen them tear through a gang of about a dozen regular MIBs who came up from the floors below."

My gaze went to Keeley. He moved with apparent ease, but I noticed lines of pain around his mouth, and the unnatural way he held his arm. He had to be about at the end of his strength. Once again, I was overwhelmed with a desire to tend his wounds, and make him comfortable.

And bury my face in his neck to breathe in deeply of his delicious scent, possibly biting the tendon on the top of his shoulder that suddenly seemed to hold an unholy fascination for me.

I wondered about this odd man whom I had evidently been ready to marry. Although he seemed familiar on some level, for the most part he felt like a stranger.

At that moment he turned to ask Mac, who was next to him, "Where is the tour bus?"

Mac pointed at the Moon Cave parking lot, which was a short distance away. "It's the big green monstrosity there."

Without seeming to realize he was doing so, Keeley hesitated a moment until I caught up with him, taking my hand in his before we continued to weave our way around cars and a couple of other tour buses.

The feeling of his fingers on mine brought me both reassurance that I hadn't known I was needing and a strange sense of wistfulness that formed as a small, hard ball in my chest.

How on earth was I was going to make up my past behavior to Keeley?

And assuming I managed that miracle, did that imply we had a future together?

22 JUNE 1889

Jenna:

Please return my coat.

Yours,

Keeley

JUNE 23, 1889

Dearest Keeley,

You said I looked good wearing it. Besides, I like it. It smells like you. I think I should keep it.

XXO,

Jenna

24 JUNE 1889

You did look good wearing it, mostly because you were not wearing anything else as you stood straddling me on the bed, but that doesn't mean I'm going to give you my favorite coat. Please return it immediately. I'm cold without it.

Yours,

Keeley

NINE

"I have questions."

Keeley looked up from where he was studying the lock on the front of the small lockbox, and noted Jenna looked simultaneously annoyed and adorable.

He fought the urge to take her into his arms and kiss away the slight frown between her straight brown brows, instead mentally shaking his head at his errant emotions. He had no future with her. He had to keep that uppermost in his mind. "If they concern the subject of whether or not your hairpins will be able to open this, the answer is no. This is a different type of lock, and I will need actual lockpicks to deal with it."

"You can borrow mine," Mac said as she marched out of the bathroom, heading for the door that Jenna, during the brief tour of the small house where she lived, had indicated led to the backyard.

"You have a set of lockpicks?" he asked, a little surprised.

"Doesn't everyone?" She waved at the two men who currently sat on Jenna's couch watching a TV. They had risen when she started to leave, but sank back down when she pointed at the couch and said sternly, "No. Anton! Dima! You boys sit and stay. Watch the TV."

"They aren't dogs, Mac," Jenna said, her annoyed expression fading long enough to pin back her friend. "They're human beings, and should be treated with respect, although we clearly need to have a talk about the fact that you decided to make yourself a couple of helots."

"That is a conversation I would very much like to be a part of," Keeley said, his attention returning to the small silver fireproof case in front of him lest he give in to his body's urges and kiss Jenna silly. "The explanation you gave me on the ride here seems questionable at best. I have no doubt that my blood plays a role in the creation of helots, but if it was as easy as simply mixing it with saline, they would have no need for me."

Mac was shaking her head before he finished. "I told Jenna these weren't the same type of slaves. For one, these guys consented to be Thrall Babied. And for another, they retain their own will. Don't you guys?" She called the last sentence to the men on the couch.

"Yes," they both answered in unison.

Jenna watched them for a few seconds before asking Mac in a near whisper, "Are they going to—for lack of a better word—pop back to normal MIBness?"

She pursed her lips and thought, then gave a half shrug. "Swan—he's the guy on the forum who said he worked with the vamp program—didn't mention them doing so. He just said it was more like they were very easy to persuade, but they weren't the same as the true slaves."

"What do you think?" Jenna asked Keeley, obviously worried about Mac's experiments. Keeley knew how she felt, although it did ease his mind that the men had agreed to Mac making them her male harem.

"About them?" He turned back to the small metal box. "Since I have never heard of a partial helot, I assume what she says is a possibility, even if it seems unlikely to me. But I have limited knowledge of what the madmen were doing, and right now, I'm more concerned with getting this box open."

"One set of lockpicks coming up," Mac said, and hustled out of the door.

"What do you think is in there?" Jenna asked, clearly interested. "Info about what drug they gave you?"

"That, and hopefully details about exactly what steps were needed to take an average Dark One and make him a walking time bomb. If we are very lucky, it will also contain the names of those people they forced me into turning. Not that there is a hope for changing them back, but perhaps we might be able to locate them and free them from the monsters who are obviously using them for heinous purposes. Why does your friend keep her lockpicks in your backyard?"

"Hmm? Oh, the she-shed is back there," she answered with a vague wave toward the door. She gave him a look he had a hard time interpreting.

"The what, now?" he asked.

"She-shed. It's really just an oversized shed that came with the house when I bought it, and which Mac promptly claimed for her combination home and laboratory. It has electricity, but no plumbing, so she uses my bathroom and kitchen. Er … I'm just telling you that in case you were planning on staying. Were you?"

He thought of asking if Mac was entirely sane, but after a glance at the heads of the oddly subdued men that were silhouetted against Jenna's TV, he decided it was a moot point "No, that wouldn't be wise," he answered, ignoring the dirge his dick sang to itself about his intentions to put as much distance as possible between it and Jenna. Guilt pricked him, causing him to add, "I am grateful to you for helping me, though. As soon as I ascertain if the information about the drug they used on me is in this box, I will ensure your safety, then leave you in peace."

"Ensure my safety?" Her expression matched the disbelief in her voice. "What on earth are you talking about? How am I unsafe?"

"Your very existence is a danger," he said sternly, wondering if she was just as heedless as she had been in the past. It was one of the things that had caused friction between them, although he hadn't known then that she was adventuring through time. He frowned at that thought and asked, "How long have you been without your memories?"

Her cheeks pinkened, something that intrigued him. "Eh," she said, waving a hand in a vague gesture. "A while. The interdict was evidently reapplied in 2011, but it was in place before that. But I'm confused about what danger I'm in. The MIBs don't know where I live."

"If they find out you are immune to the enthrallment, I assure you that they would be on your doorstep before you knew it." He studied her face, unable to keep from adding, "Since I am the one who put you in this position of vulnerability, it's my responsibility to see to your safety. It may require you to relocate."

"Whoa, now," she said, seating herself next to him. "Look, I get that you feel guilty about what happened, but it wasn't your fault. You were drugged out of your gourd. Plus, it's not like anything bad happened as a result—I'm very much not a Thrall Baby. And finally, there's the fact that I'm not some weak, feeble little thing that can't take care of herself. I've done just fine on my own all these years."

Keeley was unable to keep from pursing his lips at that last comment. The first one he dismissed—whether or not she felt he was responsible, he would never be able to live with himself if he did not see to her protection.

That had nothing to do with the fact that she was the only woman he had ever loved, and who even now stirred desires in him that he had assumed were long dead.

He ignored that last thought. "Your competence is not at issue—you don't know the Revelation. If the madmen found out that something in your genetic makeup left you immune to the enthrallment, they would go to extreme—and highly unpleasant—lengths to capture you. We will discuss steps that must be taken to ensure your safety just as soon as I see what's inside this lockbox."

"I'm going to let that whole discussion of you being Mr. Protective go because it's so unreasonable," she said with obvious dismissal, rising to move over to the kitchen before adding, "I just hope there's something in that box that has info about the drug they feed you to make you bitey."

"You don't need the drug itself if you have the antidote," one of the two men on the couch said casually.

Keeley turned an astonished look upon the man. Anton, he thought Jenna's friend had called him. Awkwardly, he rose and moved to stand in front of the man. "What did you say?"

Anton leaned to the side in order to look around Keeley to the TV screen. "I said that you wouldn't need the Thrall-making drug if you had the antidote. Was that a Gwyneth Paltrow commercial, Dima? You know I love Gwyneth Paltrow."

"No, was hamburger ad," Dima answered. He had a pronounced Russian accent, but appeared to be just as fascinated with the TV as Anton. "I like American hamburgers."

"I bet Gwyneth Paltrow likes them, too," Anton said, nodding.

Keeley rubbed his forehead with his noninjured arm. He wasn't normally prone to headaches, but he seemed on the verge of having one now. "What antidote? There is no antidote. At least, not for being a Thrall. The only end to a Thrall is destruction."

"The antidote is for the helots, but the director used it to reverse a Thrall, so I imagine it's good for both," Anton said, scooting down the couch and making an annoyed sound until he leaned far over the arm to see the screen. "I'm sure that was Gwyneth Paltrow on that commercial for lady products. She has a glow about her that you can't mistake."

"So does supersized burger and fries," Dima said, licking his lips. "Happy glow. Happy burger."

"Tell me about this antidote," Keeley demanded, first stepping to the side to block the view of the TV, and then, when Anton simply shifted the other way, grabbed the man by the collar and lifted him from the couch. "Now."

"An antidote? For the slaves?" Jenna moved around to stand next to him, confusion in her eyes. "You mean there's something to undo what you did to me?"

"I didn't do anything to you," he told her, frowning. Just her being next to him made his body want to do things he had no right to think of any longer. "Or rather, I tried to, but given your unique makeup, it didn't take. Tell me about this antidote. Where is it? Have you knowledge of it yourself, or is it just a rumor? Who made it?"

Anton, who had been making strangled noises while attempting to pry Keeley's hand off his shirt, gargled and turned red until Keeley loosened his hold and set the man on his feet, although he kept hold of his shirt. "I don't know where it is, but I know they used it when you were first brought in and changed. You attacked one of the Alpha Level members, and they had to rush the antidote from San Francisco before too much time had passed."

"An Alpha Level member?" Keeley frowned in thought, digging through memories of the hellish time when he'd been turned. His rage was out of control then, and given the amount of missing time he couldn't account for, he suspected he'd been sedated for long periods. He had a vague memory of being brought forward in the early days, his hands and feet manacled, and more or less paraded before a group of dispassionate men.

Dispassionate until, as one of the guards shot him up with the bloodlust cocktail, he managed to break free from one of the wrist manacles, using the chain to throttle the guard. All hell had broken loose then. The intended victim had enough wits to escape along with all but one of the monsters, and although the man begged and pleaded for the others to unlock the door and release him, he didn't stand a chance when the bloodlust took hold of Keeley.

"That was not intentional," he said slowly, the familiar stab of guilt and shame piercing his thoughts despite the knowledge that he was not to blame for the situation. "I thought they abandoned him as a demonstration of how the slaves were made. But they reversed it?"

Anton, who had been craning his neck to look around Keeley, nodded, his attention focused on the screen. "Paris said they had a little more than five hours before the change was irreversible. They flew out the chemist with the antidote, and got to the Alpha just before he was turned. Paris said they were lucky it worked on slaves, because it was intended to reverse what you are. Dima, do you have the remote?"

"There's an antidote," Keeley said softly, exhaustion so prevalent in his mind that the words seemed to echo inside his head before he could understand the importance of them.

"Who's Paris?" Jenna asked, moving closer to Keeley. He felt her warmth as a balm on his tormented self, and for a moment, he swayed toward her, his body reacting even if his mind determined otherwise.

"He's the one with the antidote," Anton answered, his expression rapt as he gazed at the TV.

Keeley gave him a little shake to regain the man's attention. "You're certain that there is an antidote? A Thrall antidote?"

"That's what Paris said." Anton tried to get away, but Keeley held him tight.

"What role does he play in the organization?" he asked.

"He's the director of the research department, of course," Anton said with obvious indifference. "He and the chemist come out from San Francisco every few months, and then we are sent out to bring in more subjects for the tests."

"Tests?" Jenna rubbed her arms, her expression displaying the same sense of distaste Keeley felt. "Do I want to know who the subjects are, or what the tests consist of? I don't want to know, do I?"

"I highly doubt it, but I very much wish to. This chemist you mentioned—is that the person responsible for the antidote? For the cocktail they use to bring on the bloodlust?"

Anton shrugged again. "I don't know. They don't talk much about the chemist. I've only seen her twice, when they were trying to make more of you."

Keeley's blood seemed to freeze in his veins. "They made more Thralls? How many more? Where are they?"

"They tried, but didn't succeed," Anton said, craning his neck when Keeley chewed over this new information. "That definitely was Gwyneth-ish, Dima."

"No. Cartoon," Dima answered.

"What happened to these other Thralls?" Keeley asked, still chilled with horror at the idea of others being tormented as he had been.

"Dead," Anton said succinctly.

"The madmen killed them?" he asked.

"No. They offed themselves. Went nutso-cuckoo, from what one of the other guards told me, and damn near tore themselves apart."

"How horrible," Jenna said, her eyes wide.

He knew just how she felt, and released his hold on Anton's shirt, moving back to the table where the lockbox sat. "That and so much more. It makes it even more imperative that I open this box."

"To find the antidote? Or information about the Thrall-making stuff?" she asked.

"Both," he answered, picking up the box and trying the lockpicks on it again. "I fear I'm close to the Breaking, not that I know if this antidote would actually work. Regardless, I want to know how they changed me, if for no other reason than to keep them from doing it to others."

"Breaking? Breaking what?" Jenna asked.

"Everything," he said, and, after a moment's thought, told her in explicit detail the inevitable end of Thralls.

"Jeez Louise," she said, her eyes round. "So you're … what, a ticking bomb?"

"More or less," he said, ignoring the need to comfort her. It was far better she should know the truth about him, and why he could not protect her himself.

"Hoo. OK. I can see why it's doubly important you find out where the antidote is." Jenna returned to the table, standing silently beside it for a few minutes.

Keeley wondered about that. Jenna, while possessing a mind he found delightfully quixotic, was never one to indulge in silent introspection. And yet here she was, obviously doing just that.

Irrationally, he was mildly annoyed by that fact. That she continued to have an effect on him was undeniable, and yet she shouldn't. He was long over her.

Dammit, he didn't owe her anything. She might be his Beloved, but she'd abandoned him once, and although he knew now that it hadn't been her fault as he'd imagined for more than a hundred years, the self-righteous, wounded part of his ego warned that there was nothing to stop history from repeating itself.

It was far better if he kept her at arm's length, he told himself with a satisfying sense of martyred nobility. He'd find someone to protect her because he could do no less, but that was it. Even if he wasn't likely to turn into a raving monster, he needed to keep his distance. He'd barely survived her betrayal the first time—he knew a second would destroy him completely.

Without thinking, he said, "The previous version of you never hid her thoughts from me. She told me everything she was thinking or feeling. I find this determination you have of keeping yourself private from me irritating. The old you never did so. The old you didn't wear inscrutable expressions I found impossible to read."

Jenna blinked a couple of times, opened her mouth, closed it, then opened it again with another little shake of the head. "Just when I think I'm getting a handle on everything, you go and say the most outrageous things."

"I am not outrageous," he said, gathering dignity about himself. "I'm simply pointing out that in the past, you were not secretive and mysterious."

"How am I being secretive and mysterious?" she asked, exasperation evident in her voice.

He felt mildly aggrieved about that, too, aware of just how ridiculous he sounded, but unable to keep his emotions in check.

"And that's another thing that the old you never did,"

he said, just as if she'd been privy to the mental argument he was having. "I was always in control of myself around you, even when you tempted me with your delicious legs, and your round thighs, and those hips that sang a siren song whenever you walked, and your breasts that fit so perfectly in my hands. …" He stopped, aware that it would soon be apparent to anyone just how arousing he found her presence.

"You are really cranky, aren't you?" she said, taking him by surprise once again. Rather than calling him out for his unreasonable comments, she looked concerned, and put a hand on the back of his neck. "Do you feel hot? I wonder if you have a fever and it's making you feel out of sorts with the world. Does your shoulder hurt?"

"No," he lied, enjoying the coolness of her hand on his flesh, then, diving fully into martyred mode, added, "Cease touching me, woman. I neither want nor need your attentions."

"Maybe I should look at your owie again," she said, sounding thoughtful as she eyed his collar. "It didn't look like it was doing much healing when I peeled my bra off it earlier. I wish you'd let me call a doctor, since it's in too awkward a spot for you to tend it yourself."

"I am immortal," he pointed out, trying to gather both his wits and dignity about him again. He seemed to lose both whenever she was near him. "I'm not going to die of a little scratch."

"A *scratch* that went down to the bone and likely almost severed your shoulder joint," she answered, but her voice was filled with sympathy.

"It will heal," was all he said, but he had to admit to himself that he was somewhat disconcerted to see that although the bleeding had stopped, the wound hadn't closed up in the manner to which he was used. Dark Ones, as a rule, healed quickly. But here it was more than two hours since he'd been stabbed, and not only had the wound not sealed; it still hurt.

Jenna watched him for a moment, then abruptly spun on her heel and marched out to a small kitchen. It was on the tip of his tongue to apologize for his boorish behavior, but he hesitated, not wanting to give her power over his heart again.

You really need to get over yourself.

Keeley sat upright as the thought wafted through the pain-wrapped awareness of his mind. Had he just heard a thought from Jenna? Dark Ones frequently could communicate thusly with their Beloveds …

"No," he told the box still in his hands. "I'm not a Dark One anymore. Thralls can't mark people like that."

"Like what?" Jenna asked, returning with a white cloth wrapped around a package of frozen peas. "Here, let's tuck this on your ouchie. I know you should put pressure on a puncture, but maybe the cold will take down some of the swelling, and put you in a nicer mood. I also brought you this."

He eyed the bottle of painkillers and shook his head. "I wish it would provide me relief, but it will not. I am a Thrall. Mortal-based medicines have little-to-no effect on me."

"Oh." Her expression turned crestfallen. He felt like a heel for disappointing her. "That's a shame. Although … I saw those MIBs give you a shot. You said that was some drug cocktail that made you all bitey."

"Those chemicals would be lethal to a mortal should they be administered to them," he said, tipping his head to the side so she could place the cold compress on his shoulder. It felt like heaven, and for a moment, he allowed himself the pleasure of drawing comfort from her need to tend him. "They were not medicinals under any definition of the word."

"Wow. That's seriously screwed up." Her voice was soft and airy, and he was very aware that although she'd placed the compress, her hand remained on his arm. She stood near enough to him that he could feel her warmth of her body.

He closed his eyes for a moment, and wished like hell that he could throw folly to the wind and take her to bed, sating himself in her heat.

"You smell—" Her voice choked to a stop, causing him to slide a glance up to her. She cleared her throat, and said,

"You smell really good. I want … Keeley, I know this is going to seem horrible in the extreme, but I have no idea why I want to do this, but seriously, if I don't, I think I'm going to go insane."

"Do what?" His breath hitched in his chest as she bent down over his shoulder, shifting the compress to expose the wound, her breath warm on flesh that was now chilled. His body felt as tight as a bowstring.

"I just want to—" She made an inarticulate noise and, to his amazement, dipped her head, her tongue gently touching a spot on his shoulder where a thick drop of blood had sluggishly formed.

He froze, a familiar sensation filling his mind, the red haze of hunger followed immediately by a spicy flavor that he had always thought of as a heavily mulled wine.

"Goddess," Jenna moaned, and suddenly, she was there in his lap, straddling his legs as she sat facing him, her lips caressing his partially healed shoulder. "It's so … it's just so … I want to bite you, Keeley. I want to taste you." *All of you.*

He felt just as if he'd been turned to stone. His brain, exhausted by the bloodlust, escape, and damage to his arm taking its toll, was left wondering if he truly had gone insane.

"Would it gross you out if I licked you?" she asked, squirming on his lap, her body moving against him in a restless manner that he all too clearly remembered.

"No," he said, fighting a battle both to understand what was happening and to keep himself from stripping Jenna right there and claiming her as his body demanded.

"So good," she moaned, her mouth moving over his shoulder, her tongue seeming to be made of fire as it gently touched his damaged flesh. "This should be gross as hell, but it's just … it's so … and I want to … want to …"

Bite, he said, aware he was speaking without words, but unable to keep from reveling in the sensation of her mind brushing against his. Although it was her emotions he was feeling, he knew them well. *Go ahead, Jenna. Feed.*

Feed, yes, that's what I want to do, she said with a moan into his mind. *It's overwhelming.*

Pain stung a spot at the base of his neck, causing him to jerk with the sensation, his mind filled with a rush of erotic thoughts. He clutched Jenna's hips, fighting his need even as he tried to make sense of what was happening.

Jenna's thoughts were tangled, a confusion of concern, chaotic, desire, and a bone-deep satisfaction that he remembered from the time before he'd been changed.

Somehow, she had gone from being his Beloved to becoming a Moravian, the female version of a Dark One.

"I brought both sets of lockpicks because one is—holy shitsnacks! Jenna, what the hell are you doing?"

Jenna jerked back from Keeley, her expression first surprised, then horrified as she looked down at him. "What? I—goddess! I was—I felt—and then somehow it was so good—"

"You were biting him?" Mac set the lockpicks in front of Keeley, her gaze filled with disbelief that quickly faded into speculation. "You had your mouth on his wound? That's seriously unsanitary, Jenna. Like, the kind of unsanitary that requires a visit to a mental health professional."

"You're bleeding!" Jenna's eyes widened as she stared at the spot on Keeley's neck where she'd been feeding. She stood up, backing away two steps, one hand to her mouth. "Oh my god, I *am* mentally deranged! I bit you! I licked your owie, and then I bit you and—"

She wobbled a little like she was going to faint. Keeley was on his feet and holding on to her, the feeling of her in his arms so satisfying, he ignored the wetness of blood dribbling down onto the front of the lab coat.

"You're not mentally deranged, and it was not unsanitary," he reassured both women, adding to Mac, "Jenna was, in fact, healing my wound. If you look at it now, you will see that her attention to it has caused the healing to accelerate."

Both women stared at his shoulder.

"It does look better," Jenna allowed. "Wow. That's odd."

"Yeah, but that is bleeding like a stuck pig," Mac said, pointing to his neck. "I can't believe you bit him that hard, Jenna. You've never been into kinky sex before."

"That's it," Jenna announced, her eyes almost glowing with fervor. "I'm a danger to myself and others. I have to be locked up in the nearest loony bin. Go now, Keeley. Save yourself. Mac will lock me in my bedroom until the men from the wacky house can come and get me."

Keeley sighed, and gave her a little squeeze. "'Wacky house' is, I believe, viewed these days as a problematic term. Regardless, I will repeat myself in saying that you are not to blame, and you most certainly are not deranged. You were simply acting under impulses that are new to you."

"You're stuck-pig bleeding," Jenna said, straightening up the better to glare at him. "Of course I'm deranged! You don't know what you're saying. It's probably the loss of blood."

"It's not," he reassured her.

She snatched up a handful of tissues while she spoke, and pressed them onto the side of his neck, while at the same time urging, "Sit down before you pass out. I'll hold this on to your neck to keep you from bleeding out while Mac calls for help."

"Lick me," he said, trying hard not to laugh at the absurd turn his life had taken. Was it really only a few hours ago he had been begging with any deity who would listen to end his existence?

She reared back like he'd given her the most profane insult. "I *beg* your pardon?"

"Lick where you bit me. It will close the wound."

"It will?" She glanced toward his neck again, her pupils dilating. He knew well the response, knew just how arousing feeding had been … at one time in his life. After the madmen had changed him, it had become only a nightmare. "I … it's wrong. …"

"You're not going to—ew! Jenna!"

"Do not dissuade her. It will be the only thing that will close the wound she made," Keeley told her, before gently pulling Jenna closer, mindful not to press her against the blood that dripped down his chest. "Just lick it so that I might find some other garment to wear."

"OK, but if this doesn't work, I'm going to call the home for the mentally bewildered myself," Jenna answered, her breath soft and warm on his neck. He braced himself for the rush of pleasure, but even then, the gentle swipe of her tongue on the wound convinced his penis that as far as it was concerned, all was forgiven, and they really should pick up the threads of their former relationship so it could get busy bringing them both pleasure.

"That is seriously strange," Mac said, her face a few inches from where Jenna, her eyes closed, an expression of bliss visible, still steamed his shoulder with her breath. "It's gone. It's just gone like she'd never bitten you. I'm not a germophobe, but still, that's … weird."

"It's not weird," Keeley told them both, moving back a step lest he hoist Jenna in his arms and carry her off to the nearest private location. "It's perfectly normal for Dark Ones and Moravians."

"Dark One? Isn't that another word for vampire?" Mac asked, her eyes widening. "You're a vampire as well as a Thrall? Holy macaroons!"

"I was a Dark One, yes. I am no longer. Jenna was my Beloved, but now …" He watched her for a moment as she gave a long, trembling breath. "But now I believe rather than being made into a helot as are the mortals the madmen force me to make, she has instead become a Moravian."

"Which is what?" Mac asked.

He watched Jenna closely. She first frowned, then looked thoughtful. "You think I'm a female vamp now? I admit that biting you was … hoo! I mean, it was good, and your blood tastes like the most incredibly spiced drink, but I don't feel like a vampire. I don't have pointy fangs or anything."

"Moravians are the female versions of Dark Ones," Keeley answered, the exhaustion that he'd kept at bay suddenly swamping him. "They do not suffer the same effects as the males. They can go out into the sunlight without harm. They do not need to confine themselves to a blood diet. With few exceptions, they possess their souls."

"That is seriously cool," Mac said, buffeting Jenna on the arm, her face alight with excitement. "My bestie is a badass female vamp! And I thought the guys in the vamp experiment group were going to be impressed by my Thrall Babies. They'll go batshit over this."

"I don't feel any different—" Jenna started to say. Then suddenly, she was at his side, one arm around his waist and her shoulder under his arm. "You poor thing. You've been through hell and back again what with the drugs the MIBs gave you, and the damage to your arm, and me biting you so hard you almost bled to death. I don't have a spare room, but you can lie down on my bed and get some rest."

If you take me to your bed, I assure you that rest is the last thing either of us will get.

"Don't be silly, you're too hurty to do anything—" She stopped and turned a stunned face to him. "Wait. What did you say?"

I may have been wounded, and I may be suffering from the aftereffects of the bloodlust serum, but that just means that my control has been strained past its normal level of tolerance.

He expected her to react in the same dramatic fashion that he remembered well, but to his complete surprise, she simply met his gaze for half a minute, then nodded. "I don't know how you did that, but then, I also don't know how you biting me could make me a badass female vampire, but I'm going to assume the two things are connected, and move past them. Let me show you where you can rest."

"Not yet," Keeley managed to say despite his body's demands. It was a struggle to even sit down and extract a few of Mac's lockpicks before pulling the lockbox to him. His limbs felt as if they'd been cast in lead. "I want to see what's in this first."

Mac moved to stand on his other side. "Dibs on any tech you find in there. Especially if it's woo-woo tech."

"What the hell is woo-woo tech?" Keeley asked, his eyes on the box as he slid the lockpicks in.

"You know." Mac waggled her fingers at him. "Woo-woo. Alien. Or maybe alternate reality. The guys on the Dark Web forum who sell Russian decommissioned weapons are very big into alternate-reality theories. Oh. That's anticlimactic. There's not even so much as a syringe full of the stuff they are going to dump in our water to make us all zombies."

Mac spoke the last few words upon peering into the box when Keeley opened it. He stared down at the two somewhat battered flash drives, his hopes rising at the sight of them.

"Oooh," Jenna said, watching as he examined the drives. "Let's hope they have what you want on them."

She slid over to him a thin laptop. He inserted the first drive, quickly scanning the contents before yanking it out.

"That was fast," she said, coming around to stand behind his wounded left shoulder. Mac moved into a flanking position on his other side so she, too, could see the computer screen. "What was on there?"

"Pornographic videos, judging by the titles," he said, plugging in the second drive. His spirits, momentarily so high, had plummeted at the sight of *Mrs. Claus Gets Her Stocking Stuffed* and *Deck My Balls* videos. "Let's hope this one is … ah."

"Ah?" Mac asked, leaning over his shoulder to squint at the screen of the laptop.

"Those look like pictures," Jenna commented, also leaning close. His cock was instantly aware of her nearness, of the indescribably satisfying scent that was pure Jenna as it sank into every iota of his being. "Are they porn as well?"

He mentally grumbled at himself for being so easily distracted, and pushed aside the need that had been his constant companion since she had disappeared from his life. He opened the first picture, quickly scanning it. "Screenshots of text messages, it would appear," he said, clicking through a few more of the pictures.

"From the guy named Paris," Jenna agreed, her breath tickling his ear.

Unable to stop himself, he turned his head until his lips almost touched her cheek. Likewise, she turned to look at him, her nose bumping his.

Her eyes dilated again. He felt a smug, very male sense of satisfaction at that. Until he realized he was doing so; then he said the only thing he felt would end the untenable situation. "Why are you so close to me?" His lips brushed hers as he spoke.

"I was just asking myself the same question," she answered, once again taking him by surprise. He had never felt so out of his depth with a woman before. He had no idea what she was thinking or what she'd say next, and the sensation left him feeling as if he was floundering at sea with no ship on the horizon. "And then I decided that maybe Past Jenna and Past Keeley knew what they were doing, and it would behoove me to get to know you better."

"You guys know each other?" Mac asked on his other side. He turned to look at her. She was resting her chin on his shoulder, an interested look in her eyes. "Is that why Jenna was going on about your chest, and hair, and manly stubble?"

"I didn't mention the manly stubble," Jenna pointed out. He turned back to look at her, unable to keep from tipping his head back just a little so that her lips fluttered against his again. She smiled, the gesture warming him despite the pain and tiredness that possessed him.

"I like stubble," Dima commented from the couch. "My boyfriend—my ex-boyfriend Sonny—he had stubble. The feeling on my thighs …" He gave a little shiver.

"Oooh," Jenna cooed, her breath caressing his face. "Stubble on inner thighs."

His cock hardened to a point where he thought he might have been able to use it to hew a few trees. In a desperate attempt to distract himself, he craned his head to the right and past Mac to the two men. "Do you know anything else about this man named Paris?" he asked Dima. Anton seemed to be engrossed in the TV and paid them no attention.

"No. He is big man, high up in organization," Dima said, his eyes now on Mac. There was a slavish devotion in them that reminded Keeley of a particularly needy puppy.

"Where did you get them?" he asked Mac, switching mental gears.

"What? Oh, them. From the lobby where you guys were being held." Mac frowned. "I told you that, didn't I? I have a distinct memory of telling you that. Jenna, your boyfriend looks a bit flushed. Is he feverish? Maybe you should get him to bed."

His cock twitched at the thought. Keeley had never felt as martyred as he did at that moment.

"I've been trying to get him to bed for what seems like hours," Jenna said as she straightened up.

Keeley and Mac turned identical expressions of surprise on her. To his delight, her cheeks grew a bit pinker, and she waved a hand in a vague gesture. "That is, it's obvious he's about to drop after the attack."

He glanced again at the screenshots, then removed the flash drive from the laptop and, with an effort, got to his feet. To his horror, he weaved for a few seconds. Instantly, Jenna was there, her arm around him again. "I don't need to be put to—what are you doing, woman? Unhand me."

"You're going to lie down for a bit. Stop scowling, Keeley. It's clear to everyone that you're about ready to fall over." Somehow, she managed to get him across the room to a closed door. "This is my bedroom. The bathroom is just there. Feel free to take a shower if that blood is making you feel icky, and then I really think you need to get some rest before you topple over."

"I'm not going to do anything so ridiculous," he said, but the effort it took to simply speak made him thankful that she had more sense than his penis.

He had a horrible feeling if he gave way to its demands and tried to seduce Jenna, he'd fail in a spectacular manner that neither of them would forget. "I will avail myself of your shower, however."

She eyed his shoulder but, since the wound had finally closed, said nothing other than she'd fetch a man's shirt that she normally used to sleep in.

He eyed himself in the bright lights of the bathroom, not liking the face that looked back from the mirror. His jaw was dark with whiskers, his cheekbones stood out in stark relief to the gauntness of the rest of his face, and pale lines appeared when he tightened his lips against the exhaustion.

"You look like you could do with a few good meals," Jenna told him, handing him a soft blue shirt. "I can see all your ribs."

"The madmen kept food from me in order to enhance the bloodlust," he said with a matter-of-factness that sounded harsh to his ears.

"Can you eat? Food, that is?" she asked, her voice as soft as the worn cloth of the shirt. He had an almost overwhelming desire to smell it, sure it carried her scent. "I'd be happy to make you something—"

He shook his head before she finished. "In that, Thralls are like Dark Ones."

She was silent for a moment, her gaze moving over his bare torso. He felt the examination as if she'd been stroking him. "Then can I feed you? I don't know the rules about Moravians and such, but if I can eat normal food, then it seems to me that I could keep my blood factory running to help you out when you needed it."

"You can," he said, closing his eyes for a few seconds, unable to keep the wry smile from twisting his lips. "But if you did so now, it would just end up with me attempting to make love to you, and despite my body's complete willingness to give it a try, I believe your assessment of the stresses of the day is correct, and I would not satisfy either of us."

She smiled, and he felt a slight glow in the dark corners of his being. "Part of me thinks that jumping into bed with you is just a fine idea, but sadly, the sane part says that we should apply the brakes a bit until we figure out just what's going on. With you. And me. And … us," she finished, making yet another vague gesture.

He nodded, feeling close to the point of dropping and falling into insensibility, too tired to tell her that although she might be different from the Jenna he knew, in one respect she was similar—both Jennas needed wooing rather than a quick seduction.

"That or perhaps *I* want to seduce *you*," she said, turning and moving out of the bathroom. "Get some rest, Keeley. I have a feeling you're going to need it."

She smiled into his mind. It was a long, slow smile that remained with him until he lay down in her bed, holding her pillow, and allowed himself to drift off to sleep.

He suspected he was going to need a lot more than a little rest to keep up with the woman who still held his heart.

A heart that was breaking with the knowledge that he had to leave before he destroyed everything.

JULY 3, 2011

Lemmas:

I don't know what bee got up your butt bonnet, but I don't have time to keep meeting with you to explain some trivial violation of an archaic rule that no one even knows exists except you. And I suspect that's because you peruse the Weaver rule book just so you can slap me with demerits.

Regardless, no, I will not join you at the Council House tomorrow. I have more important things to do. Weaver things.

Sincerely,
Jenna

JULY 3, 2011

Keeley, you sexy, sexy vampire! Let's have a Fourth of July picnic tomorrow to celebrate! You bring your adorable self, and I'll bring the fried chicken.

Smooches,
Jenna

JULY 4, 2011

Jenna Walker Boyle

I am in receipt of a letter from you addressed to someone named

Keeley, who is evidently a Dark One. While congressing in what is obviously a sexual manner with a being of dark power is not in violation of your terms of service with the Weavers' Guild, I will make a note of it in your file.

What is more concerning is the date of your letter. According to my records, you have not been given any cases in which you should be traveling to the year 1889. Just what, exactly, are you doing in England at that time? The Council would like a full explanation tomorrow at three p.m.

Yours in Weaver Sisterhood,

Lemmas

4 JULY 1889

Jenna, love, I suspect you sent me a letter intended for someone named Lemmas. I am returning it forthwith. Shall I see you tonight? I have a new coat that you might like to see.

I miss your breasts. And thighs. And the secret, hidden parts of you that never fail to make me insane with desire.

Keeley

TEN

"So, that was a hell of a thing." Mac was sitting at my small dining room table, Keeley's pilfered lockbox in front of her, once again closed as she manipulated the picks in the lock, obviously practicing her lock-picking skills.

I frowned. "What was? Do you mean me coming very close to jumping Keeley's bones even though he was clearly about ten seconds away from passing out, or the fact that I'm now a bloodsucker?"

"Both. Neither. Maybe the latter more than the former." She looked up. "You wanted to have sex with him? He's all …"

"Dark? Troubled? Hurting and needy and sexy as hell?" I asked, rubbing my arms. I was still trying to come to grips with the emotions that roared through me at Keeley's nearness, and felt more than a little adrift on a sea of strangeness.

"Scary, I was going to say. He's so …" She gave a faux shudder. "So cold."

"Cold? Keeley? Are you insane?" I would have thought she was pulling my leg but for the serious expression in her eyes as she met my gaze. I shook my head. "He's filled with passion, and great, big surges of emotions. And the man could substitute for a space heater the way heat rolls off him. I swear, I just about break into a sweat when I get close to him."

She pursed her lips. "That's because you've evidently got the hots for him, and yes, the pun was intentional. No, don't bother telling me how fabulous he is. If you say he's a seething pool of fiery emotion, I'll take your word for it. What are you going to do with him?"

I blinked a couple of times at the question, more to give myself time to think of an answer than because I didn't understand. "I don't know that I have a say in what he does," I finally answered. "He told me we were engaged more than a hundred years in the past, and he thought I left him on the altar."

"Did you?" Mac asked, moving past all the trivialities of my statement, and focusing on the important point.

"Yes, but not intentionally. It seems the people I worked for got their knickers in a twist because of some time travel, and they wiped my memory." I waited to see what she'd do with that morsel of information.

"Harsh," she said with a wrinkle of her nose, returning her attention to the lockbox.

"You don't think it's odd that I'm an amnesiac time-traveling she-vampire?" I finally asked.

"Odd? Not really," she said, chewing on her lower lip as she jiggled the lockpicks.

"Mac!" I said, more than a little bit frustrated.

She looked up, her eyes wide. "What?"

"Why aren't you freaked out? It's not every day you find out your best friend is something straight out of a Netflix paranormal series!"

She thought about that for a few seconds, then gave a little nod. "True, but you've always been a bit off-kilter. I mean, for one thing, you're a Midnight Walker. And for another, you can blip. And your boy toy is a slave-making walking time bomb. So I'm not freaked out. Just kind of buzzed, because it means we can do so much more if you are a superhero."

"I'm hardly that," I said, wanting to laugh at the matter-of-fact way she dealt with my new reality. "And the Midnight Walker thing is just a weird quirk of my family. None of them can turn blue. Not any longer, that is. I read a medical report that said my family had a genetic trait that limited oxygen in the blood, and inbreeding kept it strong in the family for a few generations. Luckily, by the time I was born, the family had stopped marrying their cousins and brought in some beefier genes."

"That didn't stop Jack Rayburn and the *Mysteries Abound* people from swearing your family was loaded with alien DNA," Mac pointed out.

I slumped back in my chair. "I wish I could remember my family, but thanks to the Weavers, all that has been wiped out. All I know is what I read in the medical paper."

"Badass she-vamp with alien DNA," Mac said softly, poking at the metal box. "Some people have all the luck."

I laughed and was about to comment that I didn't think being part of a family feared a few hundred years before because of the blue tint to their skin made me lucky, but just then a noise from my pocket signaled an incoming text. "Great. Lucy says that Britt's phone was in Vegas, but has been moving west at a fast pace. She thinks Britt must be on a plane."

"No surprise there. That kid is loopy."

I glanced at the two men in the living room, but they were happily engaged in watching a retro TV channel. I watched Mac fussing with the lockpicks for a few minutes before I said, "Lucy says I don't need to chase Britt down, but I feel responsible for her being on the run, out of the reach of her family."

"She's nineteen, almost twenty," Mac pointed out. "She's not an idiot, no matter what Lucy says, and Britt's within her rights to do what she wants, even if you and her mom don't think it's smart."

"Yes, but Lucy is worried. And I can't help but feel it was my fault that I was captured by the MIBs, after all."

"Meh. You're not responsible for Britt's actions. If it makes you feel any better, text her that if she ever needs help, you're there for her. That's about all you can realistically do."

"I guess so," I said, picking up one of the lockpicks and absently tapping it onto the table.

"You just like to worry," Mac said, clicking her tongue when the box refused to open.

"If I do, it's because I have a reason. Namely, you."

"You don't need to worry about me. I'm in a class by myself," she said placidly.

I laughed. "You are, but that's not what I meant. I knew once I'd been captured that you would do something, and given your new set of explosives, the resulting destruction was inevitable. What if the police find out it was you who blew things up?"

"They won't," she answered, still focused on the lockbox.

"How do you know? You can't know."

She gave me a disappointed look. "I can, because I set the whole thing up to look like a natural gas explosion. Didn't you see all the gas company trucks at the gates?"

I wasn't wholly reassured, but decided I'd just have to get Mac out of the area for a while. "Thank the goddess you didn't hurt anyone."

She made a sound that came perilously close to being a snort. "You know I'd never do that."

"Yes, but accidents happen. And then the Krebbs people will sue me for the damage. You don't think they will, do you? I don't have any money. I mean, I do, but it all goes to keeping us fed, and the tour bus running, and the tour itself competitive with the three other tour companies in town, and oh my god, they're going to bankrupt me, aren't they?"

The last few words came out as a wail.

Mac, used to my more-frequent-than-I-liked panic moments, gave yet another quelling look. "No one was hurt, and no one will know my role in today's adventure. You're worrying about nothing. And even if they did find out, you can countersue for kidnapping. Not to mention the human rights abuses that fairly oozed out of that place. Welp, I can't get this open, but I never did sign up for that lock-picking class I wanted to take a few summers back. Thank god Keeley's skills are better than mine. Think I'll hit the hay a little early. Boys! Enough TV. It's time for beddy-byes."

She stood up as she spoke, gathering up the military messenger bag she used as a purse. My eyebrows lifted as the two former MIBs obediently rose and trotted after her when she headed for the back door.

"Do I even want to know what you're going to do with those two in the small space afforded by the shed?" I called after her.

She paused at the door to grin, then was gone. I looked at the clock, decided it was too early to go to bed despite the stresses and strains of the day, and sat down to try my hand at the lockbox. Two minutes later I threw down the lock-picks in disgust and, with a long look at my closed bedroom door, went to my office and spent a few hours trying to track down which flights out of the area Britt was likely to be on. After a few phone calls, including one to Lucy, who sounded remarkably calm despite the disappearance of her daughter, I decided there wasn't anything else I could do that night. "Let me know when you can pinpoint her location," I told Lucy. "I'll head out there to try to reason with her."

"I don't know that it will do any good if she turned on you so viciously," Lucy answered, "but I'd be grateful for any attempt to make her see reason."

I peeked in on Keeley, but his form lying on top of my bed was solid and unmoving, so I closed the door and, after a significant struggle with my libido, took myself off to the couch in my office. "Things will look better in the morning," I told my sense of guilt and frustration. "They pretty much have to, because I don't see how they could be much worse."

I just hate it when fate takes my attempts to cheer myself up as a personal challenge.

The sun wasn't even up when my rumbling stomach woke me up. After quick ablutions and the consumption of yogurt, fruit, and two slices of sourdough toast, I couldn't stand the uncertainty any longer and carefully cracked open the door to my bedroom.

The room was a solid mass of darkness, but as a little finger of light snaked in from behind me, I heard the rustle of cloth.

"What is it?" Keeley's voice sounded rough and thick, as if he'd just woken up.

"Sorry, didn't mean to disturb you. I just had a horrible worry while I was eating that your wound might have opened up again, and you were lying here dying, too ill to call for help. You're OK?"

The light next to the bed clicked on as Keeley sat up, his black hair tousled in a way that made my stomach tighten with desire. He ran a hand over his face. "I told you that I can't be killed. At least, not like that. Is that clock right?"

I opened the door wider, stepping into the room. "It's five minutes fast because I'm always late to things otherwise. How do you feel?"

He swung his legs over the edge of the bed, and glanced at his shoulder before lifting the edge of the collar. "It's healed, thanks to your … attentions."

I hesitated a minute, called myself an idiot because it wasn't like I was going to fling myself on the man if I was in the same room as him, and sat down on the bed next to him. "Yeah, about that. I don't think I get how this whole thing—"

He'd shifted to pick up his shoes while I was speaking, resulting in his leg pressing against mine. For a moment, we both froze, the contact filling my head with a number of mental images that were both strange and highly enticing, and then I was on my back with Keeley looming over me, his mouth moving along my collarbone, pressing hot kisses into my flesh.

"Keeley, I don't think—oh goddess yes, right there." I writhed beneath him as his mouth moved on my neck, sending ripples of pleasure down my suddenly highly charged body. On top of all that, a sharp need that I remembered from the day before started to push my desire higher. "I just don't think we should—" I stopped, arching up when his fingers moved across my breasts, which until that moment had been existing in quiet contentment inside my bra.

Now they were strident little hussies who immediately wanted out and into Keeley's hands. And mouth. And rubbing on his bare chest.

"I won't do anything you don't want me to do," Keeley murmured into my shoulder as his tongue swirled a path down to my collarbone, and further south to where I was even now struggling to get out of my T-shirt, camisole, and bra.

I didn't stop to wonder about why or how things had gotten to this point—all my good intentions to keep a distance from him went out the window as I gave in to the need that had simmered deep within me ever since I'd been thrown into Keeley's cell.

"You can do that again, for one," I said on a moan as I arched up against his mouth, the heat of it making my breasts grow heavy with desire. I tugged on his shirt until I pulled the tail of it out of his pants, sliding my hands under it to feel the warmth of his chest. For a moment, I stilled, concerned by the heat that seemed to simmer along the delicious ripples of muscle. "You're awfully hot, Keeley. Are you feverish? Should I get a doctor?"

"At this moment, I wouldn't care if I had one foot in the grave," he murmured into the underside of one of my hussy breasts, rubbing his stubbly cheek on it in a way that damn near had my eyes rolling back in my head.

I stopped touching him and watched him with concern. It took him a minute, but eventually he glanced up, then, with a smile that quirked up higher on one side, added, "No, love, I'm not ill. Just warm thinking about you."

The term of endearment made my insides go all squishy, and I gave in to the almost overwhelming urge to bite him, nipping his good shoulder and saying, "I'm a bit heated myself." I reapplied my hands to his chest, now bare since I'd managed to get his shirt off. Just as I had the day before, I wanted to do more than give him a love bite, but mindful of the situation, I glanced at his hurt shoulder. To my relief, he was right in that it was looking much better than it had the day before. There was a jagged red line that looked a bit angry still, but the wound had sealed up just as Keeley had said it would. "Are you sure your shoulder is up to this?"

His head dipped in answer, taking one needy nipple into his mouth, making me moan nonstop before he turned his attention to the other, his hands busily working away to remove my jeans. "Very much so despite the knowledge that this is insanity, pure insanity."

"The purest," I agreed, wondering if I should ask permission before biting him.

You can do anything you want, including drinking from me.

But you were hurt. Your owie still looks a bit annoyed with the world.

I'll survive, he answered.

That was all I needed to hear. The deep, soul-burning desire in me to possess him drove me into biting his good shoulder, part of my brain still slightly shocked that I could find something so taboo as biting him satisfying on a primal level, while the other part reveled in the taste of him at the same time I wriggled against him, my body primed and ready for his attentions.

He sucked in his breath as I licked the bite mark, gathering onto my tongue a few drops of his spicy, heady blood. Pain pierced my neck for a fraction of a second as he bit me in return, his mind filled with the most erotic thoughts I had ever in my life experienced. They were so carnal, I thought I was going to go up like flash paper as he fed, his pleasure somehow mingling with mine until it drove me to the edge of an orgasm.

"Weaver, have you seen Mistress this morning? She told us to wait in the house, but she has been gone for more than an hour."

A little swirl of air that accompanied the voice had Keeley leaping off me, his body blocking me while he faced Anton, who stood in the doorway. I peered around Keeley's naked ass, wondering how he'd gotten out of his pants so quickly, but decided that wasn't important. I snatched up my camisole and held it in front of my bare chest while frowning at Anton. "What the … no, I don't. I thought she was out in her shed with you guys … er … doing whatever it is you were doing. There. Together. The three of you."

Anton frowned. "The mistress said to wait. We have waited. Dima has gone to look for her, but she is not in the love shack."

Uncomfortable with the idea that Anton was getting an eyeful of Keeley even if the latter didn't mind, I grabbed a pillow and held it in front of his crotch, all the while I struggled with the urge to lick the line up his back. "Huh?"

You do that, and I won't care who's at the door, Keeley warned.

"The love shack," Anton said, making an annoyed gesture. "Mistress said that is what we should call it. We had a most pleasant time there."

"Er …" I peered around Keeley. "I'm not entirely comfortable with the idea of you guys going at it while you're quasi Thrall Babies. You do know you have the right to say no, don't you? Just because Mac wants you to do something doesn't mean you have to. She is very big on no means no, so if you ever feel uncomfortable, just say so, and she'll respect that."

Did you just give him a consent lecture? Keeley asked.

Yes, but only because I was a bit weirded out that Mac was having sex with them while they were under her influence.

It sounds to me like it was consensual. Mac is correct in that they don't at all appear like the other helots.

Anton's eyes widened. "Of course. Mistress told us that last night. We all agreed to safe words. Also, Dima does not normally enjoy women, and I have never partaken of a man in a sexual sense, but we had the choice to say no. Mistress said she would respect our decisions. But now she's gone and we cannot find her to have another pleasant love shack experience. Dima has purchased some massage oil to enhance the experiences. Especially the part where he enjoys for me to insert—"

"Yes, that's probably way too much information for this early in the morning," I said quickly, relieved that they weren't being coerced, and more than a little desperate to get back to biting Keeley while he drank from me at the same time.

Keeley moaned in my head, his mind filling with thoughts of our bodies twining around each other in ways I didn't think were physically possible.

Oh, they are. We might need a pulley system and some stout silk ropes, but they're very possible.

"Out!" I almost yelled, then realized how rude that sounded. "That is, please leave. I don't know where Mac is, but she's very resourceful, and probably went to get fur-lined handcuffs or some sort of suspension sex system, and will be back soon."

"We have two sets of the handcuffs, and rigging up the sex swing was one of the first things we did last night," Anton said, frowning. "Where has she gone?"

"I don't know, and right now, I can honestly say that unless she's in danger, I don't care," I answered, drawing a finger down Keeley's back. He stiffened, and sucked in a huge quantity of air.

"But—" Anton started to say.

"You heard the lady," Keeley snapped, taking a menacing step forward, causing me to lurch behind him in order to keep his crotch covered by the pillow. "Leave!"

"Fine, but if something happens to Mistress, she said you would be responsible for us," he told me, then spun around and marched out of the room, thankfully closing the door behind him.

"Oh, great. Now I'm a Thrall Baby guardian," I muttered, making a mental note to have a long chat with Mac in the very near future.

Keeley sighed. "What would it take to expunge the phrase 'Thrall Baby' from your vocabulary?"

I giggled, and tossed the pillow back onto the bed, stroking a hand down his chest when he turned to face me. "I don't know. Maybe if you let me bite you again, I could see my way clear to forgetting it?"

"You can bite me any time, any day, anywhere," he said, his lovely gray eyes alight with passion.

I smiled a wicked smile I didn't realize I had in my repertoire, and allowed him to press me back down onto the bed, quickly resuming his exploration of my boobs. "I'll hold you to that, you know. Keeley, is this wrong?"

"No, this is a breast," he said, rubbing his cheek against the once-again wholly interested breast in question.

"Dangerous, sexy as sin, and with a sense of humor, too," I said, giving his hip a little pinch. "You know full well I meant, is us indulging in sexy times wrong? I didn't intend to do this. Whatever we had in the past aside, I don't know you. In my worldview, we just met yesterday. I've never let things get this far with someone I've just met—"

The words stopped in my throat when he stroked a hand down my belly to my pubic mound, then curled a finger inside me.

I damn near shot up off the bed. *That is not fair!* I said, panting into his mind. *Do it again!*

He did, and just as I pulled his hips over me, needing him inside me, there was a light tap at the door.

"Weaver Jenna, you know where are Mistress and Anton? I went to store and bought slippery oil for Anton, so that he does not mind riding sex swing, but he and Mistress are gone."

"Does your door not have a damned lock?" Keeley growled into my mouth before leaping off me, once again standing so that his body was blocking the view from the door.

Yes, but it's broken, and I've never bothered to get it fixed. What the hell is going on?

I assume there is some sort of friction regarding penetration via a sex swing—

No, not why are they getting massage oil; where is Mac? And now where has Anton gone?

"We don't know where either is," Keeley told Dima, moving swiftly to the door, adding before he slammed it, "And we don't care."

"Unless something dire has happened," I said, a slight niggle of worry seeping into the pleasure that fairly hummed through my body.

Keeley sighed, then opened the door again and said brusquely, "You may return and tell us if neither appears in half an hour."

Dima made a face but nodded. Keeley shut the door and looked around, obviously searching for something to use to block it.

"There's no one else in the house," I pointed out, and scooted up the bed so there was room for both of us to frolic. "Now, about my misgivings regarding us getting it on so quickly—"

"We were soul bound," he told me, giving up after eyeing my dresser, a massive piece in heavy oak. He marched back to the bed, his penis fully aroused, an annoyed expression on his face that made me want to laugh. "You were going to marry me. We engaged in sexual acts many, many times. There is no reason not to do so now."

A whisper crept across my mind, so nebulous I wasn't sure if I had imagined it. *Take what you can now, before all is lost.*

"You are the only man I know who can look disgruntled and aroused at the same time," I said with a little laugh, resigning myself to the fact that no matter what my life had been in the past, right now I wanted Keeley with a need that bordered on obsession. I had to have him, or my body might just explode into a million frustrated pieces.

I feel exactly the same way, he said, sliding his arms under my legs and taking them with him when he crawled up my body. I felt him mentally hesitate a moment. *Are you taking some form of birth control? I do not have any condoms.*

Yes. I get a shot. You don't have any venereal—

No.

Oh, good. Neither do I. Full steam ahead, mon capitaine.

"I'm going to do more than steam your *capitaine*," he murmured, making my toes curl with anticipation.

I welcomed him into my depths with a moan of the sheerest pleasure, my intimate muscles rippling happily with the invasion. "Wow, you're—hoo! Keeley, you didn't look huge, but man alive—oh, goddess yes, that little lunge is the very best thing I've ever felt—you seem to be extra large. Just how big are you?"

He had been kissing his way up my chest to my neck all the while his hips worked away in a fashion that almost had me seeing stars, but paused to frown down on me. "You want measurements? Now?"

I licked his chin. "No. It's just that my inner girl muscles are a bit strained taking you on. They're kind of quivering with the attempt to cope."

He closed his eyes for a moment. "I like the way they quiver. Especially when you wiggle. And flex your legs. Christ, don't do that, or I won't last."

I couldn't help but giggle at the desperation in his voice. "That is something my gynecologist has me do to keep my pelvic floor strong."

"If it was any stronger, it would rip my cock off. Do it just one more time, and then let your girl muscles relax while I take over."

I Kegeled, I wiggled my hips, I wrapped my legs tight around him and bucked wildly upward every time he thrust into me. I was a mindless blob of ecstasy, and one part of my mind that could still think pointed out something.

Oh, yes, there was a hell of an orgasm that seemed to flood my body with heat and a desire to merge myself with Keeley in a way I hadn't known was possible, but as I arched up in a gasp of pleasure when the orgasm overtook me at the same time he bit my shoulder, I was aware of an emotion that blossomed with slowly unfurling tendrils.

It wasn't an emotion that made sense, and yet at the same time, it was absolutely right.

Keeley's mind was filled with the pleasure of his own climax mingling with the bone-deep satisfaction of drinking from me, but hiding below that, there was a shadow, a sorrow that seemed to leach into his pleasure.

The emotion was gone before I could try to pin it down. I worried about it for a minute, but decided that my inner self was anticipating trouble where there was none.

Besides, my heart wanted to focus instead on all the warm fuzzy feelings that filled me. It would be all too easy, I told myself, to fall for Keeley.

His combination of need and passion was a heady mix, and I had a feeling I wouldn't last long against it.

"Keeley," I said, his conversation finally having filtered through the sensual fog in my mind. I realized that his unique sense of humor was partly responsible for the depth of my emotions, and I stroked his back, marveling that something so simple as a quirky mind could capture my heart so completely. "Were you this funny before?"

He groaned into my mind as his body shifted, rolling onto his back and taking me with him until I was splayed across his body.

How is it you can think at a time like this? I worked and slaved to drive you beyond mortal bearing, not that you're mortal to begin with, but still, I put every ounce of effort I possessed into pushing you into the most exquisite moment of pleasure, and yet here you are, talking just like you didn't have the most breathtaking orgasm.

I giggled. "I did have a breathtaking orgasm, which you must have known because no sooner did my girl muscles go to town on you than you were yelling things in another language and doing those short little hard thrusts that make me think I'll be walking funny for the rest of the day. Regardless, were you?"

Was I what?

Funny. Amusing. Entertaining.

I have no idea how to answer that. I don't believe I am known for my comic abilities, no.

"Well, you are funny. I like your mind, Keeley. You look all scary and intimidating, and then you say things that make me go all squidgy inside because you tickle my fancy."

He cracked open one eye and waggled an eyebrow. "I'd be happy to tickle your fancy again if you give me ten minutes to recover."

"See, that's just exactly the sort of thing—"

The door opened, and Mac strode into the room, her phone in her hand. "Hey, Jenna, I got the weirdest message from one of my contacts—holy cheeseballs!"

With a martyred sigh, Keeley yanked a blanket from where it had slid to the floor with our exertions, and flung it over me.

"I won't say that I'm surprised, because the way you guys were steaming each other up last night was a huge clue that things would be getting hot and heavy sooner rather than later," Mac said, leaning against the door. "But still, I'm a bit taken aback. You don't normally jump the bones of a man you've just met."

"That's because Keeley is no ordinary man," I told her over the edge of the blanket.

"You don't have to tell me that twice," she said, giving him a long look. "And I'm going to want to talk to you about that—"

"Later," I told her, making shooing motions with one hand. "We're otherwise engaged in pillow talk, so shoo. Leave. Begone."

"But I want to tell you about what I saw on the Dark Web—"

"Begone!" I said louder.

She grinned, saluted, and turned on her heel.

"I'll get the lock fixed," I told Keeley, smiling despite the fact that even through the now closed door, I could hear Mac telling one of her love toys that some people just didn't appreciate the zing an audience brings to lovemaking.

He considered me for a moment, his expression unreadable before he smiled a long, slow smile. One that warmed me to the tips of my toes.

Life was starting to look up. Despite everything that had happened, I had a feeling the future was going to be bright.

Which all just goes to show why I will never land a job as a fortune-teller.

ELEVEN

To: Roxy, Ellis

Guys! We're still in Nevada and the Thrall has been spotted! Or at least that's what Merrick thinks, and I don't see any reason to doubt him.

To: Tempest, Ellis

Oooh! Spill all. But be literary about it, because I've been reading these to Richard, and he's dying to hear the latest installment of As the Tempest Turns.

To: Roxy, Ellis

Love to Uncle Richard. And of course, I'll do this properly.

Hey.

Hmm?

You've been radio silent. What's going on?

We're at the Revelation facility. Han has just smashed one of the guards against the wall. Ouch.

Ouch? Are you hurt?

No, but the guard who jumped Andreas is. I'm willing to bet his collarbone is broken. He's whimpering.

Awww. Maybe you should call a doctor after you guys are through there?

Tempest, these men are trying to kill us. I appreciate the fact that you dislike us harming anyone, but I draw the line at being decapitated just because breaking someone's collarbone would upset you.

Good point. Still, let me know when you're done, and I'll make an anonymous call to the emergency services to go check up on them.

He sighed in my head. I may have giggled.

So far we haven't—

You haven't what?

Merrick?

Someone just blew up the building.

WHAT? Are you OK?

Of course. We're several floors below the surface, but it was definitely an explosion. We're going to check it out.

Cheese on rye, man! If the Revelation people are trying to blow you up, get out of there!

Merrick?

Merrick! Don't you no-contact me now! You know full well I'll stop looking up helots and go find you!

I know this, yes. It pains me greatly, but I'm aware of the fact that you'd put yourself at risk because you believe you are impervious to harm. No, do not lambaste me with all those thoughts I can feel you thinking. We haven't been blown up. We saw … I don't know who he was. I thought at first he was a Dark One, but he wasn't. I think it was the Thrall. Hold on. We're going after him.

Don't get too close! He might be contagious or something!

You are beyond silly, woman.

But you love that about me. Well? Did you find him?

Merrick?

Don't make me cheese-on-rye you again!

Sorry, we were chasing a woman, two Revelation men, and a gaggle of women who were with the suspected Thrall.

Wow. Sounds like an action movie. Did you catch him?

No. He escaped with the women and two Revelation people. Clearly, he has a group helping him. But we'll find him. We'll find them all.

To: Tempest, Roxy

If your life isn't made into a Netflix special, Tempest, I am going to want to know why.

JULY 5, 2011

Lemmas:

I'm doing a pro bono project to help a Dark One. Yes, the one who is delicious and sexy and gloriously handsome, and just so happens to live in 1889. OK, it didn't start that way–if you will notice from the records, I had a job to take one of the Otherworld Committee back to 1889. I popped open a portal for her, but she was a bit hesitant, never having traveled in time before. So I went with her to show her it was safe. Since her business was going to take her a few days, I had to stay there. In 1889. And during the five days it took for her to do whatever it was she was doing to the bad guy she was after, I met a really nice man named Keeley. After I came back to the present time, I felt bad because I kind of left Keeley without giving him back a book he gave me. So I popped back a few times to wrap things up. I wouldn't want to mess up anything in the time spectrum, right? Anyway, it became clear that Keeley needed me, and since Section 58, Paragraph 119, of the Weavers' Rule Book says I am allowed to dedicate up to thirty hours a year to pro bono cases that I find worthy of my help, I did so.

Because Keeley is all that and a bag of chips.

Jenna

TWELVE

"—and of course, I don't believe everything Antoinette tells me, but, Jenna, I'm telling you, this girl knows things. If she says there's a European cartel behind the MIBs, then you can believe it." Mac was curled up on a chair while I paced back and forth in front of the table where Keeley sat looking again at the non-porn files on the flash drive.

I glanced over at where Dima and Anton watched Mac with slavish devotion, and pinched my lower lip in thought as I continued to pace. For some reason, I felt both wired and overly warm, as if I'd been exercising for an hour solid. *What do you think?* I asked Keeley.

About this reference to San Francisco? I believe I'm going to have to go there and see the lab and this man named Paris for myself, he answered, printing out one of the screenshots. *I don't remember meeting him, although if what Anton says is true, I must have. It was likely during the early days. I have few memories of that time because I was heavily drugged.*

No, what do you think about what Mac said about the MIBs having their source in a group in Europe? Vienna, to be exact.

He shrugged. "It's entirely possible. The madman who captured me was definitely from a German-speaking country, but that doesn't help our situation much. It is the Revelation office in San Francisco that contains the antidote mentioned by those two."

"Huh?" Mac asked, looking confused by missing part of the conversation.

I waved that away and wandered over to the front window to stare out at my unassuming neighborhood. "I have to say that I see Keeley's point, Mac. As interesting as it is to know who is behind the MIBs, it doesn't do much to help us find the people responsible for turning him into a Thrall, and getting our hands on the fix. Assuming this antidote thingie is a fix."

"Yeah, but that's not what Antoinette was warning us about," Mac pointed out. "She just said that there's more going on with the Men in Black than we thought. There's like a super level of MIB-dom, and those guys are seriously badass."

My smart watch pinged a warning that my heart rate was higher than was normal for me. With an irritated *tsk*, I pulled the watch off and tossed it onto the table. "So long as they don't bother us, I don't care how bad their asses are. Well, the answer is pretty clear—we're going to have to go to San Francisco and investigate the Revelation office to see what's what with that antidote, and anything else we can find."

"We?" Keeley looked up from where he was reading the screenshots. His brows pulled together, his eyes darkening. "There is no *we*."

Pain stabbed through me with a sharpness that almost took away my breath. "You ass!" I told him. "You great big giant ass!"

"Dude!" Mac said, looking daggers at him.

"Whoa," Anton said to Dima. "He didn't just say that."

"He did," Dima said. "Not smart. Very much not smart."

Keeley's lips thinned. "What are you all on about?"

I raised my eyebrows at him in a meaningful way that after a few seconds he understood.

"Ah." He came perilously close to rolling his eyes, but stopped short of the actual act. "It's not that at all. I wasn't referring to our ... er ... intimate acts, Jenna. That is wholly different and completely separate from the business with the Revelation."

"Is it, though?" Mac asked, tipping her head to the side to consider him. "You guys seemed to be pretty ..." She made a gesture with both hands. "Entwined. And Jenna said that you have a past, even if she can't remember it."

"The key words there being she can't remember our past involvement," Keeley said evenly, but I felt a shadow behind his words, an emotion that confused me. It felt like despair. "In Jenna's view, we have just met. She hasn't had time to become emotionally involved to the point where she can't be separated from me."

"Boy, you just keep digging that hole deeper," Mac said with a shake of her head.

Dima and Anton shook their respective heads as well.

"I left him at the altar," I said with righteous martyrdom, the irony of which didn't in the least bit escape me. "If that doesn't indicate we had an encompassing relationship, I don't know what does."

"Right, so we go to San Fran. *All* of us," Mac said, pulling out her phone. "I'll check flight times."

Keeley took a deep breath, his expression tight, but deeper emotions seeped out: irritation, sadness, determination ... and a tiny kernel of gratitude.

The fact that he was grateful that I didn't intend to abandon him again wrung my heart, and melted my ire at the fact that he was clearly determined to protect himself from being hurt again. Tears pricked at the backs of my eyes.

"Even if I agreed to let Jenna accompany me—and it's much too dangerous for her to do so—there is no way in hell I'd allow you and your sexual playthings to go as well. It's going to be hard enough to get into the Revelation offices without having a sizable group," he said.

"That's a good point," I said, telling my inner self to stop being maudlin, and instead focus on a way of saving Keeley from the horrible men who ruined his life. I resumed my pacing and lip pinching.

"You don't seriously think you can keep me out of your adventure time," Mac asked indignantly.

I gave her a look that told her she should know better. "Of course not. Keeley doesn't realize how resourceful you are in a tight place. If he and I go to San Francisco, you will have to come with us."

"*If* we go to San Francisco?" Keeley frowned again, which just made me want to run my finger along his eyebrows to smooth them out. He'd suffered so much, it made me want to give him nothing but comfort.

And lots and lots of steamy hot lovin'.

What was that?

Nothing, I answered, and hoped he had heard only a whisper of my thoughts.

He shot me an unreadable look before continuing. "I assure you that it is necessary I track down any avenue regarding the situation the madmen put me in, and a solution therein."

"No, I'm not saying you shouldn't try to reverse things if you can," I said slowly, my mind churning through an impossible idea, one I knew I shouldn't be considering at all. And yet, it offered such a beautiful solution to the problem that faced us. "Not that I'm sure you can be de-Thralled. But it did occur to me that there is more than one way to tackle the issue."

"What other way? If you are intending on returning to the building in which I was held captive, allow me to dissuade you of that idea. The lab there was cleaned out. A return search would hold no value."

"I love it when you talk Victorian," I couldn't help saying. "Almost as much as I love your fancy accent. Where was I?"

"Is good accent. Is sexy," Dima said, casting Keeley a speculative glance. I paused in my path past the latter to put a hand on his uninjured shoulder, and gave Dima a look that hopefully made it clear I'd staked my claim.

Keeley snorted in my head before saying aloud, "We

were discussing my trip to San Francisco to locate the antidote and confront Paris."

"You know," Mac said slowly before I could answer. She'd been lounging in the chair absently watching Keeley and me, but now she sat up, her gaze on nothing in particular. "We have a bigger problem than you getting the antidote."

"We do?" Keeley's brows pulled together again. "What would that be?"

"Technology," she said, waggling her eyebrows at me. "I never thought I'd find myself saying this, but I think in your case, it might just be your biggest enemy."

"Do you mean the creation of the antidote?" Keeley asked, his expression shifting. "Hmm. Yes, I see what you mean. We will have to take the chemist as well. And anything in his lab."

"Not good enough," Mac said, shaking her head at him.

I could feel Keeley's frustration rise, but right at that moment I realized what Mac was talking about. "Crap. You're right, Mac." I turned to Keeley and explained quickly. "You won't know this because you've only had limited time with modern computers, but there's a thing called the cloud. It's a virtual storage center, for lack of a better explanation, where people can upload any sort of file. And once it's uploaded, you can't delete it. Not only that, but other people can have access to it all over the world."

"That's not entirely true," Mac corrected me as Keeley's shoulders slumped. I wanted to hold him against the sudden swell of futility that welled up inside him. "The part about not being deleted, that is. Someone—say, for instance, a talented hacker—could go in and corrupt or remove the part of the cloud hosting the data. And then search out any backups and destroy those, in effect wiping out every last file."

Keeley stopped slumping, his shoulders squaring. "And you are a talented hacker?"

"No," she said with clear regret. "But I sure as hell know one who can get into any system. He's expensive, though. Like, seven-figures sort of expensive."

"Contact him," Keeley said without batting so much as an eyelash. "Give him the name of the Revelation. See if he can destroy their cloud and remove all data regarding the antidote and whatever cocktail they use to trigger the bloodlust. Anything to do with Thralls."

Do you have that sort of money? I asked, more than a little surprised.

Yes.

I considered him with new respect, wondering what he'd done over the last one-hundred-plus years to amass that sort of a fortune.

Mac had her phone out even before Keeley finished speaking. "On it."

Keeley continued making notes on the printouts of the messages, while I sorted through what I wanted to say. I paced a few steps away, then turned and gave him a long look. "This all sounds very expensive. And there's no guarantee that Mac's hacker can do what she thinks he can do."

"Trust me, he can," she said without looking up.

I waved that assurance away, feeling like action was what was needed, not a reliance on whether others could do the job. "There's another way. We can circumvent this whole thing."

"Circumvent what?" Keeley asked.

"This," I said, gesturing toward Mac. "The hacker. You going to San Francisco to get the antidote and beat up Paris. Finding the chemist. All that. There's no reason to spend all that time and energy, and huge wads of cash. We'll simply make it so you aren't a Thrall."

"What do you—" He stopped, his expression turning first wary, then forbidding. "No."

"Hear me out," I said, picking through the ideas tumbling around in my mind, trying to place them in a logical order. "If I zap back through time—"

"No. That is not a solution," he said sternly, getting to his feet. Absently, I noted that he no longer held his hurt shoulder higher than the other, more proof that he had healed as he had claimed.

"—before you were turned into a Thrall—"

"Jenna, you aren't listening to me," he said, taking me by the arms. His eyes were a pale gray, like an early winter morning.

"—then the whole situation will be avoided," I finished. "I can warn you to avoid the men who turned you. Thus and therefore, there won't be a need for you to get the antidote, because you won't be a Thrall. It's simplicity itself."

"Not to mention all the Thrall Babies you won't make," Mac said, nodding her head. "That's a very good idea, Jenna. But what about you guys? Will you be able to hook up again?"

"It is *not* a good idea," Keeley rumbled, his jaw set. "It is the epitome of the opposite, as a matter of fact."

"Well, I'm going to have to find him to warn him about the baddies wanting to make him a Thrall," I said after a few seconds' thought. "When were you changed, Keeley?"

"In 2001," he answered with obvious reluctance.

"Damn. That's just before they wiped my brain. The first time, that is. The second time was in 2011. It just means I'll have to Back to the Future it."

"Back to the—oh." Mac's eyes widened as she thought it over for a few seconds, then nodded. "Smart."

"What does an eighties movie have to do with the insane idea that you can stop the inevitable?" Keeley demanded to know, his arms crossed.

Something about his irritability melted me even more. "It's a plot mechanism," I explained, wanting badly to kiss him.

That I would not mind. You time traveling is another matter, he said in a decidedly grumpy tone.

"When Marty McFly wanted to clue himself in to something that he did in the past, but his present self didn't know, he arranged for a message written in the past to be delivered later in time. So what I will need to do is pop back before you were Thralled, send you a message with the info about where you were at that particular time and place, and then have it delivered before the date and time so you can avoid the Men in Black. Yes, I think that will do nicely. A law firm would suit, do you think?" I asked the last question of Mac, since Keeley was continuing to shake his head at me.

"Probably. My godfather was a lawyer. I can ask my mom where he was in 2001, if you want, but honestly, I bet his firm would do it," she answered. "They were shady as hell. They probably did mysterious future messages all the time."

"I feel as if I'm not speaking, and yet I can plainly hear myself," Keeley said in a conversational tone of voice before giving me a little shake. "Jenna, much though I appreciate you offering what you believe to be a solution to this situation, it is unfeasible."

"Why?" I asked, ignoring the obvious.

He just cocked an eyebrow at me.

"OK," I admitted, the obvious refusing to be ignored. "There is the problem of the interdiction. But the fact that I was able to blip around the Men in Black during our dramatic escape from their clutches tells me that it's not worth the paper it's written on. So to speak."

"Regardless, violation of the rules bound to you is not to be considered. You yourself said you were in trouble for using your abilities without knowing just what they were. I imagine the punishment for doing so in full possession of your faculties would be far greater."

I pointed at his mouth. "You can talk all the fancy talk you want in that plummy, BBC sort of voice, but it's not going to make me want to strip off every bit of your clothing, and molest you with my mouth."

Keeley froze, his pupils dilating.

"OK, it will, but I am a strong, independent woman who has full control of her libido, and if I say there's no licking of your delicious self right now, then no licking there shall be."

"Jenna," he said warningly, pushing aside a bunch of erotic thoughts that I more than wanted him to dwell over. "You are being overly flip about a serious matter."

"I am," I agreed. "And do you know why? I'm pissed as hell. Those Weaver people took away my powers over something stupid. I am not a doormat, Keeley, and I won't put up with that. I want my powers back, and by the stars above us, if I can get around the interdict and use them, then that's what I'm going to do."

His eyes were grave, but I felt the worry deep inside him. It warmed me that he cared so much. "I understand your desire to use the power you were born with, but did you ever consider that in addition to the punishment already bound to you, there is an overwhelming likelihood that the interdiction won't allow you anything but the most minor of abilities?"

"Oh," Mac said, clearly disappointed. She plopped down at the table, and idly sifted through the printouts Keeley had made of the screenshots on the flash drive. "Dammit, he has a point. And it was such a good idea, too."

I know you want to help, he told me, allowing me to feel the concern he felt for my well-being, as well as the gratitude that I wanted to save him from ever becoming a Thrall, *but this is not the answer. The past is the past. We can't change it.*

"But we can, don't you see?" I said, leaning into him and allowing my lips to caress the corners of his mouth, my hands sliding up his chest in a manner that had his breath hitching. "And before you argue that it goes against the laws of nature, which I can tell you're about to do, consider this: you tried to Thrall Baby me, but it didn't work. That means that not only was I meant to be there to find you, and save you, but also, we can take it a step further—because I'm now a she-vamp, something in my genetic makeup was fundamentally changed by you. And if *that's* changed, then there's a very good chance that the interdict can't deal with my new, altered self. I don't know for certain, but I'm willing to bet you that Jenna 2.0 can do a time blip just fine."

He hesitated for a moment, clearly thinking that over. "That's just a supposition. You have no proof."

"I hate to rain on your extrapolation parade, but there's also the issue of the time paradox. If you change the past so Keeley wasn't made a Thrall, that might seriously impact the future," Mac pointed out.

I shrugged. "Only so much as he won't have disappeared, and won't have enslaved people. That's got to be for the better, since they won't have gone missing, and their families won't have lost them."

A pang of pain shot through him. Wordlessly, I offered him comfort.

"I have a question," Mac said, raising her hand. "Just what is this Revolution group—"

"Revelation," Keeley corrected.

"What is this Revelation group making all the Thrall Babies for? I mean … what do they do for the baddies?" She watched Keeley with an avidity that made me feel prickly.

"Whatever they want them to do. Capture people—mortal and immortal—for their experiments. Steal. Kill. Make money." Keeley's lips tightened. "They look like normal people but have no will of their own. Whatever their masters tell them to do, they will do it. Because they used mortal beings, there are no ties back to their group, so if the helot is caught while carrying out orders, the Revelation writes off that helot and sends the next in to do the job."

"Wow." Mac's eyes narrowed. "That's just seriously evil."

"They don't even protect their own people?" I asked, the prickling sensation growing.

"Why would they?" Keeley answered. "To the Revelation, the helots are dispensable. They've forced me to create more than one hundred helots, so I have no doubt they are willing to sacrifice a few in the furtherance of their goals."

"OK, I get that, but let's go back to the question of Jenna going back in time to warn Keeley so he doesn't become a Thrall. What if one of the people he took out of circulation was evil?" Mac asked, her expression troubled. "What if by making them a Thrall Baby, he kept them from being a serial killer? Or worse?"

I thought about that for a few seconds. "I would say we're just going to have to risk it, but I agree that's a pretty strong point. What if we tracked down every Thrall Baby—"

Keeley sighed heavily in my mind.

"—every helot-to-be," I corrected, "and made sure they weren't doing heinous things in their freedom?"

"I suppose," Mac said with obvious reluctance. "Although it seems to me you're willing to potentially sacrifice a lot just to save Keeley. No offense intended, naturally."

Keeley made an abrupt gesture. "As I agree with the desire to save the helots I changed, I have taken none. What Jenna proposes is simply not reasonable, however."

"I'm now a Moravian as well as a Weaver," I pointed out. "I can pretty much do anything I want, and I just bet you that includes zipping through time again."

"Not to mention you're a Midnight Walker," Mac said, circling something on one of the printouts. "So there's the alien DNA making you different."

"My family doesn't have alien DNA," I scoffed. "We just have a weird chemical thing that means that sometimes we turn blue. I've never done it, though," I added quickly at Keeley's widened eyes.

He relaxed.

"Not since I went through puberty, that is," I added, and flashed him a wide grin.

His expression remained stoic. "Your alien DNA aside—"

"It's not alien, just a bit weird."

"—unless you have become a genetic researcher since the time when I knew you, it's impossible for you to say whether or not the changes wrought upon you by me have changed your Weaving abilities."

"There's only one way to find out for sure," I said, a heated wave of happiness washing over me, driving away the prickling sensation. "I'll simply try to time travel. If I can't do it, then we know that I haven't changed on a genetic level, and we'll go with you to San Francisco to find the antidote. If I can … well, it means the interdict is rubbish, and Abbott and her Weavers can't blame me if their magic is crap."

"I don't think that's the best avenue to finding out how things lie with you," Keeley said, and, releasing my arms, gathered up the printouts.

"I get that, but, dude!" I said, unreasonably wanting to stamp my foot. "They wiped my brain and effectively took away my powers. I'm not going to just roll over because *they* made a mistake."

Keeley cocked his eyebrow at me again.

"I know, I know," I told the Eyebrow of Much Questioning. "I evidently did something wrong that put them in the position to mess with me, but that doesn't negate the fact that I was basically punished twice—first by them taking away my powers, and then by them wiping my mental hard drive. Just think how you'd like it if someone came along and wiped out every memory you had."

"That would totally blow," Mac said, winking at Dima. He beamed at her. "Hacker is on, by the way. I'm supposed to give you the account number of an escrow company that will hold your payment until the job's done. He said it might take up to twelve hours."

"Thank you," Keeley told her before narrowing his eyes on me, obviously giving my comment consideration. "I admit that it was an exceptionally harsh circumstance, and I don't believe you could have done anything so heinous as to deserve to have your memory removed, but the fact remains that you are still bound to the interdiction. The best thing is for you to remain here. I will contact you after I've been to the Revelation's headquarters and ascertained whether or not they have the antidote."

The heat inside me built up while he spoke, giving me a sense of near delirium. Time seemed to slow, just as if I were watching a movie made in slow motion. I turned my head away from Keeley, my movements sluggish even as the heat inside me caused little pinpricks of sweat to break out along my hairline.

Time travel, I thought to myself, trying to picture what that looked like. An image rose in my mind's eye of a steel gray–blue cloud hanging a few feet above the ground, the shape of it ever changing as it twisted upon itself like an endless taffy machine. "Portal," I whispered to myself, my skin hot as I mentally reached out and adjusted the warp and weft that was our plane of reality.

Keeley started to turn toward me, obviously reading my intentions, a protest starting to take form in his head even as I focused my attention on the motes of light that began to gather before me, spinning and twirling and lengthening until a twisting Möbius gray shape resolved itself.

My back itched as perspiration formed there from the heat that continued to build inside me, until I felt as if I were standing in an inferno. Even as I reached a hand out toward the portal, taking a step forward, a cold draft of wind rippled across my back.

And just like that, time seemed to snap back into its normal cadence, causing me to stumble at the same time Keeley said in my head, *Jenna! Do not*— He stopped to stare past me, surprise flickering across his face.

I spun around to face a fiercely frowning Lemmas.

"What is this?" she asked, her eyes moving from the portal, which hung impossibly in the air, slowly and endlessly spinning upon itself, to me. "How did you do that? The interdict—"

"Is worthless," I said, the heat inside me turning to elation. I felt almost giddy with power. I felt like a combination of every comic superhero rolled together. There was nothing I couldn't do!

On the contrary, there are a great many things that are beyond your reach, but that is not what's important right now. What is important is this fever I feel in you. Are you ill? And who is this woman?

Lemmas. She's one of the people who got pissy at me. Don't worry about it, though. I'll take care of her. I didn't even wonder at the bravado that filled me.

Lemmas sucked in an irate breath at my words, her voice as cold as flint when she replied, "I see that I was grossly mistaken in your depth of character. You may rest assured I will not be so again. Jenna Walker Boyle, in the name of the Weavers' Guild, I hereby condemn you to exsanguination."

I swaggered forward, about to tell her what she could do with her threats when suddenly the heat within me that had given me such a sense of power fizzled to nothing, leaving me empty and weak.

Keeley caught me when I staggered to the side, concern filling my head. *What is wrong? Did she do something to you?*

No. I'm not sure what happened, but I don't think it had anything to do with her. "Look," I told Lemmas, moving from Keeley's side even though my legs were a bit wobbly. "I know you feel I need to be punished, but this is important. I swear to you that I'm not doing any of that joyriding you mentioned. This is to save a bunch of innocent people from being turned into slaves. So if you don't mind—"

"But I do mind," she snapped. "You have been warned. How you broke the interdict this time, I do not know, but it doesn't matter. You agreed to the terms of the punishment, and now you have violated them. I shall summon the rest of the Council members, and begin the exsanguination."

"First, I didn't agree to anything. And second, oh hell no," I said, rallying my inner strength. Before she could react, I grabbed her arm and ran the few feet to my front door, shoving her through it, slamming the door shut and locking it before turning back to the others. My mind squirreled around frantically for a few seconds before grasping at the only option we had.

Run.

Are you insane? Keeley started toward me.

No. Run through the portal.

Keeley shot me a look that spoke volumes, but I didn't have time to argue with him.

"Portal," I yelled at Mac, who had risen to her feet at the appearance of Lemmas.

Mac glanced over at me with wide eyes. "Huh?"

"Go through the portal," I answered, pointing.

She didn't hesitate. She grabbed Dima and Anton, and with a quick, "OK, but if we die, I get to come back and haunt you," she flung herself into the twisting gray object. Dima whooped and jumped in after her. Anton sighed heavily, bowed to me and Keeley, and strolled into the portal just as if it were something he did every day.

At the same moment, Lemmas, who had been in the act of texting when I had shoved her outside, evidently finished sending her messages, and returned by blipping back into the room. "I will not stand for being physically abused on top of everything else! You have much to answer for, which you will find out when Council arrives to teach you your place," she said, a furious glint to her eyes.

"If you think I'm going to let you guys de-brain me again, you're nuttier than I thought," I snapped back. "No one is wiping my memories again, let alone my powers."

"You think to fight us?" she asked, her eyes narrowing even as she started toward us. "You will quickly find that the Council is not so weak. We will see to it that you are punished for your acts this day, no matter how much you fight."

Right, this is where we throw caution to the wind, I told Keeley, taking his hand and running for the portal.

To my surprise, he didn't argue; he simply paused at it and wrapped both arms around me, pulling me up close to his body before he stepped through.

The protective gesture would have done me in if the portal had zapped us back in time as I expected.

Instead we ran into a familiar mustard-yellow wall. I blinked at it before turning to look behind me.

The tour bus sat half-sheltered by the shade of the carport. The very same carport that was just a few feet away from my living room.

"Well, hell," I said, annoyance filling me. "This is just the epitome of disappointment. I go to all the trouble of summoning up an actual portal, and all it does is move us a few feet?"

"There you are! We thought you were never coming out."

I gawked at the source of the cheerful voice that I hadn't heard since the day before, and stared in surprise at the five heads that poked out of the bus. "Wha—Beth?"

"Hi!" the tourist named Beth said, waving. "Is the adventure starting now? We all brought packed lunches, just as Mac asked."

"You'd think payin' as much as we did, we would have gotten a lunch," Mrs. Walsh drawled with a sniff. "I expect a Thrall Baby for me havin' to bring my own tuna sammy."

I turned my gawk onto Mac. I was so flabbergasted, for a few minutes I forgot the threat of Lemmas. "You told the tourists to be here? You made them bring a packed lunch?"

She grabbed my arm and hustled me toward the bus, saying quietly but quickly, "They wanted to come along. All five messaged me last night, and offered to pay big for more action. Two hundred bucks each, Jenna!"

"You brought tourists on our dramatic escape from—" I remembered at that moment that Lemmas was just a few yards away, and stopped arguing, running up the steps of the bus after Mac.

Anton and Dima were already on board, politely introducing themselves to the tourists.

"Come on!" I stood at the top of the stairs and gestured at Keeley, who hesitated. "You're stalling? Now? I don't want to be exsanguinated," I told him, and gestured again.

You wouldn't be facing such a thing—not that I entirely understand what blood has to do with a Weaver—if you hadn't been so quick to dismiss my concerns, he answered, but, to my relief, also entered the bus. *What I would really like to know is why you thought it suitable to bring along the tourists from yesterday.*

First of all, you can't blame me for what happened inside. I was trying to save us, and it just seemed like the thing to do to fix everything, I answered, secretly pleased when he smooshed into a seat next to me, his body reassuringly solid beside me. "To the airport?"

"We're going to the airport?" Madison asked. She had been filming Anton and Dima at the back of the bus, but turned back to us at the word. "Are we going somewhere?"

Keeley sighed another of the martyred sighs that made me want to giggle. "I suppose so, assuming that the Weaver Council will attempt to follow you."

"A trip!" Lolly said, clapping her hands.

"I get airsick," Mrs. Walsh intoned, moving back a few seats to sit alongside Dima. "And carsick. You're foreign, ain't you? I always did like foreign boys. I like how they talk funny. And a lot of them ain't … you know … snipped at the tip."

I thought about how angry Lemmas had been. "Unfortunately, I think they are a little pissed at me. And Lemmas might try to come after me. Although the rest of you and the tourists should be OK."

One of his eyebrows rose.

Oh, you did not just cock an eyebrow in that telling way, I said with a sniff. *I didn't book the tourists for today. This is supposed to be our day off, as a matter of fact, but Mac said they offered big money to have an adventure, so I guess they're coming with us. At least they brought their own snacks.*

Keeley tipped his head and shot me a disbelieving look.

Two hundred each, Keeley! That's a thousand bucks just for letting them ride around with us. I mean, you'd have to be crazy to turn down that sort of money.

I won't even honor that statement with the obvious response, he answered. Do you have a cellular phone I could use?

"Sure. Can you get tickets for all of us? It'll cut into the profits, but that can't be helped," I asked, grabbing at the rail when Mac put her foot down and swung us around a corner at a dangerous speed. "Mac! Let's get there in one piece!"

"Just didn't want that blippy lady to pop onto the bus with us," she answered, heading for the highway that led to the nearby town's airport.

"No," Keeley answered, and examined phone. "It's faster to simply charter a plane."

I blinked at him in surprise. "Wow. That sounds kind of expensive."

"It is." His fingers moved hesitantly across my phone.

"Er …" I spent a quick minute mentally tallying my credit card bill, and said softly, "If you are using my credit card, I'm afraid it's not quite up to private-plane-ride standards. Not all of us can afford seven-figure purchases. I can't even afford a four-figure one."

"I won't use your card. I'll use my bank account." He continued to poke tentatively at the screen. "Hopefully they haven't changed my log-in information over the years."

"Gotcha," I said before glancing over my shoulder to make sure that we weren't being followed.

Four happy, expectant faces immediately turned to me. The fifth tourist, Mrs. Walsh, was whispering something in Dima's ear, leaving him with a startled expression. Anton was watching the back of Mac's head with a look of slavish devotion that I was coming to believe was the standard Thrall Baby expression.

I cleared my throat and stood, facing the occupants before clicking on the PA microphone. "Hello again, everyone. I'm so glad you decided to join Outta This World Tours for a second—albeit unexpected—day of adventure and excitement. You will notice that we are making our way to the airport, where my … er … friend Keeley is booking us a private plane."

"Oooh!" Beth said in a near squeal. She was sitting with Lolly, who clapped her hands again.

The TikTok girls cheered. "We are so going viral with these videos," Madison told Tucson even as the pair of them lifted their phones to film me.

I turned slightly to a more flattering angle. "You are under no obligation to fly to San Francisco with us, however, so if you'd prefer to have your tour fee for today refunded, we will be happy to do so."

"The hell we will," I heard Mac mutter from the front.

I slapped my professional tour-guide smile into place. "I should also remind you that when you signed the agreement to take this tour—" A horrible thought struck me, and I leaned to the side and asked in a low tone, "Mac, did they sign another form?"

"Yes."

"Whew." I smiled again at the tourists, and clicked the mic back on. "I should remind you that the tour agreement includes a liability exclusion for any potential dangerous situations, so please be careful when around the Men in Black, a woman named Lemmas, and any odd individuals you might encounter in the course of our journey. I hope you all enjoy today's tour … er … experience, and please don't hesitate to ask if you have any questions."

Mrs. Walsh held up her hand.

"Yes, Mrs. Walsh?"

"I wanna know what sort of Thrall Babies there will be in San Francisco. Do we get a herd of them to pick from? Are they all gonna be sexual slaves like these two? 'Cause I don't want just an ordinary Thrall Baby. Not if I'm payin' all this money. I expect to have a blue-ribbon sort available."

Waves of martyrdom seemed to roll from Keeley.

Blame Mac, not me, I told him. *They picked it up from her.*

I don't even know where to begin with any of this, he commented, but returned his attention to the phone.

"We are not offering Thrall—er—helots, Mrs. Walsh," I said with another of my fake smiles.

"Actually, I told them I had enough juice I squeezed out of Keeley's shirt to make one for everyone," Mac said.

I closed my eyes for a moment, willing Keeley to not sigh into my head.

Oh, I have a lot more than sighing to do, he said, now positively dripping with martyred emotions.

You're not the only one. "I stand corrected. However, I feel it important to point out that we cannot guarantee the availability of helots. Mac might not be able to make them."

Keeley shot me an outraged look.

"More importantly," I said quickly, feeling the sting of that look, "it's very, very against common decency to make someone a mindless slave just for your own satisfaction, sexual or otherwise. Consent, as I believe you all know, is important. We do not make helots out of individuals who have not consented to do so."

"Did you consent to being Mac's boy toy?" Mrs. Walsh asked Dima.

"Yes," he answered.

"That's a shame, that is," Mrs. Walsh said, giving him a wink. "Older women know things younger ones don't."

"Mac isn't a monster," I told Mrs. Walsh. "She wouldn't have Thrall Babied them if they didn't want to be so."

Keeley flinched. I put a hand on his shoulder, and fed him warm, consoling emotions.

"I told them that if they joined me, they could take part in an exciting experiment, and they said yes," Mac said, blithely unaware of the pain she'd caused Keeley.

"Mac is much nicer than our former supervisor," Anton said, calmly removing Mrs. Walsh's hand from where it was caressing his thigh. "We knew we would be happier with her than with the corporation."

"We very happy with Mac," Dima added.

"Well. There you have it. Possible Thr—helots if they agree to the position, and Mac can make them. Does anyone wish to withdraw from the day's experience, such as it is?" I asked.

Five heads shook.

"This is going to make us a shit-ton," Tucson said, now filming Mrs. Walsh, who preened for her.

"A shit-ton of what?" Beth asked, her gray curls bobbing with the motion of the bus. "Money?"

"And followers. We'll get the big influencer accounts, the kind that go to the Kardashians," Madison answered, filming Tucson before turning the camera on herself for a little selfie time. "Oh my god! We could end up with a reality show!"

"On Netflix!" Tucson agreed, and the two girls stared at each other for a few seconds before screaming happily.

"Oh, I love reality shows," Lolly told Beth.

I sat back down next to Keeley, exhaustion suddenly swamping me as around us the tourists chattered happily. Occasionally I glanced over my shoulder to make sure we weren't being followed. Not, I told myself, that Lemmas was likely to be driving a car in hot pursuit when she could just magic her way onto the bus, but perhaps she had to know where we were in order to blip successfully.

"I don't mind if you log into things on my phone, so feel free to get any text messages you've missed while you were being held prisoner," I told Keeley. "Or is that before your time? I don't remember what was happening in 2001."

"Yes, text messaging was around, although I didn't use it much. I will log into my e-mail client, although that will be sadly out-of-date." Keeley frowned at the phone. "How do I get to that?"

"Oh, right, you probably aren't too familiar with Android systems." I spent a few minutes showing him the ways of a smartphone, then left him to deal with what I assumed were very old e-mails.

I sat back, my mind wondering and wandering, and watched as the sagebrush blurred past us when we bumped our way onto the smooth tarmac of the highway.

Was I getting some sort of a cold that occasionally left me hot with a fever, and at other times as limp as a wet rag?

What was going on with my Weaver abilities? How could I summon a portal, but not actually use it as I intended? Was that the interdict, or something else?

And most important of all, was there anything that could be done for Keeley? Was the pursuit of the antidote a potential solution to his problem, or just a wild-goose chase?

In the end, did it matter, so long as I was there to help him?

Mentally, I shook away all the questions, too tired to cope with any of them. I leaned into Keeley and gave myself up to the enjoyment of the feel, and sight, and scent, of him, my worries melting away in the pleasure to be found simply in his presence.

THIRTEEN

To: Tempest, Roxy

Any news? I'm back in Monaco, but I don't know what to tell the troupe about the whole doom doom doom situation. Should we close the theater? Is it safe for Dark Ones to be out and about? What is the dishy Merrick doing? Inquiring minds want to know!

To: Roxy, Ellis

We're heading to San Francisco. The Revelation flunky the guys interrogated said something about the HQ being there. Merrick, Han, and Ciaran are tracking down some tourist company that they think is working with the Thrall, and are en route to the tour office to see what they can find before we go to California. I've been sent to the airport to arrange for a plane, with Andreas as my shadow. And don't think I didn't have a few words for Merrick about that.

To: Tempest, Ellis

About what—Merrick keeping you out of a possibly dangerous situation with the tour people, or booking a plane? Also, can't you just do that on your phone?

To: Roxy, Ellis

Both. But mostly Merrick insisting that Andreas tag along since he—Merrick—says it's not safe in this area when it's loaded with Rev people. Regardless, yes, I could charter a plane by phone except we can't get through to the only private plane company available. Their system is messed up. So annoying. Anyway, I'll let you know—oh, sec, call from Merrick.

To: Roxy, Ellis

Update: the tour company is a bust. Or at least the office is. Merrick and the others broke in and didn't find anything in their records to indicate a relationship with the Revelation, so the guys are going to meet us at the airport, and we'll head west. Will catch you guys up with all the latest details as soon as I can!

10 JULY 1889

My beloved Jenna,

I can only assume by your refusal to see me or acknowledge my many messages and letters that you have had an inexplicable change of heart regarding me, our future, and the wedding which was to take place yesterday.

I don't know what I've done to so anger you that you have withdrawn completely, evidently going so far as to leave London without word of your destination, but whatever it is, whatever I have said, whatever act I have conducted that you find so heinous, know that I am truly sorry. I would not hurt you for the world. You are my heart. You are my life. You are everything to me. I don't know what I've done to drive you from my side, but please, please tell me what it is, so that I might undo my actions and regain your love.

It may be unmanly to beg, but I have no pride left. Without you, there is no future. Please return to me. Please tell me why you have left me. Please tell me how I have destroyed your love.

Yours in utter despair,

Keeley

FOURTEEN

Keeley was distracted by approximately twenty years of e-mail that had collected since the madmen had found him and turned him into a monster. *Twenty years,* he told Jenna, shifting so that she could slump more comfortably against him while at the same time accessing his e-mail via her phone.

Hmm? No, I'm thirty-six. Or thought I was. I gather I'm actually around a hundred.

I meant that I've been a prisoner for almost twenty years. I'm responsible for more than one hundred helots.

Not responsible, she murmured sleepily into his mind, obviously drowsy by the ride into the next town. Just the weight of her body pressed against him gave him a sense of peace that had been missing so long from his life he didn't recognize its loss.

"Wow. AOL still exists?" the young woman who was always filming things asked as she returned from perching across from him, filming Mac as she drove. "I remember my parents using it, but had no idea it was still around."

"Evidently so," Keeley said, deleting several thousand e-mails, most of which were impersonal advertisements. Every now and again he'd find one from an old acquaintance, or business concern, but for the most part, they were long past relevance. "The madmen let me use a laptop and sometimes a tablet to keep from going insane, but they refused to allow me outside access. Why is a Nigerian prince contacting me?"

"Spam," Jenna murmured, then gave a little snore as she snuggled into him.

I told you that I can't eat food. "You are going to the Marysville Field Airport, yes?" he asked Mac, verifying that the plane he booked was going to be ready within the hour.

"Yup. That's the nearest one." Mac glanced in the rear-view mirror, and said softly, so her voice wouldn't carry back to the tourists, "Hey, if you made Jenna a female vamp, do you think you could make me one, too? I don't have a blood fetish or anything like that, but vampires are immortal, aren't they? I'd like to be immortal. For one thing, it would freak the hell out of my friends. And for another, I could do research for centuries!"

"Are you a Weaver?" Keeley asked the woman, knowing full well she was as mortal as they came.

"No," she admitted, making a face in the mirror at him.

"Then if I tried to turn you, you'd end up a brainless, mindless helot. Not only that, you might push me into the Breaking, at which point everyone around me would be destroyed."

"My Thrall Babies aren't brainless or mindless," she pointed out, clearly ignoring the important part of his statement.

Keeley glanced back to where her two helots were chatting with the tourists, but simply said, "The fact remains that Jenna is unique. All the mortals I've been forced to change were helots."

"Hmm," Mac said thoughtfully, chewing that over for a few minutes before adding, "Maybe when you drank from Chez Jenna, something changed inside you."

He looked up from his thousands of e-mails. "Changed how?"

She shrugged. "I'm not a geneticist, but it seems to me that if Jenna's makeup is so different, and you drank her blood, then maybe her genes changed you."

Jenna murmured something unintelligible next to him. He moved slightly so she could rest more comfortably against him. He thought about what Mac had said, wondering if her speculation had any reasonable validation. "It is something to investigate further," he finally said. "I don't think we can say either way without looking closer at what the madmen did to me, and we can't do that without the drugs they used to make me a Thrall, or the antidote that keeps their victims from turning into helots."

"Experimentation is a good thing," Mac said with a waggle of her eyebrows.

"I am not desirous of entering the state of Breaking, but even if I was, are you willing to risk becoming a mindless helot?" he asked.

She made a face in the rearview mirror. "Yeah, good point. OK, we'll save that for later."

The Marysville Field Airport wasn't large by any sense of the word, but it did have two airplanes available for hire. Luckily, one was still available when Keeley booked it. He emerged from the bus, automatically sticking to the shade as he helped a still-sleepy Jenna down the stairs, watching with a sense of resigned martyrdom when the five tourists happily followed them.

"I'll just go check that the plane is ready for us," he said, mentally frowning at the slight flush that warmed Jenna's cheeks. "Would you prefer waiting here, or in the terminal?"

"Oh, inside," she answered, fanning herself.

"Amen to that," Mac said as she and the two quasi-helots followed her out of the bus.

"It's as hot as Satan's taint out here," the old lady with the sour face said, giving him an appraising glance that he had no trouble interpreting.

He put his arm around Jenna.

"Cold drinks for everyone," Jenna said, adding mentally, *Well, you can have yours body temperature. You feel hungry to me. Did you want to … er … dine, for lack of a better word?*

Later, he answered. "Are you sure you're feeling well?"

She hesitated a few seconds before answering, "I'm not unwell. Just a bit warm. I'm probably a bit dehydrated, but a couple of lemonades should take care of that."

He nodded, and hurried off to find the office of the private airlines, habit keeping him to the shade although Thralls, he had been told, did not suffer the same level of damage from the sun as Dark Ones. "The one and only benefit to what the madmen did to me," he muttered to himself as he pushed open a door reading MOTHER FOKKER AIRLINES.

A man in a long coat and a hat stood at the reception counter, his voice bearing a faint German accent as he spoke. "—you certain there is no way you can accommodate my request? My friends and I need to get to San Francisco as soon as possible."

"Sorry, but as I, like, *just* got done telling you, we only have two planes, and one is out in Arizona right now, and the other is booked, and will be leaving shortly," the woman behind the counter told the man.

"I would be willing to pay more than the regular fee if you would delay the customer," the German said.

"Sorry," the woman repeated, picking up her phone, clearly dismissing the man. "If you'd gotten here an hour ago, I could let you have it, but there's nothing I can do."

"I'll double the rate," the man insisted. "It is extremely important that my friends and I reach San Francisco as soon as possible."

Keeley leveled a look at the back of the man's head, thought about saying something rude, but decided that his confinement for the last twenty years in the company of nothing but madmen and their henchmen had left his social skills shriveled and atrophied.

Instead of giving in to his inner snark, he approached the counter and said, "I'm Keeley Moore. I believe you have a flight booked for my party."

At his voice, the pushy man at the counter spun around and stared at him in obvious surprise. An odd sense of rage filled him as he jerked backward just as if the other man had punched him. Keeley had no idea who the man was, but the fine hairs on the back of his neck stood on end.

"You!" the man said, and before Keeley could ask him who he was, the man pulled a familiar-looking small black device from his pocket and thrust it into Keeley's chest, right over his heart.

"T-T-Tas—" Keeley hit the floor when his muscles locked up, agony crawling through his head leaving him breathless and speechless. His body curled up on itself, the muscles straining against themselves, leaving his mind filled with wave after wave of pain.

Keeley? What the hell?

Jenna! She must have sensed his emotions. Keeley tried to rally his brainpower enough to shut out Jenna, but his mind was locked in a cycle of wrenching, twisting pain.

Above him, the man was speaking in German, clearly talking into a phone. "Merrick! I found the Old One. No, right here at the airport. He was trying to escape, but I Tasered him. Christos, there's Tempest. She's sure to want to help. Get here as soon as you can. I'll get him onto the plane, but he'll come out of it soon enough, and I'd prefer to have you here since you are familiar with the Revelation."

"Andreas?" The small bell over the door jangled softly when a woman's voice floated past Keeley. "Did you get the plane? Merrick says he and the others will be here in about fifteen minutes—whoa. Who's that rolling around on the floor?"

Keeley desperately tried to relax his cramping muscles. He willed his body to a state of calm, praying he exuded that sense to Jenna, lest she come to find him—

The door was flung open with such force that the bell slammed first into the wall, then went flying across the room with a discordant sound. "Keeley! Oh my goddess, what's wrong? Are you hurt again?"

Before he could do so much as roll over, he was aware of Jenna's presence, warm, delightful, filling all his senses with the wonderfulness of her being.

"Urk," he said, trying to speak, but unable to get his jaw to unlock.

"What the hell did you do to him!" Jenna roared, her sandals moving into his range of vision. One part of his brain, the part that could still function, was amused to note just how annoyed her toes looked. The other part, however, was horrified that she would put herself in what was obvious danger. *Rn,* he thought at her, his synapses not fully working.

Huh?

"Excuse me? Who are you?" the newly arrived woman asked.

"Did you touch him?" Jenna asked in a snarl, the threat in her voice simultaneously warming him to his toes and further frightening him. *Run,* he managed at last to say. He might have no idea who the German man was, but he was clearly not a friend.

Are you insane? What did these people do to you?

Tsr.

"You bastards! How dare you Taser Keeley!"

Slowly, he felt the cramping in his muscles begin to lessen. He managed to tip his head back, desperately needing to get Jenna out of danger. *Leave. Can't … work.*

"Who are you?" the man with the hat asked, grabbing the other woman and pulling her to his side. She pulled her arm from his grip with a jerk and a small frown that drew her auburn brows together. "Are you with the Old One?"

Oh, no one touches my once-fiancé and gets away with it, Jenna growled in his head, and stalked forward to poke a finger into the chest of the German man. "Who I am is none of your damned business, but you are so going to pay for what you did! In fact—"

Jenna stopped speaking for a few seconds, and Keeley could feel her mentally reel. *Um. How are you doing?*

Hurt. But better.

Not able to walk?

No, he answered, fighting to move an arm so he could shift himself into a sitting position.

Right. We'll just have to do this the woo-woo way.

Do what? No, Jenna! Do not do anything that you will regret. Panic filled him at the thought of Jenna putting herself at risk on his behalf. He damned his body's weakness, struggling to move his limbs, pushing down the red haze of pain that wrapped around his brain.

Here's the thing. … I've seen this guy before. He's one of the guys who we saw in the hallway after you escaped, and later he was with a group who was chasing Mac at the Krebbs place. I have to get you out of here.

Keeley fought his body's urge to remain locked in a fetal position, and managed to half lift himself from the ground. "No," he said, his voice sounding as if it were made up of gravel.

"I know you," the German said, narrowing his eyes at Jenna.

"You do?" She moved back a step, one hand moving to clutch the purse strap that crossed her torso.

"Yes." He turned to the other woman. "Have you seen either of them before?"

"Me?" The redhead examined first Jenna, then Keeley before shaking her head. "No, I haven't. Do I know you?"

Jenna moved closer to Keeley. "Nope. Never seen you before." *Right, we're going to have to do this the hard way.*

Christ, Keeley swore. *If I begged you to leave—*

Dude, she said on a mental snort.

His shoulders would have slumped if they hadn't been drawn up almost to his ears.

"Maybe you saw her in Italy, at your uncle's house?" the German asked. Keeley had a suspicion the man was annoyed by the woman's answer, but he was too caught in his own nightmare to do more than wonder what the madman was up to. "Perhaps you have seen pictures of them? How about just the man?"

"I said no," the woman answered with a little pull of her eyebrows. She gestured toward Jenna. "I've got an excellent memory for faces, and I haven't seen either of these people before, so stop trying to make me say otherwise. What do you have against them, anyway?"

"Does the word 'asshat' ring any bells?" Jenna said softly, her eyes focused on the floor. Keeley had a feeling she was drawing energy into herself.

"This is the Old One we have sought, and the woman was at the laboratory yesterday," the German answered, his jaw tightening.

Keeley, his body screaming in protest, got to his knees.

If you can't move, then I'll just have to get rid of these two.

You can't. You'll bring down the wrath of the Weavers again.

Pfft, she said with a mental snort that expressed so much. *I'm not going to send them back in time or anything big. Just move them out of our way so we can get you to safety. Let's see. I think if I just …*

"I don't know what's going on here," the woman who accompanied the man said, looking from Jenna to Keeley, "but it's obvious that the man on the floor isn't doing well. Andreas, why don't you help him up onto a chair, and we'll have a little chat until Merrick and Han get here."

"You touch him and I'll … I'll—" Jenna stopped, obviously stymied by a suitable threat.

Love, do not do this. By dint of grabbing the seat of a nearby plastic chair, Keeley managed to more or less haul himself onto it, albeit listing heavily on one side.

"You'll do what?" the red-haired woman asked, her eyes bright with interest, apparently not in the least bit worried.

Jenna waved a hand before helping Keeley into a fully upright position, gently brushing her hand down his shirt to straighten it. "Well, I don't know, exactly. I don't have much call to threaten people, so I'm not really used to pulling up threats at a moment's notice. Besides, it's probably in violation of some rule or other, but you can take it as read that if you try to hurt him again, you'll be a very sad panda."

"I do love pandas," the woman said in an aside to the German man. "Especially the babies. They're just so darned cute."

He stared at her as if she had a panda dancing on her head.

"Sorry, it just struck me how much I liked them. Maybe we should start over, not that I think we really had a start to begin with," she said, holding out her hand to Jenna. "Hi, I'm Tempest Keye."

"No," Jenna said, shaking her head. "I'm not falling for that. You guys are Men in Black even if you're not wearing the shades, plus you hurt Keeley. There will be no sharing of names. No polite chitchat. No discussion of how adorable baby pandas are when they roll around sucking on their toes. This is good-bye."

"What—" the woman started to say, but before she could get more than the one word out, Jenna's hand flicked at nothing, causing the same swirling portal to open that Keeley had seen at her house. Jenna grabbed both the German man and the red-haired woman, and spun them into the portal.

Keeley sighed, and willed his legs to work, accepting Jenna's assistance when she slid an arm under his shoulder and helped hoist him to his feet. "I wish you hadn't done that," he said after gritting his teeth against the residual pain.

"Stop fussing. They likely just got ported out to the back of the building. Come on, let's get out of here before they figure out where they are. Left foot. Right foot. Left foot. That's it, you got it."

"You should leave me," Keeley said, his voice as gritty as his mind felt.

"Wow, are you really lacking so much self-confidence that you'd fish for compliments that way?" Jenna shook her head again as they made their way out the door. "I wouldn't dump a friend in this circumstance, and I'm certainly not going to abandon you. Which way is the plane, do you think? Behind the office? You stay here and recover, and I'll go see where the gruesome twosome got blipped."

"I'm really growing tired of saying no to you," Keeley said in what was almost a conversational tone. "Not to mention I wasn't asking you to bolster my sagging ego."

Jenna leaned him up against the side of the building, pressed a fast kiss to the corner of his mouth, and was off before his mind could register both.

He thought of giving in to the pain and crumpling to the ground, but decided that although his ego might be in need of a bit of polish, it wasn't so far gone that he wanted Jenna to see him incapacitated a second time. With a square of his shoulders, he pushed himself away from the wall, and tottered around the corner of the building.

He staggered to a halt at the sight that met his eyes. A plane was in the process of being fueled, the man holding the fuel nozzle watching with obvious interest as the madman was being swarmed by four of the tourists, one of the younger ones standing back filming the whole thing, while yelling out encouragement.

Mac and her helots raced in the opposite direction, clearly off to fetch the bus. Jenna, Keeley was not in the least bit surprised to see, was yelling at the madman with the hat, her hands gesturing wildly. "That's our plane, you asshat! You can just get the hell away from it—oh! You did not just push me!"

That last was in response to the red-haired woman pushing her way in between Jenna and the madman, but due to the sour-faced tourist swinging a substantial-sized purse at the madman at that exact moment—but clipping the redhead instead—the latter was sent flying into Jenna.

The madman's fingers tightened into fists as he looked to the skies for a few seconds. Keeley had a moment of commiseration despite the situation; the past two days with Jenna had left him seeking divine intervention several times.

"Hey!" the redhead snapped, and shot the tourist a fulminating look. "That's assault! I could have you arrested for that."

"Ha! I like that. This is elder abuse, that's what it is," the sour-faced woman said, sniffing, and clutching her bag to her chest.

"It most certainly is," another tourist piped up, this one

with gray hair. She pulled out a pad of paper. "I'm going to take your name and report you."

"Report me to who?" the redhead asked, rubbing her arm.

"I haven't decided yet, but you can be sure I will report you to someone. Come, Lolly. Let us go to the airline office and report these two people."

One part of Keeley's mind wanted to laugh at the expression of outrage on Jenna's face, but the other part, the one that had fought so hard to survive even when his mind cried out for destruction, warned him the situation was untenable. If there was one madman present, there were more nearby. He had to get Jenna and the others out of there before the madmen forced him into the Breaking.

"Look, I did not push you. That crazy lady walloped me with her bag," the redhead was now explaining to Jenna, still rubbing her arm. "Grape juice, what do you have in there? A couple of anvils? Andreas, will you stop trying to pull me behind you? Only Merrick gets to do that, and even then, he gets pinched on the back when he does so. Now, listen, if everyone would calm down, we can discuss this whole plane thing like reasonable human beings. My husband is on his way here, and—"

His stomach tightened with dread. Although the last thing he wanted was to be recaptured by the madmen, he was more worried about what they would do if they found out about Jenna. Images of insufferable vivisection rose in his mind.

He would die before he allowed anyone to do so much as touch her. Fury, mingled with a bone-deep fear unlike anything he'd felt, forced his body into movement. *Jenna! We must leave! More madmen are coming.*

She hesitated for a moment but, to his intense relief, saw reason. *Right. We'll just have to drive instead of fly.* "Tourists! Retreat!"

"What?" the sour-faced woman asked, halting in midswing with her bag. "We're stoppin'?"

The two older ones had passed him, heading for the parking lot. At Jenna's words, the younger ones stopped filming and took off after them with the combative tourist in tow.

"Right. Time for another blip," Jenna started to say, raising her hands in the air.

The madman grabbed her wrist, jerking her forward even as he hissed, "Do you think we're stupid? I don't know what you did back there, but you're our prisoner now—"

Keeley was moving before his brain could even process the still-painful muscles being forced. He leaped forward in a spinning kick that would do a martial arts actor proud. It was far more flash than power, he knew as soon as his foot connected with the madman's jaw, but it served to snap his opponent's head back and send him flying backward a few feet into the side of the plane.

"Are you all right?" he asked Jenna, not waiting for her answer before he turned to face the redhead.

She gave him a long, considering look before turning the same on Jenna. "OK," she said simply.

"OK what?" Jenna asked, taking the hand Keeley held out for her. The fact that she did so automatically made something in his chest glow with contentment.

"OK, you're going to run off now. I'm not going to stop you. I told my husband that something wasn't right about this all along, and it's clear that I was right."

"If you weren't evil, I'd love to have a talk with you about how men can be so obtuse at times, and also, baby pandas, but you are, so we can't. Plus, that screeching sound means that we need to be going. Also, the bus needs a brake job."

"I'm not evil, but I'm starting to see why you think so," the woman said, giving them a smile.

"He's getting up," Jenna told Keeley, nodding toward the madman. "I know running is probably the last thing in the world you want to do, but—"

He tightened his fingers on hers, shoved down the scream of pain from his legs, and lumbered back toward the low building that served as a terminal.

Waves of heat shimmered from the tarmac in front of them as they ran, making the scrubby ground beyond the paved area waver in the midday sun. To the left, a horrible screech sounded; then suddenly, a familiar big green shape emerged from behind another building.

Jenna yelled and waggled her free hand, her face red with sun and exertion when Mac pulled the bus to a stop in front of them with a squeal of tires on hot tarmac. The door opened and Mac yelled, "Hurry! The MIBs just pulled into the parking lot!"

"We know, we heard more were on the way. Those bastards Tased Keeley. Stop being chivalrous—you first." Jenna more or less shoved Keeley up the stairs, hot on his heels as he collapsed down onto the nearest seat.

"Do they have the plane?" Mac asked as she jerked the wheel, slamming her foot down on the gas pedal. "Hold on, everyone!"

"Are those the bad guys?" the gray-haired tourist asked, peering out of a window as a couple of men in dusters and hats headed toward the terminal.

"We should run them over," the purse woman suggested.

"Mrs. Walsh!" Jenna said even as she toppled into Keeley's seat, falling over him and knocking his chin with her elbow. "The Outta This World Tours does not condone the running over of anyone, even if they are evil cohorts bent on tormenting innocent Keeleys."

"I wouldn't tell if you didn't," the woman answered.

Jenna righted herself. "And, Mac, yes, unfortunately the plane is out of our grasp. I blipped one of the MIBs and his girlfriend out, and they ended up in the hangar with the planes. Are you OK?" The last was addressed to Keeley, who rubbed his chin.

Yes. Did you hurt yourself falling?

"Not in the least." She gave him a lopsided grin that sent warmth through his aching body. "You make a lovely cushion, although I feel bad about smacking you in the face with my arm. You poor thing. Your hair looks annoyed as hell."

Keeley thought about running a hand through his hair, but it seemed like way too much effort.

Jenna shifted on the seat and, with a gentle hand, tidied his hair. He closed his eyes, wanting nothing so much as the ability to lie down with Jenna at his side, her presence a balm that he desperately needed. Then he remembered that he needed to leave her, and his spirits sank again.

"So, we're driving to San Francisco?" Mac asked, turning onto a highway that a sign indicated would lead to an interstate freeway heading west.

"It'll only take four hours, so I guess so," Jenna answered, glancing behind her.

Keeley managed to slide his arm around her, needing to comfort her. *I want quite badly to tell you that you need have no worries that I will allow any of the madmen to harm you, but since you just more or less rescued me from them, I fear such a statement would sound pompous at best.*

I love it when you talk all formal and Victorian, she said with a giggle into his head, and put a hand on his leg in what he secretly hoped was a possessive gesture. It was as if her fingers were made of fire. Heat sank deep into him, kindling a desire that never seemed to go out. "Everyone needs rescuing now and again, even big, bad Thralls. But I have some questions."

"So do I," said Mac, glancing in the rearview mirror.

"Me, too," one of the younger women said, arranging herself sideways on a seat. "Who was that German guy? He was seriously hot."

"The subs are going to love him," the second young woman agreed, her gaze on her phone. "I got some great video of him. Mmrowr."

"Ladies," Jenna said in what Keeley thought of as her professional tour-guide voice. "We do not thirst over Men in Black. They are the enemy."

"Everyone loves a bad boy," the first one said.

Keeley could see heads nodding in the rearview mirror, even those of the helots.

"Well … I admit he was handsome—" Jenna cleared her throat and slid Keeley a glance. "But not drop-dead gorgeous like some men sitting right here."

"Thank you," Dima said, glancing over at her. "But I am taken. Twice."

She sighed into Keeley's head.

I appreciate the fact that you seek to restore my somewhat tattered pride by lavishing me with compliments, but it is not necessary. I am conversant with my appearance, Jenna. I am not unpleasant to look at, but certainly do not deserve such praise. He thought for a moment, and then, unable to keep from asking, continued, *Did you really find the madman handsome?*

Oh, yes. But I wasn't trying to restore your pride or bolster your ego. You are gorgeous, Keeley. Your jaw is a work of art. Your shoulders make me feel girly as hell. And your chest … well, like Tucson said, mmrowr.

"What I want to know is how did the Men in Black know we would be at the airport?" Mac asked. "Or were they just there getting their own flights out? And if it was the latter, why? They have a landing strip at the Crabs."

We're talking world-class mmrowr. The sort that makes me want to touch you all over.

"Jenna?"

I have no problem with that idea, he told her, trying not to sound as lascivious as he felt.

"Earth to Jenna!"

Good, because it's up next once we get to a hotel—Jenna glanced over at her friend. "Hmm? Yes, I was listening." She snuggled into Keeley again. He was more than a little distracted by the feeling of her so soft and warm, the scent of her twining itself around him before sinking into his blood. Emotions that he'd thought long dead burned to life again despite his attempt to ignore them. "But I have no answers, and a couple of questions of my own."

She felt so right, so natural next to him. His heart mourned as he mentally went through his list of people whom he might contact to see to Jenna's future safety. First, he'd tackle the antidote and Paris, and then, he'd find someone to protect Jenna, and would retire into the background.

Alone again.

"What're your questions?" Mac asked while Keeley was busily considering and dismissing various acquaintances, which shifted to a consideration of how to keep her from becoming involved with his investigation into the Revelation's San Francisco office. He had a feeling she was not going to like being left out of that.

You got that right whispered so softly in his head that he wasn't sure it was really there.

"For one, why that MIB named Andreas kept referring to Keeley as old. You're not old, are you?" she asked.

He glanced over his shoulder, but the tourists had gathered toward the back of the bus, the two older ladies and the helots having set up a makeshift table from a cooler, where they were playing cards. The three younger women were all engrossed in their phones, the small white devices he remembered were called earbuds visible. "I was born in 1851 in a small town outside of Dublin."

"Jeezumcrow!" Mac said, the bus swerving sharply before she righted it again. "You're over a hundred and seventy years old?"

"He's not old," Jenna said, rubbing the back of her hand across her forehead.

Once again, he was aware of an odd tiredness in her that pulled at him, and wondered if he could convince her to rest in a hotel room while he slipped out to find the Revelation headquarters.

"I am by mortal standards, but not by those in the Otherworld," he answered.

"You look like you're in your late thirties," Jenna protested. "You don't even have any gray hairs, which is more than I can say. Where that Andreas got off calling you old … well, I suppose it doesn't really matter what he or that pushy Tempest said, so long as they don't bother us anymore."

Old One, he said slowly, rolling the words around in his

mind. There was something familiar about them, some vague idea that seemed to elude focus, sliding around in the shadows of his memory.

Hmm?

The German—Andreas—he referred to me as 'the Old One,' not as old.

Is there a difference?

I think there is. I have a memory—a very vague memory—of something my father's mother told me. She was a Beloved, my grandfather's mate, but she had very nearly been killed centuries before. My grandfather rescued her—it's how they met.

Jenna sat up, her interest clearly piqued. "Wow, your grandparents were centuries old? How many centuries?"

"Five or six hundred," Keeley answered, still probing his memories of a time when he was a child listening to tales from his grandam.

"Holy moly. Are they … they aren't still alive, are they?"

"No. My family is all dead. My mother died in childbirth, and my father did not survive her death. My grandparents raised me for a short while, but they perished when the ship they were on sank on the way to North Africa."

"It's like you're a walking history book," Mac said, and, glancing at her two helots, added, "I don't suppose they are like you, Keeley?"

"Not unless they were immortal to begin with, and given their status as normal workers for the Revelation, I suspect they are not."

"Rats," she answered, and returned her focus to driving.

Jenna gave Keeley's thigh a little squeeze. Instantly, he grew hard and hunger roared to life inside him.

"Whoa," she said softly, fanning herself while her pupils dilated in response to his reaction. "That's seriously … whew! It's like you're a pheromone factory."

He struggled against the temptation she posed. "San Francisco is bound to be dangerous for you. I know you won't agree to it without what I suspect will be a lengthy and wholly frustrating argument, but it would be infinitely safer for you to remain at a hotel while I attend to the Revelation and Paris, assuming he is there."

"Dangerous how?" she asked, surprising him because she didn't dismiss the idea of staying out of the way.

"It is a major city. There are portals there—not, I suspect, that the Weavers who are bent on punishing you would need access to them if they are able to open their own. It is, however, a major Otherworld hub, and if the Weavers hire thief takers or their ilk to find you, you would be at an increased risk to be seen should you accompany me."

"Smooth," Jenna said with another of her fingers-of-fire squeezes to his leg. "Very smooth."

"Enough to keep you at a hotel?" he asked, hope evident in his voice despite his attempt to keep it hidden.

"Nope. But it was a very good try. You get a gold star for the day for the effort." She yawned, stretched, and, to his extreme unhappiness, slid off the seat. "I think the couple of blippings I did today wore me out. Is everyone OK back there? No one wants off before we go to San Francisco?"

"We're fine," the gray-haired woman said without looking up. "Maude and I are going to take these two boys for everything they have."

"Including their pants," said the sour-faced woman.

"Hey! No strip poker until it's Jenna's turn to drive," Mac called from the driver's seat.

"Lolly? Tucson? Madison?" Jenna asked the ladies.

All three removed one earbud and looked at her with obvious question, then assured Jenna they were fine.

"In that case, I'm going to take a wee nap. Mac, wake me up when it's my turn to drive."

"Will do," she called as Jenna claimed the seat across from Keeley, scrunching down into it with her back to the window.

Keeley frowned to himself, not liking the sensation of exhaustion he was feeling from Jenna, but knowing she would be offended if he lectured her as he wanted to. Instead, he made a mental note to keep a closer eye on her lest her newly refound abilities were taxing her too much, and pulled out her phone to continue sorting through e-mails.

He had to find a way to keep Jenna safe while the hacker destroyed the Revelation's records, and he tracked down Paris and the antidote. After that … well, he'd deal with leaving her then.

It would kill him to walk away, but there was simply no other choice to be made.

FIFTEEN

Something was definitely wrong.

"You OK?" Mac asked two hours later when we were partaking of a rest stop. Although Keeley maintained he didn't need to use the facilities, he followed the two helots into the men's room to wash up after his adventure rolling around on the floor of the airline office. "You look like something Jeff Goldblum created in a lab, which then got mingled with his DNA, and caused him to later go on a murderous killing spree before being squashed under a large press."

"I love that movie!" Lolly said, popping into the restroom to fill a water bottle. "Young Jeff Goldblum—does it get any better? Jenna, are you sure you don't want to share some of my chicken? I really did buy enough for you and Mac. Although I didn't realize your boyfriend was going to be with us."

I looked up from where I was washing my hands, and glanced at her in the mirror. "I don't want anything, and I know Keeley won't, but thank you again for thinking of us."

"Mac?" she asked, glancing at the woman in question as Mac brushed her teeth.

"Nope. The boys bought some sandwiches at the airport—we're going to practice feeding each other."

Lolly looked as baffled as I felt by that statement, but she toddled off without comment.

I pursed my lips at my friend. "You really shouldn't say things like that around our customers. And thank you for telling me I look like a human/fly hybrid. I feel a bit off, if you want to know the truth."

"A bit off how? A couple of hours ago, you were all but sucking Keeley's tongue out of his head." Her eyes widened. "You don't have a disease, do you? Like … like mono, but vampire-based? Something viral? Can I get it? Will it change me without making me a Thrall Baby? Man, I didn't know I wanted it, but now that I think about being immortal like Keeley, it's really starting to appeal to me."

I glanced around the women's room, but it was thankfully empty. "I'd tell you that you're the oddest person I know, but I've said that far too many times to have any impact left in the statement. No, I'm sure it's not mono, or even vamp mono. I'm just …" I stopped, having a hard time sorting through my thoughts. They were jumbled together like my grandmother's buttons in a Mason jar. "I think I'm having a reaction to Keeley. Or rather, to when he first bit me back in his prison cell. I go through waves of feeling exhausted, so tired I can hardly keep awake, and the next minute I'm hot, little beads of perspiration along my forehead sort of hot. Then whammo! I'm filled with energy, and feel like I could take on the world without breaking a sweat. Except, I'm already sweating." I rubbed my temples. "It's all very weird."

Mac watched me for a moment, then wet a couple of paper towels and held them out to me. I pressed them against my burning cheeks, trying to keep from moaning at the sensation of cold.

I had a horrible feeling that Keeley might pick up on my emotions if I dwelled on them too much, and the last thing he needed was to worry about me.

"Yeah, but that's kind of his job, isn't it? I mean, if you guys truly are a couple."

I stared at Mac. "What?"

"Worrying about you." She handed me another wet paper towel. "That's what being together means."

"I really must be out of it if I said that aloud without realizing it," I answered somewhat indistinctly while I wiped my face with the wet towel.

"You *are* together, aren't you?" she asked, still watching me closely.

I waggled my hand. "I don't know what we are other than in trouble with the Weavers, and the MIBs, and probably the county for blowing up the Krebbs lab. I'm trying to take things one step at a time, and right now, the next step is to find this antidote that Keeley needs so badly."

"Listen to yourself," she said, shaking her head. "*He* needs the antidote, so you're making sure he gets it. *He* would be upset if he knew he made you sick with his bitey powers, so you're keeping that from him. You, girl, are most definitely a couple. Which makes me very happy, because I've been worried about you for a long time."

"You have not," I said, smiling and touched despite my protestation. "You've never liked any of the men I was involved with."

"That's because they were all dillweeds," she said, baring her teeth at herself in the mirror before making a face. "The point is that Mr. Mad, Bad, and Handsome to Know is important to you, so what are you going to do to keep him in your life?"

I patted my damp forehead again before drooping over the sink and cupping a handful of water to splash on my cheeks. "I'm doing everything I can, Mac."

She obviously heard the plaintive note in my voice, but ignored it, walking alongside me when we left the restroom and headed back toward the bus. The tourists had claimed two picnic tables and were enjoying their alfresco lunch. "Yeah, and that's the problem."

I paused and squinted at her, the sun dead in my eyes. "What do you mean?"

"That you don't have the best track record. Oh good, the boys have lunch set out. You sure you don't want anything?"

"I'm sure," I said, pulling her back when she started forward, noticing even as I did so that Keeley was waiting for me in the shade next to the bus. "Not until you explain that 'track record' comment."

She wiggled her arm free after giving me an exasperated glance. "Dude. Lunch first. Baring of souls later."

I bit back a rude word as she strode off to join her two boy toys, and returned to the bus to curl up on my seat. Twenty minutes later, the tourists were back on board, and another round of cards was under way. Madison and Tucson were recording snippets of video to their phones, details of their thoughts and feelings about the morning's events, which I assumed they'd incorporate into later social media releases. Lolly had a large medical book out and headphones on.

I looked at Mac when she marched up the steps of the bus. "Right. You've eaten. Everyone is busy. Now you can explain what you meant by your snarky comment."

"I simply meant that you doing your best is exactly why we're here right now."

Keeley glanced from Mac to me. "Is something amiss?"

"No. Yes. I don't know. Maybe? Mac is just being Mac." I got up, hesitating at the driver's seat, since it was my turn to take over.

"I'll drive," Keeley said, wearing an expression I couldn't interpret.

Do you know how to drive a bus? I asked.

Yes, he replied, surprising me.

Really? When did you learn to do that?

World War II. I was a medic, he answered.

Wow. Seriously?

Seriously. I served in both World Wars in a medical capacity. I didn't feel right taking the lives of mortals, so I worked at saving them when they were injured.

"OK, let's put a pin in that for a discussion at a later date," I told him, and handed him the keys to the bus, watching him for a second while he familiarized himself with the intricacies of driving it.

Mac sat sideways on a seat, her back to the window while she tapped at her phone. I sat across from her, giving her a gimlet look that she flat out ignored until, after I cleared my throat twice, she asked, "You need a cough drop?"

"No, I need an explanation. Namely, why do I feel like you're blaming me for something?"

She tipped her head toward Keeley. "Do you really want to do this now?"

"I didn't start it," I said, feeling myself puff up with indignation despite feeling as weak as a newborn.

"No, but you are peeved," she pointed out.

"You bet your booty I am," I answered, and I slumped back against the window of the bus, the heat from the sun making the back of my neck tingle. "I know the signs—whenever you have something unpleasant to say, you go into full procrastination mode and avoid talking about it. Stop dancing around this, Mac, and just spit out whatever it is you want to say."

She glanced back toward Keeley before making a face at me. "OK, but if you make me say things that piss off your boyfriend to the point where he won't make me immortal, then I'll haunt you to the end of my days. Or, rather, afterlife."

"That's passive-aggressive, and you know it," I told her. "Not to mention you're assuming I'm immortal to the point where I'm hauntable. Which I don't know if I am."

"You are," Keeley said, swearing softly when someone in an SUV cut him off. "Also, I can't make anyone immortal. Not without them becoming a helot."

I cocked an eyebrow at Mac, and continued waiting until she gave a sigh.

"I don't know why you can never let unpleasant things go, but if you really want to do this, we can. You feel like I'm blaming you not because I am—friends don't blame—but because you're feeling guilty about putting Keeley, and the boys, and possibly me, in danger. Every time you try your best, things get worse. Infinitely so."

"I what?" Irritation made my voice sharper than I liked, so with a quick glance to make sure all the tourists were occupied and not listening to us, I cleared my throat again and said in a much more reasonable tone, "Are you nuts? I do not make things infinitely worse. I don't endanger anyone. I've never heard such a load of crap in my life!" *Can you believe what she said?* I asked Keeley.

It seems most unlike her, he answered, leaving me with an itchy feeling. I wanted him to reassure me that she was being outrageous and uncalled-for, but didn't want to come right out and demand that, so instead, I focused my attention on Mac.

"I'm not the one who captured Keeley and turned him into a slave-making monster," I told her before glancing over at Keeley. "Sorry. That came out harsher than I intended."

In the rearview mirror, I caught sight of his lips twisting in a slight grimace. "I've been called worse."

"The fact remains that I am not to blame for all the shit that's happened to us," I said, glaring at Mac.

"Oh really?" Mac set down her phone and started ticking items off on her fingers. "You went to get Britt from the Crabs, and ended up getting an interdiction slapped on your head, and got your boss pissed at you."

"After which you bombed the place," I answered, feeling that was a point for our team.

One, Keeley allowed.

Mac grinned. "It was good, wasn't it? Where was I? Oh, index finger: then, rather than minding your manners and doing what your boss said, you tried to use your power again, and got that Lemmas chick on your ass."

"That was not my fault," I protested. "I'm not responsible for how Lemmas or any of the Weaver Council reacts. Or overreacts, in that case."

"Then you used the very same power again at the airport, with the result that we're here now rather than flying in expensive private-jet comfort, with not only your Weaver gang trying to find you, but more MIBs." She shook her head. "That's just not good, son."

"I'm not your son, and stop being so unreasonable," I said, irritation making me feel prickly. "Just because there were a few unfortunate events—"

"And the daddy of all fuckups is Keeley," she said, pointing at the man in question.

"—that I wasn't at all responsible—wait, what?" I gawked at her, an actual full-fledged gawk. It wasn't a pretty thing to see, but Mac had seen worse. "What about Keeley?" *What about you?*

Erm ...

To my surprise and no little dismay, regret was present in his mind, regret that I knew centered around me.

What? I demanded to know, feeling alternately hot and ice-cold. My palms started sweating at the same time I shivered, goose bumps rising on my arms. *Why are you thinking about distracting Mac? Why are you feeling awkward?* "WHY DO YOU FEEL SAD ABOUT ME?"

"I don't feel sad—" Mac started to say, but I interrupted her.

"Not you, him!" I said, pointing. "He feels all shades of unhappy and I want to know why."

"You want to tell her, or should I?" Mac asked him.

Keeley obviously thought about that for a moment, because he said with a sigh, "I suppose I should. I suspect you will just make her more angry than she already is."

"Someone better tell me something," I said with a desire to snort in annoyance.

"Naw, I won't let you take the fall for this. I stirred her up. I'll finish it," Mac told him.

I flexed my fingers, and wondered if I'd get in trouble if I teleported Mac a hundred miles away from here.

Yes.

It might be worth it, I muttered into his head, knowing full well he could feel the real affection I had for Mac.

We might occasionally drive each other nuts, but I knew absolutely that she had my back, just as she knew I had hers.

Mac pointed her phone at me. "The daddy of all fuckups is the fact that you got Keeley into this mess to begin with. Don't give me that look—you told me just last night that it was because you were visiting him in Victorian times that your boss got pissed at you, and they wiped out your memory. You left Keeley at a church, waiting to marry you. Worse, you left him for more than a hundred years not knowing what happened to you, or why you dumped him, or even where you were. And then the Men in Black got him. It's all because you were … what did you call it? Joyriding through time?"

I sat silent, too stunned by her accusations to do more than feel a strange sense of displacement, almost as if I were separate from my body.

Jenna, Keeley said, his voice gentle in my mind, but I could feel the regret that still filled him.

You think she's right, don't you? I asked, a sense of betrayal biting deep into my soul. *You think I'm to blame for everything?*

No. I think that you bear some of the responsibility for having your memory wiped, although not all of it. The Weavers extracted an extreme punishment, one far beyond your so-called crime.

My eyes filled with tears. I could bear Mac's assessment of my character because I knew she was occasionally wrong about things, or just didn't see them as I did, but for Keeley to believe I was the cause of all his woe was hard to deal with.

I do not blame you, love, he said, the words sweet, but they fell on barren ground. *You are as you are, just as I am what I am. Circumstances beyond both our control have affected our lives. What we were does not matter so much as what we are now.*

"That sounds very New Agey, but at the same time wise," I said, my gut churning with unhappiness.

"It is merely the wisdom that comes from being a prisoner for twenty years," he said evenly, by his jaw tightening with every word.

"I don't know what he's being wise about—I really wish I could listen in on your convos when you guys go mental—

but if he's being smart, then listen to him. Jenna." Mac put down her phone and gave me a look that had far too much pity in it for my liking. "I'm not trying to pick on you. I just don't want you to mess up what could be a lifetime of happiness because you're too caught up in an image of what you want life to be to see what is facing you."

"I want to help Keeley," I said, stiffening a little. I knew she hadn't meant to insult me, but her words stung nonetheless. "I don't see how trying to help a man who has suffered—yes, I will accept partial blame for that suffering, although Keeley himself agrees that the Weaver Council overreacted to me spending time in the past to visit him—I don't see how trying to help him is screwing things up."

To my extreme annoyance, she just shrugged and continued with her phone. "It's your life, babe."

The rest of the drive to San Francisco was quiet, with everyone obviously absorbed by their own thoughts. Keeley had insisted that we regroup before we made plans with regard to the MIBs, so we stopped at a hotel that had enough vacant rooms.

"This would have bankrupted us if Keeley hadn't offered to pick up the bill by transferring money to my account," I told Mac in an undertone as I handed out room key cards. "As it is, it'll take a long time to repay him. Next time, would you please ask me before you take on unscheduled tours?"

"Bah. They'll tip big. I can tell," she said, smiling benignly as the tourists all headed for the elevator.

"They'd better, because I can't expect Keeley to spring for more than one night for everyone," I grumbled.

"I hope my room has a Jacuzzi. Did you ask for a Jacuzzi?" Mac asked when I handed her a key card.

I tipped my head at her. "What about me says I can afford several rooms, let alone one with a Jacuzzi, in downtown SF?"

She grinned and patted my cheek. "I thought it was worth a shot. Come along, my guy harem. Let's go see if this king bed has the staying power we need."

"I'm going to need several B vitamins, some oysters, and spicy peppers," Anton said, trailing after her.

"And chocolate. Is very sexy, chocolate," Dima added.

"I'd be worried about Mac getting in over her head, but she's never been a head-above-water sort of person," I told Keeley, watching as the threesome got on the elevator, Mac having a hand on each man's ass. "I just hope that the Thrall Babies don't lose their smutty desires someday, and leave her. She takes breakups really hard."

He didn't answer, which had me watching him as he poked around on the burner phone we'd picked up at a strip mall we'd come across in the suburbs.

"You know," I said softly, smiling to myself when his brows pulled together over some intricacy of the software, "I didn't mind you using my phone."

He glanced up, for a moment holding the phone protectively to his chest. The gesture reminded me of a child receiving a rare gift, and made me determined to make sure he had all the technological toys he wanted. "I appreciate that, but now that I am free of the madmen, I believe it would be efficacious for me to also have a mobile device. What is Bluetooth?"

I explained it to him briefly while we made our way to our rooms, located directly across the hall from Mac.

Keeley said nothing when I claimed the first room. "It has more sunlight, since it faces south."

He simply moved through the shared bathroom to a second, larger room.

"So, what's the game plan?" Mac asked when I tottered into Keeley's room and collapsed onto a tall wingback chair. Dima and Anton were visible through the open doors, sitting on the edge of the bed in Mac's room while they stared at a TV. "You guys going to have a quickie, then we'll all go tackle the baddies?"

"We are not the quickie-having sort of people, not that it's any of your business," I said, summoning up enough energy to look down my nose at her, which wasn't easy given my slumped position on the chair. "We might have been 'up against a wall in a fast one' sort of lovers in the past, but as Keeley has so sagely pointed out, the past is in the past, and that shouldn't influence us now."

Keeley gave me a look with one eyebrow raised in obvious speculation.

Wow. We were *against the wall sort of people?*

Sometimes. When you pushed me past what I could bear. He thought for a moment. *And when you were what you referred to as Needy McNeederson.*

Images of just what that entailed danced through my imagination. I shifted in my chair, and wondered if I couldn't rally enough energy to pounce on Keeley.

Mac grinned. "Fair enough. What's the plan, then?"

"The plan is for you and Jenna to stay here while I gather some information about the Revelation headquarters," Keeley said, still poking at things on his phone.

"You can't dump us here, you know," I told him, waving a languid hand toward Mac. "We're not stupid, even though one of us has implied the other is to blame for everything. No, I'm not going to rehash that again, Mac. You said what you needed to say. I agree with some of it, and I'm going to make sure that my blipping and tossing people through those weird twisty portals doesn't end up biting us in the butt. Regardless of that, we're not going to be left behind, Keeley."

He stabbed at his phone with renewed intensity, but said nothing.

I can feel you thinking things, you know.

Hrmph.

You're adorable when you're grumpy, by the way.

"How about this—I think we could all use a break after the long ride, and since it's likely going to be easier to tackle the Men in Black when it's not daylight, why don't we get some food, maybe a little rest, and then regroup at"—I glanced at the clock next to the bed—"nine? It'll be close to getting dark then, which will let us skulk around much more effectively."

"I like skulking," Mac said, her expression brightening. "I always did want to be a spy. But the mad-scientist career track just seemed much more lucrative, and less likely to end up shot through the back on a street in some exotic Eastern European town. I'll go tell the tourists that they're on their own until nine."

"Mac, I don't think we should get them involved," I said. "It's too dangerous. Besides, my liability insurance doesn't cover skulking and tackling potentially dangerous villains."

Keeley made a *tch*ing sound in the back of his throat.

"Bah," Mac said, waving away that concern. "They love that sort of thing. Why else would they have paid two hundred bucks per person just to go around with us? Madison and Tucson are off their gourds with happiness, and Mrs. Walsh keeps asking me if I can make her a Thrall Baby of her own. Right, I'm off. I'll update the tourists, then have a quick dinner, and then put in a little time with the boys to work out the resulting kinks from the road trip, following which we'll all have some high-level skulking. See you at nine!"

"There's a camera in this phone?" Keeley asked, turning it around a few times to examine all the various bits and pieces of it.

"Yes. And stop thinking that you'll slip out when Mac and I aren't looking, because we aren't going to let you go off on your own to tackle the Men in Black."

He looked up at that, and I felt his gaze searing a way down to my soul, making me feel oddly vulnerable considering that he could stroll into my head at any time he liked. "Why do you feel so strongly about this?"

"About helping you?" I asked, thinking for a few seconds before I made a moue. "I'm not quite sure. There's something needy about you that calls out to my inner nurturer."

"Needy!" He sat up straight, and squared his shoulders. "I object to that term. I am not needy. I am like any other man—other than the fact that I'm a Thrall—and I have needs, yes, but I am not needy."

"Sorry," I said, wanting badly to giggle, but knew that would offend his delicate sensibilities. "That came out wrong. It's just that there's something about you that makes me want to …"

The sentence trailed away when I made a vague gesture, unsure how to explain the tangle of emotions that lay coiled inside me.

"Kiss me?" he asked, the gray of his eyes darkening. "Touch me? Have me touch and taste and lick you?"

A faint prickle along my spine warned that I was shifting from a limbs-of-leaden-weight state into the so-hot-I-could-probably-fry-an-egg-on-my-cheeks phase of whatever illness I'd gotten from Keeley. I shivered with the erotic promise in his eyes. "It goes without saying that I'd like to kiss you, and stroke all those long expanses of flesh in ways that make you pant and demand I impale myself on you."

Ghostly memories danced through my mind, little flickers of the image of our bodies moving on each other in a rhythm as old as mankind.

"Oh, yes," he said, his pupils flaring. I had a feeling he was also reliving those moments. "Those were some very good times. That one where you were upside down was a bit awkward, but still enjoyable. Ah, now, the one you are just thinking about was especially good. I never thought I'd like to be confined by the wrists, but the way you tormented my cock—"

That was all it took. One minute I was starting to feel warm, and the next I was on Keeley's lap facing him, my legs clasped around his hips, while passion scorched along my veins. "You can't bring up memories like that to me without making me seriously Needy McNeederson."

His chuckle was rusty, and the sound of it made my stomach feel as if it were filled with fireflies. "I never did understand that reference—Jenna!"

I didn't wait for him to finish his thought. I couldn't. My head was filled with his emotions, a red haze of hunger and desire that mingled with mine, the desire … no, *need* …

to taste him overruling any shred of common sense I might still cling to. I bit the cord at the base of his neck, not hard enough to break the skin, but enough that his body tensed beneath me.

Sex? he asked, his hope and desire and wanting spilling onto me.

Oh, hell yes, I cooed into his mind, and in the next second, the air was filled with various garments being pulled from our bodies and flung hither and yon.

I should be researching the Revelation building. …

"Later. I'll just feed you … oh, yes, that nipple likes you to do that … I'll just feed you and then I'll have room … Keeley! Mmrowr! … I'll have room service send up a burger for me, and then we can meet with—holy hellballs, man! How many hands do you have? Gods, yes, do that thing with your thumb again."

His thumb brushed against flesh made sensitive by his magic fingers.

I squirmed with delight; then the words he had just spoken penetrated the lust and need that twisted tightly around me, and I moved back a smidgen, just enough to stop the fingers from sending me flying.

Keeley, who had been nuzzling my breasts, looked up, his gorgeous eyes now smoky, his pupils huge.

"You let me do bondage on you?"

"Bondage?" His brows pulled together for a few seconds, then smoothed out as he gave me a heavy-lidded look that could have steamed cauliflower. "Ah. The hand restraints. Yes, that was very good, as I mentioned."

"Right. I know we've just reconnected, and honestly, regular ole nooky time would be fine with me, but suddenly, I have this image in my head of you tied down, and me frolicking all over your body. And much as I want your fingers—which are probably illegal in several states—to continue, I really want my turn tormenting you."

"Restraints," he mused, clearly thinking this over. I slid off his legs, intent on finding something I could use to tie him down—or at least his hands—when suddenly a Keeley-shaped blur zipped past me and returned, and I found myself on my back, my hands pulled up around my ears, tied together with the belt from his jeans.

"Wait, I said I wanted to tie you down—glorioski, man! With your tongue?"

The belt wasn't tight around my wrists, certainly loose enough for me to pull my hands from it if I had so wanted, but when he dipped his head to lave his tongue along my inner thighs, I clutched hard at the thin leather, and gave myself up to the sensation.

You can have your turn later. Right now, you are my smorgasbord of delectable, quivering woman. Does it hurt if I do this?

He bit the spot he had been licking on my inner thigh, a second of sting immediately melting into pleasure so great I arched up, almost pushed over into an orgasm.

Ah, he said, his mind filled with male satisfaction. *So you like that.*

I… I panted into his mind. *I will exact my revenge, sirrah, and it will be lengthy and merciless. Oh goddess, how can feeding you be so erotic? Bite the other thigh. It feels left out.*

He chuckled aloud, and did as I asked. I tried hard to analyze the biting sensation, feeling it was important I understood just what it was he was doing.

There's pain, I told him, ripples of pleasure skimming my skin like silk.

He paused in the act of feeding.

But that fades almost the second I realize it, and then … hoobah. I wish you could feel what it's like.

I have.

"Really? When was that?" Jealousy stabbed deep before I could quell it.

Amusement filled my mind. *You would be jealous of yourself, love.* His tongue swirled over the spot on my thigh before he moved higher, kissing a path up to my belly, avoiding my personal party zone.

"Huh? And also, hey! You missed ground zero."

"You're too close," he murmured into one hip before giving it a love nip, his hands spreading upward, to my breasts. "I wish to have time to torment you until you're mindless with passion, and that means I have to pleasure you in other areas. Unless you've become multiorgasmic since we were together?"

I had been about to protest that I was the best judge of just how close I was to grabbing the brass ring, but decided that his ability to read my emotions—coupled with the fact that I was, in fact, perilously close to falling into an orgasm—was a valid point. "Fine, but that's only because your fingers and mouth are the most amazing things ever. Why am I jealous of myself?"

"You bit me yesterday," he murmured, the light stubble from his cheeks making my breasts demand all his attention.

"Your brain is lust-riddled, sir, because it was just a few minutes ago that I bit that delicious tendon that goes down to your collarbone. It's a sexy, sexy tendon, and I couldn't resist."

"You also bit me yesterday, and fed from me." His voice was muffled as he was first nuzzling my breasts, then tormenting them with long, toe-curling sweeps of his tongue.

"I did?" My toes uncurled as I tried to rally my wits enough to look through them.

"Yes." He released one thoroughly pleasured nipple and glanced up at me, a strange hesitancy in his mind. "You don't remember?"

"Not really. Was it while we were at the laboratory?"

"No." He propped himself up on his elbows, his chest pressing into mine in a way that was extremely distracting, the soft hairs on his chest teasing my already sensitive nipples. "We were at your house. You put a cold pack on my wound."

For a moment, panic hit me hard. Was I now losing my memory? Was it part of whatever illness I had? Just as I was about to go into a full-fledged hissy fit, the mental image of our actions the day before returned, followed immediately by relief. Perhaps all the blipping I'd done had left me tired, ending in a brief lapse in memory. "Oh, that's right. I'd forgotten about your owie since it healed up so fast after you had me lick it for you."

Another odd hesitation rose in his mind, but as I wriggled my hips against him, twining one leg around his, his attention was returned exactly where I wanted it—to me.

"Since you are wholly and completely at my mercy, not that I have any when it comes to pleasuring you, I believe I will go back and investigate those areas you so badly wanted me to visit earlier," he said in that plummy English accent that never failed to make my insides feel soft and squishy. His breath steamed over my personal parts, but I had stood just about as much as I could take.

"Right, you might be sexy as sin, and twice as enjoyable, but you, sir, have way too many Victorian sensibilities. I am a modern woman. I don't like to be tied down and pleasured to the very depths of my soul. Well … I do, but not without my turn. And that is now."

He grumbled in my head when I slid my hands out of his belt and pushed him over onto his back, straddling his penis, which was standing up and waving at me in an obvious attempt to get me to notice it. "I might have been born in the middle of Victoria's reign, but I assure you that I am anything but stuffy—Christos! How are you doing that?"

"Lots and lots of pelvic floor exercises," I said more than a little breathless, since the act of sliding down onto his very persistent penis all but stripped the air from my lungs. "The threat of old-lady bladder pads is great. Good god, is there an end to you? I have limits, Keeley. My vagina doesn't go on forever. There has to be an end to you. Goddess, there's more? Ung. OK, I can handle this. Seriously, we're not at the end yet? Are you part horse or something? Oooh, yes, please, do that swivel again."

He swiveled.

I moaned.

Things went a little crazy at that point. My rhythm shifted until it was off beat. His hips bucked wildly. We both panted, and moaned, and quivered with utter delight as we raced to the finish. And later, much later, once my brain rebooted and came back on line again, I tried to identify just what happened.

"It's like one moment, everything's fine, we're enjoying ourselves, and you're swiveling, and I'm engaging all my inner girly muscles in an attempt to get you to moan nonstop, and then holy cats in pajamas, you let me see what you're feeling, and that spins around what I'm feeling, and then when you bite me, it's just all way too much. My body goes up like dry tinder into the orgasm to end all orgasms." I patted the part nearest my hand, which, given that I had collapsed down upon his heaving chest, was his bicep. "I seriously hope you don't get better, sexually speaking, because I don't think my heart could stand it if you did. I'll have to go take spin classes or start swimming, and I hate both of those things."

He laughed—he actually laughed—which made me push back off his chest enough that I could frown down at him.

"Why are you giving me that decidedly disgruntled look?" he asked, wiping the edges of his eyes. My inner Jenna melted at the fact that I'd tickled his funny bone. "You have nothing to frown about, woman. I have pleasured you to the tips of your delightful toes, and well beyond that. Your girly muscles were exceptionally proficient, which was demonstrated by the fact that I not only moaned, but also groaned, shouted in ecstasy, and, I have a horrible suspicion, once or twice grunted in sheer incoherent rapture. You will please remove that expression and replace it with one more befitting a woman who enjoyed the many fine swivels I performed."

"Your swivels get an 'A plus plus, would buy from again' rating," I told him, and bit his chin. "I'm frowning because I really don't want to have to get a gym membership just so I can keep up with you sexually. I don't want to be the one to let down the team, Keeley, but I really dislike gyms."

He chuckled into my head even as he gave one butt cheek a pinch. "You're a Weaver, Jenna. You're not mortal, and you won't have a heart attack from lovemaking, although I may well if you continue to use those inner muscles on me."

I smiled into his collarbone as I snuggled back onto his chest, too boneless to do anything but lie in a puddle of satisfied Jenna. "That makes no sense, and we both know it."

His body relaxed underneath me as his breathing deepened. I slid off him, determination driving the postcoital need for a nap away.

You're leaving?

Just to soak in the tub. I'm feeling a bit meh after the long ride on the bus, and I think a long bath will help. I waffled for a few seconds, unsure if I should tell him my suspicion.

Sleeping on the bus isn't the most comfortable exper— He stopped and opened his eyes, the black brows slashes above them. "Why are you feeling guilty?"

"Who, me?" I grabbed up his shirt and put it on, suddenly feeling far more naked than was normal in such a situation.

Why are you filled with contriteness? What is it you feel will hurt me? He sat up now, his gorgeous chest right there in front of me, but for once, I admired it with only half my attention.

The other half was wondering how to tell him.

"Tell me what?" His voice was rough with emotion, worry mingling with pain, and a sense of abandonment that had me instantly sitting next to him, my arms around him.

"I'm not leaving you, Keeley."

He froze, and after a moment gently moved out of my embrace, icy reserve now tipping his words with frost. "I am delighted to hear that, but I suspect that is not what you are so hesitant to tell me."

Pain laced with loss was engraved so deeply on his soul that for a moment it stripped my breath, and in that moment, I understood the contrary mixture of traits that made up Keeley— everyone he had loved had abandoned him, his parents and grandparents by death, and later me. He loved, and sooner or later, everyone he loved left him … or at least that's what it had felt like to a little boy whose family had disappeared, leaving him a stranger in the homes of mortals.

"And then I came along. Oh, Keeley," I said, my eyes burning, the hard ache in my throat making it difficult to speak. "I'm so sorry. I didn't know Abbott and the others would remove all memories of you. I didn't know that I would be punished for being so in love with you that it didn't matter what trouble I'd be in just so I could be with you."

He blinked, but the coldness in his manner remained. "I am not quite sure why you have brought up that old history now, but it is, perhaps, a discussion left for another time. What is it you're hiding from me, Jenna?"

I took his hand in both of mine, and gently bit his thumb. "I think I'm … changing."

His brows pulled together. I wanted to smooth the resulting furrow between them. "Beyond becoming a Moravian, you mean?"

"Yes. No. I don't know, really," I admitted, the strange heat and energy that had driven me into jumping his bones earlier now fading into a gray miasma of lethargy. The ache in my throat still made it hard to swallow, but I wasn't sure any longer for whom I wanted to weep. Perhaps both of us.

Tell me, he commanded, twining his fingers through mine. The gesture, along with the genuine concern that I could feel inside him, warmed me.

"When you bit me back at the Krebbs … when you tried to make me a Thrall Baby—"

He sighed into my head.

"—and then when I didn't turn into one, but suddenly there you were all handsome and irresistible, and chock-full of blood, and you said I was a she-vamp, which was OK so long as it didn't complicate things, but now …" I had never been a lip-biter, and I didn't want to start that habit, but my lower lip didn't have much choice when I caught it between my teeth.

"Now, what?"

"Something has happened to me." I explained quickly how I went from exhausted to feverishly full of zip and vim. "The only thing that's changed in the last couple of days has been the reapplication of the interdiction, and you trying to helot me. I can't imagine why the interdiction would suddenly turn me weird, when I've had one in place for over a hundred years without consequence. Which means it has to be your bite." I searched his gaze, hoping against hope to find something there that would reassure me.

His gaze dropped to our joined hands, leaving me feeling bereft. "You are not a helot," he said after a few minutes' silence, his words emerging with a slow cadence that left my stomach feeling leaden. "You're not even close to the quasi-helots your friend made. A Thrall has no power other than that. . . ."

I watched him as the sentence trailed away. I could feel him thinking hard, shifting through impressions and half-remembered comments, my sense of frustration matching his. "No," he said with a sidelong look to me that I couldn't interpret. "I don't see how it could be something from me. I have fed from you several times, and if it was something in me that was making you ill, then those feedings would have accelerated it to the point where we were in no doubt of what was affecting you."

"If it's not the helot-making, then what is it?" I asked, despair leaching into my heart. "It has to be something. Just a few minutes ago, I forgot what happened yesterday. What if that continues and I forget more and more stuff? And more importantly, how do I make it stop?"

He turned to face me fully, speculation lighting his eyes. "I do not know much about my people—my former people—but perhaps what you are experiencing is simply the manifestation of becoming Moravian. Your body has changed to allow you to gain nourishment from blood—perhaps that, or the fact that you are feeding me, has drained you of energy, leaving you to experience periods of lethargy."

"And the manic times when I'm all hot and feel like I could do just about anything?" I asked, not quite sold on the idea.

He rubbed his chin. "You are immortal. Your body must move into regenerative times to compensate for anything that's threatened your well-being, including me feeding from you. It may well be your own immune system operating at a higher level than you are used to."

"I suppose that makes sense." I thought about it a bit, then decided that as Keeley had experience in that area, and I didn't, I'd go with his explanation. *The fact remains that I still want a hot bubble bath. I don't think there's room for us both, or I'd invite you to join me.*

He stretched out again on the bed. "Enjoy your bath. It will take me a little time to recover from your sexual demands. Perhaps a week or two."

Despite the mystery of what was happening to my body and mind, I giggled. I entered the bathroom, a plan forming even as I acknowledged that a needy Keeley might pull at my heartstrings to help him, but a sated Keeley showing a hidden sense of humor was nigh on irresistible.

I was in deep, deep trouble emotionally, and I knew it.

SIXTEEN

Ahhh, I sighed into Keeley's head, swishing my arm around in a tub of soapy hot water. I focused my attention on just how good that water felt, and kept my mind firmly away from the fact that I was kneeling fully clothed next to the tub. *Sometimes, a bath is just bliss.*

Do you need me to help you wash anything? he asked, punctuating the sentence with a mental yawn.

No, I can feel how sleepy you are. You take a nap before we rendezvous with Mac. You certainly deserve a rest, I answered with a mental waggle of my eyebrows.

You helped a little, he said, but the words drifted through my mind slowly.

I waited a few more minutes before entering the other attached room, softly closing the door so no click would give me away.

"And so, it begins," I told myself a few minutes later, as I waited outside the hotel for the ride I'd ordered. "This is my chance to make everything right. Things have gone sideways in the past, but that ends now. It's time to pull on your shining armor, and be the knight that Keeley needs—oh, hi. Are you Bibi?"

"I am." The woman at the wheel with lime-green hair and a number of facial piercings had a lilting Hispanic accent, a very clean car, and blessedly effective air-conditioning. "It shouldn't take us long to get to your address. You new in town? It's over by Cayuga Park, which is a very pretty park to visit. I can give you much information about it if you like."

I collapsed against the back seat, drained just with the effort to move, but relishing the cold blast of air. "I don't think I'm new here, although I couldn't tell you for certain, since Abbott made sure I wouldn't remember anything good. And thank you for the park info, but I'm good. Will you stop about a block before the actual address I entered in the app? I ... er ... want to walk the last bit."

"In this heat?" She gave me a quick look in the rearview mirror, but said nothing more than, "The sun won't set for an hour, but if you want to get heatstroke walking the streets before it cools down, that's your business."

I worried the entire twenty minutes it took to get to the Revelation headquarters that Keeley would discover that I wasn't taking the world's longest bubble bath, but hesitated to reach out to give him a mental prod. "It's far better he stay asleep," I said to myself, giving Bibi a wave as she deposited me a block from my destination. "This way I can take care of things without having to protect him, and hopefully be back to the hotel before Mac and the tourists converge on him."

Heat rose from the pavement in palpable waves, the slight breeze combining with it to make small rippling mirage puddles appear ahead of me. I don't know what I expected the headquarters of a group of nefarious agents to look like, but the smoke-colored glass building wasn't it.

"It looks more like a high-end hair salon than the home of a bunch of bad guys clearly bent on global domination," I grumbled, melting my way down the sidewalk toward the building.

"I think it looks like one of those fancy banks," a familiar nasal voice emerged from behind me when I passed a ten-foot-tall fence that delineated the grounds of the building next to the Revelation headquarters.

I spun around, my heartbeat pounding in my ears. "Wha—Mrs. Walsh? Lolly? Beth?"

"Hello," Lolly said, beaming at me as all five tourists came forward from where they'd been lurking alongside the fence. "You look surprised. Are you surprised?"

"Ye-yes," I stammered, trying to calm my heart rate. "Very much so. What are all of you doing here?"

"Helping," Beth said, gesturing to the others. "Mac said you might slip out before our meeting time later on, so we thought we'd just be in place in case you needed us."

"Skulkin'," Mrs. Walsh said, nodding, then raised her phone and snapped a picture of me. I had a mental image of just how idiotic I looked with my mouth hanging agape, and snapped my teeth together. "Mac said there would be lots of skulkin' needed, and we all's here to do it."

"Mac?" I glanced around, relaxing when I didn't see her. "She's not here, is she?"

Beth gave a one-shouldered shrug. "She said she had some things to do with her gentlemen friends—"

"I've got a few things I'd like to do to them, too," Mrs. Walsh told Lolly sotto voce.

Lolly giggled.

"—but that we might want to keep an eye out in case you tried to get away early. So here we are, your able assistants!" Beth's voice, like her expression, was filled with enthusiasm and excitement that I had a hard time understanding. All I wanted to do was curl up in a puddle of melted Jenna, and here were my tourists ready for action.

Those last couple of words rang ominously in my head. I shook away my weariness and befuddled state, and said in what I hoped was an authoritative tone, "Much though I appreciate your help, I'm afraid this is too dangerous a situation for you all. For one thing, we don't know how many Men in Black are inside. And for another, my insurance broker would have kittens if she found out I brought paying customers to a potentially deadly situation."

"Deadly!" squealed Tucson, elbowing her friend. "This just keeps getting better and better!"

"You film Jenna, and I'll capture anyone who interacts with her," Madison said, flexing her fingers a couple of times. "We'll get all the action that way."

"Deal," Tucson said.

I slapped my hands on my thighs. "Ladies, this just isn't feasible."

"Nonsense," Beth said, and, taking me by the arm, turned me so we were heading straight for the entrance of the Revelation building. "We won't get in your way at all, so there's no danger to us. Tucson and Madison are going to film everything, just in case we need a record for evidence. Lolly and I will be the lookouts. We'll watch for more of those rude men with hats and sunglasses, and warn you if someone is coming up behind you."

"And I'm your wingman," Mrs. Walsh said, elbowing Beth aside in order to grab my arm and pull me toward the big glass doors at the entrance.

"I really do appreciate this, but I just can't—"

"Shhh!" Mrs. Walsh said loudly. "Don't let anyone know y'all know us. It's more confusin' that way."

I tried to protest again, but she shoved me through the door. I stumbled forward a few steps, then stopped, quickly taking in my surroundings. Lining both sides of the room were banks of chrome and black leather chairs, a few tables with fanned displays of magazines, and a large chrome and glass desk smack-dab in the center of the room.

The individual at the desk glanced up when I came in.

"Er … hi," I greeted the receptionist, moving forward to the desk. They had long blond hair caught up in a bun, a black-and-white striped steampunk skirt and vest, and a large circular button in the transgender flag colors, over which a silhouette of a dinosaur was placed with the words *T. Rexes for Trans Rights*. "I'm Jenna, and I'm here to see Paris … er …" I dug through my memory, which took a few moments since my brain seemed to be suffering from the same sense of exhaustion as had claimed my body. "Sigurdsson? Yeah, I think that's it. Can I pop up and see him, please?"

Behind me, I heard the soft whoosh of the automatic doors opening and, by dint of my peripheral vision catching the reflection in the glass walls, noted that Lolly and Beth had taken up positions on one side of the room, while the two vloggers had gone to the other.

Behind me, stentorian breathing announced the arrival of my wingman, Mrs. Walsh.

The receptionist pursed their lips. "Citizen Sigurdsson is available only by appointment."

"Citizen?" I asked, momentarily discombobulated by the word.

They sniffed. "We here at the Revelation like to use gender-neutral words when possible so as to avoid stereotypes and expectations based on birth alignment rather than personal preference."

Mrs. Walsh gave one of her expressive snorts behind me, but I thought best to ignore it.

"Gotcha. I'm all for equality and all that goes with it, but regardless, I really do have to see Mr. Sigurd—er, Citizen Sigurdsson. Is there any way you could slip me into his schedule?"

The receptionist tapped on the computer keyboard, squinting slightly at the screen. "I'm afraid not. He has an appointment due in ten minutes, but that is the last for tonight. If you like, I can set you up with a time tomorrow or the following day. What did you say your name was?"

"Jenna, but tomorrow isn't going to work." I though hard about my options. I couldn't wait, but I had a feeling if I tried to force my way into the MIB's office, there would be hell to pay. More important, I would not put the tourists at risk. They might be somewhat of an albatross around my neck, but they meant well, and were trying to help.

I eyed the receptionist again. "Who is the appointment with?"

"Pardon?" Their eyebrows rose at my audacity in asking such a question.

"I might know them," I said with a lameness that made me flinch. "If I do, I could piggyback on their appointment, and everyone would be happy."

That wasn't quite true, but I decided that there was a time and place for absolute honesty, and this was not it.

"I'm afraid it's against the Revelation policy to share details like that," they said with a primness that would have made a schoolmarm happy.

Mrs. Walsh snorted again. I didn't want her getting involved with the situation, and with the acknowledgment that desperate times called for potentially desperate measures, I smiled and leaned as far over the high desk as I could. "I hope you don't mind me commenting on this, but you have such a cool skirt. Is it steampunk? I love that sort of quasi-Victorian aesthetic. Oooh, there are ruffles on the bottom."

The receptionist stepped back as I leaned even farther over the desk, angling my head so I could see the monitor screen in my peripheral vision. I thought for a moment that they were going to call for security, but instead, they gestured toward the skirt. "I hand stitched the entire hem."

"Impressive," I said, genuinely in awe of someone who could put so much work into a garment. "I've always wanted to do cosplay, but never seemed to have the time for it. Well, if there's no way for me to see Paris today, then that's all there is to it."

They looked a bit baffled when I turned on my heel and marched toward the door, being sure to not make eye contact with any of my tourists.

As I walked, I murmured under my breath the name I'd seen on the computer screen while reaching out with my mind for the weft of time and space.

For a few seconds, nothing happened. Then as if with reluctance, the world shifted ever so slightly, rolling back the clock by approximately five minutes.

"Hello," Lolly said as she and the others emerged from the shadow of the fence when I passed by it.

This time I was ready for them, and didn't argue when they insisted on accompanying me. I let Mrs. Walsh push me to the doors, and strolled in, a smile affixed to my lips.

"Hi," I told the receptionist. "My name is Hartley Benner, and I have a meeting with Paris Sigurdsson in ten minutes. I'm a little early. I hope that's not a problem?"

As the last word left my lips, pain pierced my head, a pain so sharp it left me gasping with the strength of it. I reeled forward, and clutched the edge of the desk so I wouldn't fall.

"Are you all right?" the receptionist asked, hesitating over a visitor's badge.

"Just peachy," I croaked, and grabbed the badge before they could withdraw it. "Just a bit of a migraine is all. Which office?"

"Three fifteen, but you know, you don't look at all well. Would you care to sit down? I could bring you some water—"

"No, no, that's not necessary," I said, fighting against the urge to curl up into a fetal ball and scream. Just as I thought I was going to pass out, the pain began to ebb, and I tottered forward a few steps. "I'll be fine in a minute. Thanks for the offer, though."

The tourists all looked concerned, but I turned my body so the receptionist couldn't see the gesture I made at them to stay put. Beth nodded in response, and Mrs. Walsh, now under scrutiny by Citizen Receptionist, told them she was new in town before launching into a convoluted story about finding a long-lost cousin named Aaron.

I had intended on taking the stairs up to Paris's office, since it was just two flights up, but instead I wobbled my way over to the elevator, and prayed to every deity I could name that the real Hartley Benner was held up in traffic. "Just long enough for me to take care of things," I whispered to myself, taking a few deep breaths, grateful when the pain continued to melt away.

The upstairs had a similar feel as the Krebbs administrative building layout: glass-fronted offices lining one side of the massive room, while the rest of the floor was taken up by a maze of cubicles, most of which were empty at this relatively late hour.

The five offices were occupied, however, and I couldn't help making a face at the male and female Men in Black who sat inside their glass cages, dutifully working late to impress the higher-ups.

"Sycophants," I said under my breath, thankfully feeling a now-familiar tickle of heat forming along my back. "Enjoy your last few seconds of being a slave to your own desires, because it's all about to end. Three eleven, three thirteen, ah. Here we go."

Visible through the glass wall I could see a man seated at a massive mahogany desk. Like the others, he wore a black suit and tie, although he had forgone the sunglasses, and was leaning back in his chair, his head tipped back as he spoke, no doubt dictating something.

I smiled, and embraced the prickle of sweat as it formed along my back and forehead, grateful that at least I wasn't going to have to do this in my exhausted noodle state. I flung open the door and strolled in, my odd physical state giving me a flip attitude. "So. You're the man responsible for ruining Keeley's life. Well, that just isn't going to fly. Prepare to make amends for your bad choices in life."

To my regret, Paris didn't look at all bothered by my threats. "—will have to address the issue of the Council—" He stopped speaking as I sashayed in, but didn't even bother to sit up straight. He simply glanced over to me as if I was a minor interruption, and gave me a quick once-over that was cold and clinical before frowning. "You are not Hartley Benner."

"No, I'm not. I'm Jenna Boyle and I'd like to say I was your worst enemy, but not only do I think that's a fairly cliché line—it isn't particularly true, because in a few seconds, you won't even remember me, let alone have nightmares about me. Although you really should, because, dude. You put Keeley through hell, and no one does that to my former fiancé and potential future partner without having to deal with me."

"Keeley," he said slowly, and then he did take his feet from where they had been propped up on an open drawer. "You know the Thrall. Ah. You must be the woman who attacked—"

"No time for chitchat," I interrupted. "This isn't a Bond film, and I'm not the baddie, so you don't get an expository explanation about what's happened. Say bye-bye, Paris."

He started to stand even as I reached out with both hands, using the heat that burned through me to open a portal. I had a vision of a time in my mind, a time more than a hundred years in the past where Paris would be helpless to effect his torment of Keeley. With Paris stuck in the Victorian era, Keeley would never be changed, and at last everything that I had messed up would be fixed.

"Ah. There you are. I had a feeling you wouldn't be content with the minor infraction you just conducted."

The voice that spoke was soft and feminine, and came from behind me.

I spun around to behold the sight of Abbott, with Lemmas and Marley flanking her. "Crapbeans!"

Abbott stiffened at my exclamation.

"Sorry," I hastened to add, gesturing toward Paris, who had slowly gotten to his feet and was watching with mild interest while the three women entered the room. "I didn't mean a personal insult. It was more a general statement about … well, being caught about to send this bastard where he can't do any harm. So, hi, how are things going? Everything well in your pretty house? Also, I know how this looks, but it's not what you think. He's a bad man. A very bad man."

The three Weavers looked at Paris.

He made them a bow, and smiled. I took an involuntary step back when I noticed that he had the same sort of elongated canines that Keeley had when he got all bitey. "You're a Thrall!" I said on a gasp.

"Dark One, I think," Abbott said, eyeing him with a curiously blank expression.

The urge to gawk was strong, but I resisted it. "A vampire? You're a vampire like Keeley used to be?"

He bowed again. "I am."

"You bastard!" I slammed my hand down on the desk, hurting it, but not caring. "You are one of his own people, and you turned him into something he hates. You used him to torment others!"

"I did," he agreed, and started toward me, pausing at the edge of the desk. "And you, if my nose does not lie—and it never does—are a Beloved, which is interesting. *Very* interesting. I believe you will be able to help me with a little project I am undertaking."

"Oh, hell no," I told him, and before Abbott or Lemmas or even Paris could say anything else, I pulled hard on the heat that sizzled along my veins, and opened a portal right under his feet.

"You bastard!" I slammed my hand down on the desk, hurting my hand, but not so much that it stopped me. "You were one of his own people, and you turned him into something he hates. You used him to torment others! Wait … didn't I just say that?"

Behind me, Abbott sighed. Lemmas sniffed. Marley pulled out a small notebook and wrote a few lines.

I shook my head as if that would clear it, gathered my energy, and threw a portal down at Paris's feet again.

"You bastard!" I slammed my hand down on the desk, cracking my knuckles on it. "You were one of his own people and you turned him … dammit! What is going on?"

"Alas, I suspected it would come to this," Abbott said, her voice mournful. She lifted a hand just as Paris started toward me, and drew a symbol in the air. It floated there for a few seconds, a lovely silver blue, before dissolving away, leaving Paris apparently frozen in time.

"Holy hellcats. Can I do that?" I asked, my mind squirreling around with the idea of being a more-or-less time lord. Doctor Who would have nothing on me if I could stop time itself.

"You? No," Abbott said, and looked at me with an expression that made me profoundly uncomfortable. A faint memory of a time when I'd been called before a teacher to explain misconduct came sharply to mind, but I pushed it down in order to remain focused. "However, I—"

The pain hit me at that moment. My knees buckled, and I hit the floor hard, smacking my head on it and knocking myself out for a short while.

When I came to, the pain was fading, but my entire body felt bruised, as if I'd been through an old-fashioned washing machine mangler. I was laid out on the leather couch in Paris's room, the man himself still frozen in a horrible parody of a statue. "What … eh … what happened?"

Abbott, who had been looking out of the window at the golden-orange streaks stretching across the sky as the sun began its descent for the night, turned to look back at me. "I forget just how lovely the mortal plane can be. Experiencing a sunset, for instance—it makes it worth the effort it takes to live here. Are you recovered?"

I pushed my hair out of my face and sat up, glancing around as I did so. Lemmas and Marley were no longer present. "Mostly. What happened?"

She moved over to stand before me when I got to my feet, stumbling over to a chair that I used as a support until my legs stopped being made of gelatin. Her eyes, as ever, appeared to see things that weren't visible to the rest of us. She considered me for a few minutes before saying, "You suffered repercussions for using powers that you should not have, and yet consistently prove otherwise."

"Huh?" I rubbed my forehead. I had a little bump there.

"The pain was a result from attempting to open a portal," she said, a slight exasperated edge to her voice. "Which you were not successful in doing."

"No, I can see that." I slid a glance toward Paris, but he was still playing statue. "I kind of hoped the interdiction wouldn't keep messing with me."

"It isn't. Somehow, you have broken another one," she said, examining me. "Unless ... no, I can see no signs of it."

That lifted my spirits. "Oh?"

Her gaze held mine, exuding a sense of calm that I badly wanted to embrace. Her words, however, were another matter. "I came to exsanguinate you, you know. You defied the Council, and brought shame to not just yourself but the Weavers' Guild."

"Just because I pushed Lemmas out of my house?" I tried to find a valid reason for doing so, but knew in my heart of hearts that although my act had been born of desperation, there was no real excuse for it.

Dammit, Keeley and Mac had been right all along. The situation we were in now *was* due to my hasty actions.

Abbott continued to watch me, saying nothing.

I shuffled my feet and rearranged a few accessories on Paris's desk. "And the incident at the airport, I suppose. Not to mention a few minutes ago, although I had a really good reason for doing all of those. Valid justification, in fact. More than valid. There were bad people I had to take care of." I slid a glance at her from the corner of my eye.

She stood still, her expression placid.

I sighed the sigh of the martyred. "Fine," I said, seating my wobbly self on the edge of the desk, ignoring the still form of Paris a few feet away. "I went against the rules and blipped people when I shouldn't have. I'm sorry, but you have to understand what's been going on in my life. This isn't just about the Weavers' Guild, or even me being a Weaver, it's—"

"Ah, but that does not matter," she interrupted, turning back to the window to admire the deepening orange, red, and peach of the sky. "Not any longer."

My insides felt oddly cold and somewhat clammy at her words. "The exsanguination?" I asked, swallowing back a painful lump of fear that seemed to stick in my throat.

"No. As I said, the Council came to exsanguinate you, but there is no need."

"Because you see that although I broke the rules, what I did was right and just, and made the world a better place?" I asked, hope lightening the leaden feeling of my stomach.

She tipped her head and turned slightly to pin me back with another one of those unfathomable looks.

"Sorry," I said, making a little gesture of apology. "That was a bit overdone, But surely someone as powerful as you can tell that I did what I did for a good reason. I'm not evil. Not like him," I said, pointing at Paris.

"We did not perform the exsanguination because you are diminishing."

Diminishing? Great, now I was losing the wonky bit of power that I had.

She continued, "We will have to formally remove you from the Weavers' Guild, but as you no longer wield the power of a Weaver, there is no need to exsanguinate you."

"I'm not a Weaver?" I shook my head, trying to make puzzle pieces that didn't want to fit together into a coherent picture. "But I just blipped. Three times here, and once on the ground floor, and earlier today—"

"You are not a Weaver," Abbott interrupted again, this time turning fully to face me. She brushed a spot on my forehead, a whisper-soft touch that made me feel as if a thousand gossamer strands bound to me suddenly dissolved into nothing. "You are something unique now. What, I do not know, but the fact that you are diminishing is evident."

"If my powers are fading, it has to be because you guys keep slapping interdictions on me," I protested.

Her eyebrows rose a smidgen. "Diminishing does not mean simply a reduction of powers, child. You, yourself, are fading."

Icy fingers of fear—true, unadulterated fear—touched my spine. "I'm … you're not saying I'm dying, are you?"

She just looked at me, but her gaze was shuttered.

I clutched the edge of the desk, my head swimming. "I thought I was immortal? Keeley said I was. How can I be dying if I'm immortal?"

"All beings must end," she said, her voice gentle, but at the same time with a thread of steel in it. "That goes for Weavers as well as Dark Ones. Their life spans are measured in centuries or millennia, but with enough time, an end will be reached. You are simply reaching yours sooner than others."

I desperately wanted to talk to Keeley, to have him hold me and reassure me that I wasn't in the process of dying, but a tiny kernel of truth glowed in the darkness of my soul, and my heart wept. Keeley already had abandonment issues—I had absolutely no doubt that he would interpret this as yet more proof that he was unworthy of love.

And in that moment, determination flared to life in my belly, growing to a burning need.

"If Keeley wasn't a Thrall," I said slowly, turning my eyes to the man frozen before me, "then he'd stand a chance at finding someone who would love him. Someone who could be with him for the amount of time he had left. Someone—" My voice broke even as my eyes burned, and my throat grew tight. "Someone who he could love in return."

"You would see him bound to another?" Abbott asked, her voice as light as a whisper.

No, my heart sobbed. *No one but me!*

"Yes," I said, the effort to speak making my stomach turn. For a moment, I thought I would vomit.

"It seems I was wrong about you after all," Abbott said, moving in front of me, tipping my chin up with one finger in order to gaze deep into my eyes. "I had thought you given only to instinct, listening to your heart rather than common sense, but now I see the error in my thinking."

"You weren't wrong," I said, sniffing and pulling a tissue from a box on Paris's desk. "But this isn't about me. It's about Keeley—and he's suffered so much. Ever since he was born, all he's known is sorrow." My eyes, now watery even though I was determined not to cry in front of her, lifted to hers, and I was unable to keep from adding, "And the one time he found happiness, you guys erased my memory. I don't deny that I was to blame for misusing my abilities, which threw me in his path to begin with, but what you did was unnecessarily cruel."

She looked at me for a few seconds, then inclined her head. "I regret that I did not oversee your situation myself, and thus I accept the Weavers' share of the blame."

My gaze slid over to Paris. "Does that mean you feel sufficiently guilty that you will zap him to the past for me, so that we can reset everything?"

"Alas, no," she said with a little laugh. "That would be a situation of attempting to make two wrongs a right, and I have never supported such follies."

Rage hit me at that moment, a fury unlike anything I'd felt before. I struggled for a moment to stay above it, to keep from lashing out, but like everything else in my life, it just seemed too much for me.

I snatched up a mug from Paris's desk and threw it at the nearest wall, where it smashed with a satisfying noise. "What the ever-living hell? You come here and tell me I'm dying, and that you guys are partly to blame for the nightmare that Keeley is in now, which, incidentally, is *why* I'm dying, but you won't do anything about it?"

"It is not in our purview—" she started to say, but this time, it was my turn to do the interrupting.

"This man is the cause of all the suffering that's happened since he kidnapped Keeley and turned him into a monster," I yelled, pointing at Paris.

"For which I am sorry, but you cannot lay that at the Weavers' door," she said with a flash of her eyes.

I bit back a rude remark, and switched tactics. The anger set a headache pounding in my temples, but I ignored it. "You said that Weavers serve mortals. This man, this vampire, brought about the endless suffering to who knows how many mortal beings. Stop him. Send him back in time. Zap him to the Stone Age. Hell, throw him in front of a big, hungry T. rex if you like. … Just do something!"

Abbott was silent for what seemed like an eternity. I was about to get on my knees and beg for her to intervene, since I was helpless, but before I had to grovel, she spoke. "Weavers are not servants of mortal beings, but I feel a certain leeway is merited to your request given the circumstances of your original punishment. Therefore, I will grant you the Grace of the Weavers, but I warn you, in your diminishing state, you may well have only one chance to use it." She touched me on my forehead in the same spot the thin man had placed the interdiction, but unlike this, her touch left a spot of warmth that seemed to fill me with a warm, golden light.

"Grace of the Weavers?" I asked, the anger fading quickly as the warmth spread. Unfortunately, that also left me moving straight for the wet-noodle stage of whatever illness was killing me. "Is that a spell or something?"

"You could think of it that way. Mind, I make no promises as to how effective it will be given your waning health." She moved closer to me, her gaze holding me upright despite the exhaustion that began to creep into my limbs. "Be sure when you use it, Jenna Walker Boyle. Be certain of your intent, and what actions will follow, for you will not be able to undo anything you perform under the Grace."

"Thank you," I said, turning to look with obvious intent at Paris. "My intent is pretty clear."

"Is it?" She glided away toward the door, pausing at it to ask, "Is destroying this man what you truly want? I had thought it was the happiness of the man for whom you risked so much."

"Sending him to the distant past will make Keeley happy," I said, but the words fell from my lips like chunks of lead. Everything about the idea of banishing Paris felt wrong, and yet I could see no other way to save Keeley.

"I wish I could advise you more, but …" She made an aborted movement of her hands. "You are on your own. You must rely solely upon yourself."

"You're wrong there." I took a step beyond Paris, wanting badly to punch him in the noogies for what he'd done to Keeley, but couldn't bring myself to do it. Not with Abbott watching, anyway. "My powers may be borked when it comes to portaling people back to Victorian times so they can't bring about the torment and destruction of untold numbers of people, my boyfriend included, but that doesn't mean I'm alone."

The corners of her mouth curled for the space between two seconds; then she handed me a folded slip of paper, saying, "Farewell, Jenna Walker Boyle."

A swirly gray mass formed in the air behind her, swallowing her up.

As her image melted into nothing, I unfolded the paper she'd slipped me, frowning at the one word written there. A few minutes with Google enlightened me. I glanced at the still-frozen Paris, thought for a second about sending him far, far away, but ended up bolting out of the room.

She was right in that, most of all, I wanted Keeley safe. And if I had only one chance to use the power she'd given me, then by the stars, I'd make sure that it did more than throw Paris out of the picture.

"Mac, I have something important to tell you. It's a worst-case scenario situation, but if it happens, here's what I want you to know," I said, using my phone's voice-to-text function, and dictated a handful of short texts.

"There's two ways to skin a bastard, Thrall-making vampire," I told the phone when I was finished, forcing my legs to run for the stairs. I knew from the glimpse I'd had at the receptionist's computer that the lab was located on the fourth floor. Where there was a lab, there was an antidote. Once I de-Thralled Keeley, I'd use the Grace to send him somewhere he could be happy. Only then would I be able to die in peace.

My inner Jenna mocked such a stupid idea, but I ignored her. This time I wasn't going to think with pure emotions. This time, I was going to do things right.

SEVENTEEN

Keeley counted to a hundred, then listened intently. The water had stopped running in the connected bathroom, and a few splashing noises told him Jenna was ensconced within.

He rose and quickly donned his clothing, knowing well she'd be furious when she found he had slipped out without her. "She will just have to be angry," he told himself as he availed himself of one of the taxis that sat waiting outside the hotel.

"Eh?" the driver said.

"I'm just talking to myself," Keeley told the man, wondering how long Jenna would be in the bath.

"I used to do that," the driver said in a conversational tone. "But then I heard a podcast on how too much of it meant you aren't getting enough social interaction, so I upped my chat-with-customers game."

"Indeed." Keeley paid the man little attention, his mind flitting between worry about Jenna—was she really ill? or just suffering from a change from Weaver to a Weaver who was now also Moravian?—and what he would face at the headquarters of the madmen who had so effectively ruined his life.

"Then again, there's a lot to be said with being comfortable enough with yourself that you don't have to fill every second with noise. My wife, she likes the TV on all the time, but I like to have time to let my ears breathe, if you know what I mean. Peace and quiet, without constant noise hitting you over the head."

"Quiet is underrated," Keeley agreed, wondering if he should check in with Jenna. He had no doubt he could mask his own location from her, but he had led her to believe he was sleeping, so as to encourage her to let him rest after her bath. He decided against it, then congratulated himself on keeping from her the printout with the address of the Revelation. "Even if she does find me gone, she won't know where to look."

"Slipping out on a partner, are you?" the driver asked. "I don't hold with that, myself, but I make it a policy to not judge. I am but a simple taxi driver. Say, you wouldn't happen to like a tour around the city? My wife says I need to start offering that service to tourists, and I've been boning up on all the important historical sites."

Keeley had a hazy image of what would happen once he arrived at the madmen's headquarters. They would try to stop him, of course, but assuming that they weren't equipped with any of those damned Tasers, he was confident he could handle whatever guards would be located at the building.

"Not interested? I can't say that I blame you. I mean, there's only so much you can appreciate from inside a car," the driver said.

Keeley said nothing, his mind turning over possibilities of what would greet him at the Revelation building. Assuming there were six or fewer guards, he'd be able to handle them. He'd just have to keep the bloodlust from claiming him. For a moment, he had a horrible mental image of turning a roomful of madmen, finally driving him to the Breaking and turning him into a nightmarish being without any chance of redemption.

"My wife wants me to give up the taxi and go into tour guiding, but I just don't see the point. There's only so many people who want to see the sites, but there's always people who need rides, am I right?"

Cold sweat broke out on Keeley's palms. What would happen to Jenna if the Breaking claimed him while she was in the same city? Would she be safe from him?

"No," he said, refusing to consider it. He'd simply have to take charge of the situation and not allow the madmen to push him to Breaking.

"You're entitled to your opinion," the driver said, and spent the rest of the trip in injured silence.

Keeley emerged from the taxi a few blocks from the building, filled with determination. He felt the need to get the lay of the land before he entered the building. Long experience as a Dark One had taught him to always identify exits, just in case he needed to leave via a shaded side of the building.

The building sat innocuously in a street of other buildings ranging from a plastics manufacturer to a tire-repair business. A tall white wood fence separated the latter from the Revelation headquarters, and as Keeley cautiously approached the fence, he paused at the sight of a man who had slipped around the front of the building to the far side.

"What the hell?" He didn't hesitate but walked briskly past the entrance to the far side, at which point he almost ran down the Russian Dima. "What are you doing here?"

"Shhh," Dima said, then peeked around the corner to the front. To Keeley's amazement, the helot pulled out a phone, quickly punching a button. "One came out, but was woman. Not member."

"Damn," came the voice that Keeley recognized as belonging to Mac. "Where did Keeley go? He was right there in front of me. Then he took off like a lion after a gazelle."

Dima was about to answer, but Keeley took the phone from him and answered, "What the hell are you doing here? Is Jenna with you?"

"Oddly enough, I was going to ask you those very same questions. I assume that means she's not with you, either?"

"No. She was bathing when I left."

"Huh." Mac was silent for a few seconds. "That doesn't sound like her, but given that she's been feeling puny lately, I guess it's understandable. Whoa. Dima, who is that one?"

Dima, who had been watching the front of the building, ducked back and snatched his phone from Keeley's hand. "Is one mens of Paris. One who work in lab."

"Gotcha. Anton, would you?"

"What's going on here?" Keeley demanded of Dima, who shushed him again and waved him back when he tried to get around him.

"Stay back. Mistress is gelding trees."

"She's what?"

"Pruning, not gelding," came Mac's voice from the phone. Then she gave a little giggle. "Right, that's four more added to Team Mad Scientist. You going in, Keeley?"

Keeley ignored the phone that Dima held out, and simply marched around the man, across the front of the building, resisting the urge to look in through the big glass walls, and turning at the end to discover Mac and several madmen huddled behind a large trash container.

"What is going on here?" he asked, pinning Mac back with a look that should let her know he would stand for no shenanigans.

"Oh hi," she said, and giggled. "I was just taking out some of the baddies for you."

Keeley looked from the three syringes she fanned to the five people who stood in various attitudes along the wall, and rubbed his jaw. "You made more helots?"

"I'm a Thrall Baby–makin' fiend," she said with a bright smile that struck Keeley as not being quite sane. "And before you give me crap about it, I'm only taking down the Men in Black, and they all agreed that they'd rather live a life where they aren't serving any number of nefarious overlords to spread their agenda of corruption and deceit. Right, guys?"

"Damn straight," a female helot said. "We're going to stick it to the man."

"Literally," another helot added, and flipped open a switchblade.

Keeley thought of pointing out that making an army of vigilantes might not be construed in as beneficial a light as Mac had hoped, but decided that he had other things to worry about. "What's in those syringes?" he asked, suspicious that she had taken the antidote from the lab the day before.

"Just my love-slave juice," she said, waving them around casually. "It works wonders at making Thrall Babies."

Keeley rubbed the back of his neck, wondering if he'd ever understand how Mac's mind worked. "He thought of forbidding her from attacking any more of the madmen but, upon a moment's reflection, realized that would be spiting himself for no reason.

She was doing him a service in that the fewer madmen who were located inside, the better his chances of finding what he sought.

"Just see to it that you don't enthrall anyone who is unwilling. You can restrain any of the madmen who are opposed to such actions," he told Mac, then turned and started toward the front of the building.

"Ten four, big buddy," Mac said, saluting, then added, "Oh, if you happen to see the tourists inside, please tell them that we have an après Thrall Baby–making celebration arranged in my room at midnight."

"We're having cheese fondue," Anton told him.

"And bondage for those who like to indulge," another helot added.

Several murmurs of excitement followed Keeley as he made his way to the entrance with a profound sense of martyrdom.

Of course Mac and the tourists would be here, getting in his way. He wondered again about Jenna, and was just about to reach out and see how she was, but he didn't want to risk her finding out he'd left without her. She'd be angry, but right now she was safe at the hotel, and that knowledge was worth any amount of penance he'd have to do later.

He expected to see the tourists that Mac mentioned inside the lobby of the headquarters, but it was strangely empty of people.

He strolled across the room, braced and ready for an ambush, the skin between his shoulders twitching in anticipation, but he made it to the bank of elevators without so much as a sound.

It wasn't until he turned to go to the stairs that he saw a line of chairs set against a back hallway. Six bodies lay on the floor, all madmen, judging by their clothing. In the chairs sat the five women tourists and one stranger, a man, all bound and gagged to the chairs.

"Is anyone hurt?" he asked them, torn between wanting to help them and knowing they would be safer tucked away where they were.

The nearest woman, the gray-haired one called Beth, shook her head, but said something indistinguishable, and jerked her head upward.

He moved over to see if the madmen were dead, but they all appeared to be unconscious, arms bound behind them with zip ties.

"Did you see who did this?" he asked.

Beth nodded and said something again. Keeley gave in to the pleading expression in her eyes and removed the gag.

"Oh, thank you," she said. "You can't imagine how annoying it is to be stifled like that. Yes, we saw the four men who attacked their compatriots. It must be some sort of an internal coup, don't you think?"

"Possibly," Keeley said, glancing over at the man with them. With an annoyed *tsk*, he pulled off his gag as well, asking, "Who are you?"

The man's face was red and covered in perspiration. "Hartley B. Benner, and I am not at all accustomed to being treated in this manner. I want to see whoever is in charge—"

Keeley jerked the gag back up, stopping the man from continuing. He glanced down to the unconscious men a second time, seeing nothing to indicate any reason they had been outcast and bound in such a fashion, but he supposed that there must be ranks of unhappy employees within the Revelation, just as there were in most companies. Especially so, given the enthusiasm with which Mac's helots had agreed to be changed. "In the end, it matters little why their own have turned on them. They must all be stopped. You will remain here while I go find their leader."

"You can't just leave us here!" the woman protested. The others grunted their unhappiness behind their gags.

"You'll be safer here than anywhere else," he growled, and took the stairs three at a time, ignoring the muffled cries that followed him.

The next floor appeared to be full of cubicles, but nothing indicated a lab, so he continued up to the top floor. He was immediately greeted by two guards outside a door bearing a retinal scanner.

"Who—" one of the two guards got out before the bloodlust hit Keeley. He managed to hold it from releasing fully, but allowed enough to slip his control that he sent the first guard slamming back into the wall, knocking him out immediately.

"Oy!" the second guard yelled, and fumbled with a familiar-looking device, but before he could fire the Taser, Keeley snatched it from the guard and threw it to the floor, crushing it before punching the man in the face.

His head snapped back, and he slid slowly down to the floor, leaving a long crimson smear of blood on the wall.

The scent of it hit Keeley, hunger blotting out everything in his mind, urging him to do what he had been born to do—drink.

Panic mingled with the need to feast upon the men, to punish them for their roles in his torment, and he honestly feared the bloodlust would triumph over him, but after a few minutes' struggle, he managed to leash it enough to pick up the now unconscious man and prop his face up at the retinal scanner.

The door slid open with a sibilant hiss.

"Paris!" Keeley bellowed, stalking into the room. He had little doubt that the security cameras set all around the building had alerted the madmen to his presence. "Are you so craven that you would hide from the monster you created?"

The lab was evidently arranged in three consecutive rooms. The first contained the same counters, chemical and medical equipment, and tall stools as had the one in the Krebbs campus. It was empty of people. Keeley yanked open the second door, and entered another room, this one bearing various machines that he recalled seeing at a research hospital: high-tech versions of autoclaves, chemistry analyzers, and two centrifuges amongst them. This room was also empty of personnel, which just made him growl to himself even as he carefully nurtured the fury that was driven by the bloodlust.

The third door was locked, but it gave once he kicked at the lock a few times, the door sagging inward with a wrenching noise.

The room was full of madmen.

"Five against one. Not bad odds," he said, stalking into the room, noting that the walls were lined with glass-fronted refrigerated units. Three of the five men were in the process of unloading the contents into heavy-duty medical-grade coolers. The fourth man was in the middle of saying, "I don't understand it. Everything is gone from the cloud. All the backups. All the databases. All the files. The formulas, the videos—everything is gone. Even the backups of the backups are gone. Poof. Just like they never existed. See for yourself."

The fifth man, who was looking at where the other was pointing to a laptop, glanced up with an irritated expression that faded into one of smug satisfaction.

"Ah," the man said, turning to face Keeley. He was obviously Paris. "It's you. I expected you'd show up at some point. I agree about the odds, as a matter of fact. Four men are nothing to the Beast."

Keeley kept from leaping upon Paris, but only by reminding himself that he wanted more than just revenge. He needed to get hold of the antidote. "You don't count yourself?" he asked as soon as he got the need to destroy under control.

"Should I?" Paris appeared to think for a moment, then made a wry face and straightened up, crossing his arms and watching with apparent interest when two of the madmen flung themselves on Keeley. "There is the slight fact that I am not like the others—"

Paris sidestepped quickly when the first attacker went flying backward, narrowly missing the laptop, and crashing into one of the refrigerator units.

The second flung himself on Keeley, a glint of metal in his hand, but after so many years being tormented by the madmen, he was wise to their attacks, and deflected the knife even as he slammed the man into the wall, watching with a moment of satisfaction as he slid to a crumpled blob on the floor.

"Three to one," Keeley announced, turning back to Paris, who continued to watch in apparent ease.

"Indeed." Paris considered the two men, now frozen in the act of unloading the cases, clearly looking to their boss for instruction.

To Keeley's surprise—and the men's horror—Paris waved at them and said in a voice dripping with nonchalance, "You were always very good at fighting the bloodlust. But there's no need for you to do so now. You want revenge against us? Help yourself. Take them. I won't stop you."

A red haze of need gripped Keeley, but he knew better than to believe any of the lies the madmen spewed. He shook his head, and instead moved forward, heading for Paris. "They are victims just as the innocents you threw to me. Why aren't you trying to stop me?"

Paris smiled, and Keeley felt something in his gut twist. The smile was wrong, filled not with bravado but with confidence. "Perhaps it's because I have little care for the fate of mortals. Perhaps I tired of the dictates that come down from the ones who claim to lead this group. Perhaps I believe the stories, and I know how close you are to the Breaking. Any or all would be a valid answer."

Keeley growled deep in his chest and lunged, but before his hands closed around Paris's neck, he realized two things that really should have warned him: the first was the word *mortal* in Paris's statement, and the second was the faint swirl of air that tickled the back of his neck, heralding the arrival of others.

Pain spiked into his neck, and he whirled around to find two more madmen, both wearing lab coats. A familiar burn spread from the injection, and Keeley knew without a shadow of doubt that he'd just been shot up with the bloodlust cocktail.

No, his soul cried. *Not now! Not now! Not when I'm so close to actually having a future. Not when I've found Jenna again.*

"Then again, it might be because your Beloved is being held in my office," Paris said, sidestepping again when Keeley lunged, but it was an attack that lacked true threat, as the chemicals fogged his mind with one need only: to destroy.

"I believe we'll retreat to the outer office and leave Keeley here with our friends for a few minutes while we watch from the monitors to see if the Breaking really happens," Keeley heard through the red haze that wrapped itself around him. He fought it just as he always fought, the faint cries of madmen being sacrificed dancing on the edge of his awareness, but even as he strove to keep from giving in to the chemical's demand, a stray thought flitted through his brain: Paris had Jenna.

"No!" The roar tore from his throat, anguish at the knowledge that he had failed the woman who held his heart almost as great as the pain from the bloodlust.

He fell to his knees, his body locked in a struggle with itself, desperately trying to clear the haze from his mind so he could find a way out of this hellish scenario. The alternative was unthinkable—he had to survive in order to save her from a future that would make his nightmares seem like happy little dreams filled with unicorns and rainbows.

Pounding filled his head, but he wasn't sure if it was the blood sounding in his ears, or something else. He remained on his knees, his hands fisted, his head bowed, as he fought with every ounce of his being.

"I will not … give … in … ," he said, each word costing him untold agony.

His control slipped, and he roared again, an inhuman sound that was answered by shrieks of the purest terror from the two trapped madmen. He was on them in a second, both men bashing at the middle door with chairs in an attempt to escape their fate, but Keeley knew with every iota of being that they would perish even as he, himself, would turn into the ultimate grotesque parody of what he had once been, a vampire who preyed not to survive, but to destroy.

His soul fought against the knowledge, but just as he reached the first man, a miracle happened. For a second, the bloodlust haze seemed to diminish, allowing him to see and think with reason. Keeley stared in surprise at the man he held in an unescapable grip, now begging and sobbing in terror. He looked from the man to the other one, still frantically trying to break down the door, and Keeley knew that Mac was right—Jenna had changed him on some fundamental level.

Keeley hesitated, glancing behind him where the coolers and refrigerated units sat. The antidote was there—he knew it had to be there, or Paris wouldn't have been in here.

But Jenna was at risk. Even now, Paris might be whisking her away, and he'd never see her again. Worse, he'd have to live with the knowledge that he'd let the woman he loved more than his own existence be made the same sort of victim as he had been.

He shoved the men out of the way, using the strength of the bloodlust to rip the door off its hinges, racing out of the room, the red haze continuing to fade even as he leaped down the stairs, heading for the floor where the offices were.

Jenna?

There was no response.

Panic hit his gut hard, causing him to stumble and crash into a wall before continuing. *I'll find you, love, have no fear of that. I lost you once, but I am not going to do so again. I won't let the madmen do anything to you,* he swore, pushing down the thoughts of just what he'd do to anyone who dared to harm his beloved.

No, not beloved … Beloved. He didn't know why he had fought so hard against the idea of Jenna filling that role, since it now seemed as natural as breathing.

She was his other half, the reason for his existence, and he'd die before he allowed anyone to take that light out of his life. Not again. Not ever.

As he reached the third floor, light spilled out of one of the offices, the others all dark. He snarled invectives as he ran, praying that enough of the bloodlust strength remained to rescue Jenna from whatever horrible situation Paris was keeping her in.

As he expected, the office was also full of madmen, five in number, including the German named Andreas and the red-haired woman.

All four men had their backs to him, and turned when he stopped in the doorway.

"Oh, it's you," the redhead said, moving around the men to face him, and at that moment he saw beyond her.

Jenna was bound to a chair, slumped to the side, her head hanging at what must be an uncomfortable angle.

If he thought the bloodlust had triggered rage in him, it was nothing to the sight of Jenna in the madmen's control.

A primal cry made the windows rattle, and the only thing that saved the people in the room was the fact that they leaped out of the way even as he flung himself forward, sliding on his knees the last few feet in order to snatch Jenna from the chair. Her body was warm and soft, and so right against him that he wanted to weep with the exquisite pleasure of her being.

"Awww. I do love a happy ending," he heard the woman say even as he checked Jenna for signs of injury. She had a few marks on her arms from where he'd jerked the bonds from her body, but other than that, she seemed fine, her soft breath reassuringly regular. Even her heartbeat was steady, thrumming so deeply within him that he thought he'd never separate it from his own.

"Just so you know, there are four of us here, in case you think to attack us," Andreas said.

"Ahem!" the woman said, and moved over to take the hand of one of the other madmen.

"You are not a Horseman," the German told her. "Beloveds don't count. You shouldn't even be here. Merrick should have told you that."

"Boy, you are really obnoxious," the woman snapped as Keeley got to his feet, Jenna in his arms, spinning around to find somewhere safe to put her before he took care of the madman who dared to abduct her.

The man next to the redhead laughed, and shook his head in a manner expressing mock regret. "You have a lot to learn if you believe I can dictate to Tempest."

"That's right," the redhead said, blowing the madman who spoke a kiss. "Merrick and I are a team. How is Jenna?"

Keeley, who had gently placed Jenna on a short suede couch, spun around and snarled, "You will perish for what you've done to her."

"Save her?" the woman asked, tipping her head to the side even as the madman next to her growled and took an antagonistic step forward. "No, Merrick, don't. You can see how upset he is … er … what's your name? All anyone refers to you as is the Old One."

Keeley, who had been calculating which of the madmen he would take out first, glanced at the woman, unable to believe her words.

"Keeley?" The voice wasn't his that spoke, but instantly, he was on his knees at the couch, cradling Jenna as she rubbed her eyes. "What—ow, my head—what's going on?"

Are you hurt anywhere, love? Did the bastards strike you down?

Paris and a couple of goons in green coats did—oh. Jenna spotted the others behind him, and pushed herself back until she was sitting upright. "Er … hello again. If any of you have plans to Tase Keeley, please don't, because I can only blip once, and I don't think that Abbott would want me to use something that important for a Taser avoidance."

Keeley glanced from Jenna to the men and back to her. "The madmen didn't capture you?"

"These guys?" Jenna felt the back of her head, winced, and made a rueful face. "No. It was Paris."

"You know, I really dislike being called a madman," one of the madmen told the other. This one had a French accent, and was leaning against the wall watching the scene with a mild expression of interest.

"Me, too," another one answered. "I mean, we are the good guys after all."

"Not when it comes to the Revelation," the French one pointed out.

"True," the other agreed, and both looked at Keeley.

"He's not with the Revelation," Jenna said, accepting his arm when she got to her feet. She wobbled for a second, throwing him a smile when he pulled her up close to his side. "Any more than I am. Just who are you guys? I thought you were Men in Black, but you're not with Paris, are you?"

"Assuming Paris is a person and not a capital city, no. We're the Four Horsemen," the woman answered, then, with an effort, managed to extricate herself from the man who was clutching her just as tightly as Keeley was holding Jenna. "Or rather, my husband, Merrick, is, along with his friends Han—"

One of the madmen nodded his head in acknowledgment.

"—and Ciaran—" The blond scowled at Keeley, who returned the gesture.

"—and Andreas, who is the newest member of the

Horsemen. He joined because the previous guy, Nico, went batshit crazy and ran off with my cousin Carlo."

The German said something rude under his breath.

"And I'd just like to point out that what I said earlier was right. I knew something was going on. No one who has a Beloved can be bad," the woman finished with a note of triumph.

"You're wrong," her man said, watching Keeley with a dark, suspicious gaze.

"You said yourself that she was a Beloved," the woman answered, gesturing toward Jenna.

"She is," Keeley said, and thought seriously about shoving Jenna out of the room and closing the door, so he could take care of the threat before them.

Dude, she said, laughter in her mind. *I might realize the value of working as a team rather than trying to fix everything myself, but that doesn't mean you get to go all manly-man on me.*

Please assume that I am making an innuendo regarding going manly-man all over you, he told her, never moving his gaze from the men in front of him.

To his surprise, a martyred expression flitted over the suspicious man, who sighed and said, "I meant that there are bad Dark Ones just as there are bad mortals. Nico proved that point."

"What do you know of Dark Ones?" Keeley asked.

"Whoa, you guys are vamps, too?" Jenna asked at the same time.

"Yes," the redhead answered; then she stepped forward and held out her hand. "We'll try this again since the first time, you were rolling around on the floor in agony. Hi, I'm Tempest Keye."

Keeley stared first at the woman, then at her hand, then at the man who stood glowering behind her. *What is going on? Is this a trick of some sort?*

I don't think so. Tempest says they're not Men in Black, and I believe her, Jenna answered, speculation rife in her mind. *In fact, I don't think they're our enemies at all. At least, I don't think they're allied with the Revelation.*

"Oh, come on," the woman named Tempest said, waving her hand at him before thrusting it out again. "It won't kill you to shake my hand."

Keeley thought of sighing a sigh of pure martyrdom, but he had always tried to limit the number of sighs he conducted per day, and he had a feeling he was well beyond that point. He shook the woman's hand, ignoring her when she beamed at him.

"I will admit to not being up-to-date on lore regarding the Old Ones, but I was not aware they had Beloveds," the man named Ciaran said, watching Keeley closely. "It does not change matters, however. You are a threat to the Dark Ones. You must be stopped."

"Whoa, now," Jenna said, straightening up from where she had melted into his side. "You don't get to talk to us like that. Keeley hasn't done anything wrong."

He couldn't stop himself. He sighed into her head. *Love, let me deal with this. More is at stake than you know.*

I could say the same thing to you, she answered. *I've got a lot to tell you, but we should probably deal with these guys first. Although… I'm not sure how much time I'm going to have before …*

"I don't know who you are, and at this moment, unless you are working with or for Paris, I don't particularly care what you think of me," Keeley told Ciaran. *Before what? Why do you not have time? Christos, the Council isn't here, are they?*

They were earlier. But don't worry about them. That's taken care of.

"Whereas we have a great deal to say about an Old One being in the world, putting all Dark Ones in peril," snapped Han.

Taken care of how?

He could feel a hesitancy in Jenna that disturbed him. He wanted to focus his attention on finding Paris, but he couldn't do so while Jenna remained at risk.

If I told you that I love you, would you believe me? she asked.

He turned to face her, his jaw tight. "Now? You choose now to discuss this? Woman, you are aware that the biggest threat to the mortal and immortal worlds alike is running loose in this building, no doubt setting into motion nefarious plans that will likely end in the destruction of not just both of us, but a great many innocent mortals as well? And yet you pick this moment in time to have this discussion?"

Jenna laughed into his head. *You're adorable when you're righteously indignant.*

"What are you talking about?" Andreas asked, glancing in confusion to his compatriots.

"Sounds like they're having a relationship talk,"Tempest said, and took her husband's arm, casting a look of adoration at him.

Andreas rolled his eyes. "Of all the inappropriate—we do not have time for this! You, whatever your name is—"

"His name is Keeley, and I'm madly, wholly, wonderfully head-over-heels in love with him, and if he knows what's good for him, he's going to realize that he can't live another day without me," Jenna said, looking at him with so much love glowing in her eyes that, for a few minutes, he forgot about Paris, forgot about his need to protect her from the men present, forgot everything but how deeply embedded she was within his soul.

"We don't have time for this," Andreas repeated, his fingers flexing.

"I think we should let them have a time-out,"Tempest said. "Clearly, they need a little privacy to work out some things."

"Merrick," Andreas said, appealing to the other man. "You know how important this is."

"I do, but I also know that when a Beloved sets her mind to having a relationship discussion, that discussion will be held," Merrick replied with a lascivious look at his wife.

She booped his nose.

I like them, Jenna said, startling Keeley. *Tempest knows her relationship potatoes. So to speak. So, are you going to say it, or do I have to prod you more? You can stop thinking about calling yourself Saint Keeley the Martyred, because I feel how warm and fuzzy you are inside. You're filled with love for me. So just acknowledge it already, and let's get a move on.*

He took her in his arms, unable to keep from claiming her mouth, the sweetness he found therein waking up his hunger, and driving a need to join with her before it. *I've loved you from the moment when I saw you sitting on my coat, and you subsequently refused to give it back. I loved you even when I thought you left me as all others have left me. I loved you in the depths of my despair when I sought nothing more than my own destruction. And I love you still, even when I want to shake you for putting yourself in danger on my behalf. Why are you here? Why are you not back at the hotel?*

She laughed into his mouth, giving his lower lip a nip before pulling back and saying, "I could ask you the same thing. You were supposed to wait for me so we could come here with Mac."

"She's outside, converting stray madmen into her own personal mostly-male harem," he told her, giving her one last kiss before reluctantly releasing her.

"Ooh, a male harem," Tempest said.

Her husband glared at her.

"I just said ooh," she told him.

"The thought shouldn't even strike you as interesting," he answered, turning to face her. "Not when you tell me I'm your sun and moon and stars."

"Dammit! That's so poetic," Jenna said, her lips thinning. "I wish I'd thought of it, but my mind just doesn't work that way."

"I read a lot," Tempest told her before giving her man a swift kiss.

The other men looked mildly disgusted.

"We've strayed from the point," Andreas said, gesturing toward them with a Taser. "The fact remains that the Old One and his Beloved have to be removed—"

"You so much as touch Jenna, and I'll see to it that you don't have hands to touch anyone again," Keeley warned him.

"There are four of us," Han said, rolling up his sleeves.

"AHEM," Tempest said pointedly.

"Why do you keep calling Keeley old?" Jenna asked, taking everyone by surprise, or so it seemed to Keeley. He glanced at her, unsure of whether she was trying to distract the men so he could remove her from the threat they posed.

No. I really want to know. Something is going on, and I want to know what it is before I . . .

Before you what? he asked, a nagging worry returning to the pit of his stomach. He could feel she was hiding thoughts from him. *Why are you talking in riddles?*

Me? She opened her eyes wide and blinked them a few times at him. *I'm not talking in riddles.*

He wasn't fooled in the least. "You're ending all your sentences in ellipses. I want to know why."

"I'll tell you later. Right now, I want to know why Andy there—"

"Andreas," the man corrected her, frowning at her.

"Why they keep calling you old. I mean, you're a hundred-plus years old, but if they are vamps, too, then I bet they aren't all spring chickens."

"Merrick is more than three hundred years old," Tempest said. "And he doesn't look a day over forty. A really buff forty. You should see his abs. They are a thing of beauty to behold."

"You want to talk buff, you need to see Keeley's stomach. He has an actual six-pack despite being held prisoner for the last twenty years," Jenna said, and to Keeley's surprise, she actually tugged the front edge of his shirt out of his waistband and held it up, exposing his belly.

"Oh, nice!" Tempest said, gazing at him.

Instantly, Merrick stood in front of her to block the view, his hands on his hips. "Woman!" he snarled. "You go too far."

"And you're adorable when you're jealous," she told him, her hands on his chest as she bit his chin. "Relax, I was just looking. I'm allowed to look."

"You are not," he answered, but at a waggle of eyebrows from his wife, he tempered that by adding, "I would prefer you not to admire other men. Especially ones who hold the future of all Dark Ones in their hands."

"Better," Tempest told him, then leaned around him and said, "I'll show you his abs another time. I think there are some things we need to discuss."

"Like what it is you guys have against Keeley when he's done nothing wrong to you. I mean, you're his own people. He wouldn't hurt you."

All four men stared first at Jenna, then at Keeley. "He is an Old One, a Thrall," the man named Han said at last.

"I was born a Dark One," Keeley answered, tucking his shirt in again.

"Keeley?" Merrick said, glancing at the others. "I have not heard of a Dark One with such a name. Who was your father?"

"Aldous Moore," Keeley answered, puzzled despite his need to get Jenna to safety before tackling Paris.

"No, I haven't heard that name," Merrick said. "Han? You're the oldest. Do you know of Dark Ones named Moore?"

"Ireland?" he asked, glancing at Keeley, who nodded in response. "No, the name is not one known to me, either. Ciaran, you were born there—do know of this family?"

"I was born there, but raised in Spain," the other answered, making a vague gesture. "The Moravian Council will assumedly have information about them. Text Christian and see what he says."

Keeley had been chewing over this latest wrinkle while the others discussed him. He readjusted his image of the men from being prime threats to lesser ones, and began to think of ways to convince Jenna to leave the building while he searched for Paris.

"But what does this have to do with you guys?" Jenna asked.

"Thralls are dangerous," Han told her, a scowl back between his brows. "They were progenitors of Dark Ones, the beings who bore the sin they passed on to us in order to free themselves of the stink of dark power. This one has clearly come back to destroy us all."

"Keeley wasn't born this way. That bastard Paris shot him up with all sorts of chemicals and made him into a Thrall," Jenna protested. *If I walked over and punched Han on the nose, would you have my back?*

Of course.

Even if the others attacked?

Yes, even if they all attacked. But do not do so.

Why? she asked, and another wave of fear gripped his belly when he realized the sense of fatigue that had been growing stronger had its origination in Jenna.

Because I hear something. If I asked you to go hide in a closet—

Dude, she repeated.

He sighed, caught himself doing it, and changed it into a near snort. Somehow, a near snort seemed to express more of his frustration.

"You can't make a Thrall," the man Han was saying when a voice came from the door.

"Can it be that the reports were true? My office filled to the brim with Dark Ones. And a second Beloved! My lucky day. You're quite wrong, you know," Paris told Han in his drawling voice that prickled along Keeley's skin like a burr. "Thralls can be made. Our friend Keeley is the perfect example of that. Sadly, the other Dark Ones we tried the formula on weren't so lucky, but we haven't given up. Our latest version should be much more effective. And here before me are so many opportunities for experimentation. Luckily, I hate being caught out unexpectedly. Stillson? The cooler."

Jenna— Keeley started to say, gently pushing her behind him, turning so that he blocked Paris's view of her.

Don't even think about telling me to run or hide. We're in this together. Besides, Abbott gave me a thingie.

A what? he asked, startled.

Grace of the Weavers, she answered. *It's like a big fat wallop of Weaver goodness.*

Keeley wanted badly to ask her why the head of her order would do such a thing, but there would be time for that discussion later.

Just a warning—you're going to want to talk to Mac after I use it.

Why?

He could feel her thoughts shifting so that they remained just beyond his reach. *It's too involved to tell you now. Just don't panic, and talk to Mac.*

Before he could demand an explanation, Paris spun around.

"No, not that cooler," Paris told the flunky in a lab coat who had scuttled forward. "The other one. Fetch the one with the new serum."

Insight flashed into his mind like a sunburst. *The other cooler—it has the antidote. We must get it.*

You're damned straight we must. It'll save you.

We don't know that, but you are ill. It will help you.

You distract Paris, and I'll grab it, she responded.

No. It's too dangerous—

Evidently the others had heard enough of Paris's speech to decide he was the enemy, because at that moment, all four men rushed forward toward him. Keeley made a dive for the cooler, but Paris snatched it away just as his fingers brushed on the handle.

"Stop!" Paris yelled, yanking open the lid and pulling out a handful of narrow, delicate vials. "You take one more step toward me, and I'll destroy the neutralizer. You won't have any chance of surviving if Keeley gets hold of you."

"We don't fear him—" Ciaran started to say, but a squawk from behind Keeley had the man freezing.

Keeley spun around, terror gripping him in an iron vise. One of the madmen stood behind Jenna, holding her by the neck, a syringe in his free hand. Keeley's brain stopped functioning at the sight of her, his breath caught in his throat.

I love you. I know I've told you that, but I really, really love you, Jenna told him, her eyes bright, red fever circles now evident on her cheeks. *And I want you to be happy. Very, very happy. You've been sad for so long, you deserve a lifetime of happiness.*

The terror intensified, and he knew without a shred of doubt that she was warning him of her death.

I can't live without you, he said simply, and allowed her to see the truth of the statement. *Not again.*

That is not the right answer, she said, her eyes softening even as her gaze filled him with love so profound, he knew he'd never be able to exist if she wasn't by his side. *But I've decided that I'm the only one who's going to make sure that you stay happy, so we're going to have to use a little magic.*

"You should fear him, you know," Paris said, moving carefully toward the window, keeping his body angled so that he faced Keeley and the other men. "He is really most effective when the right combination of drugs is used on him. It's just too bad that changing you lot will push him past the limit of what he can survive, but that can't be helped. The original Thralls never could find a solution to the problem of the Breaking, and sadly, neither have we. However, I see our friend Keeley is very interested in these, so I believe we will dispense with them in order to keep anyone from having hopes of escaping the very upcoming experiments that await you all."

Keeley leaped forward just as Paris flung open the window and threw the glass vials through it, stopping a few feet shy of the man, his heart sinking.

It's showtime, baby, Jenna's voice said softly in his head. He turned to see what she was intending on doing, but the world seemed to shimmer at that point, rippling like waves on a windy pond, then resolved itself back to normal.

"Stop!" Paris yelled, yanking open the lid of the cooler he held, pulling out a handful of narrow, delicate vials. "You take one more step toward me—"

Air swirled behind him even as he lunged forward toward Paris, but Jenna was faster. She snatched up one of the syringes, and before Keeley could reach Paris, she pulled the cap off the needle and jammed it into Keeley's arm, depressing the plunger.

He paused, staring down at his arm for a second.

Paris swore and dashed to the window, throwing the remainder of the syringes out it.

Why did you do that? Keeley asked Jenna even as the four Dark Ones rushed forward and quickly surrounded Paris and his henchman. *Why did you use it on me when you're so ill?*

Jenna's expression was stricken when she turned from where she'd been staring out of the window to him, her body slowly crumpling, her emotions a tangle of regret, love, admiration, and sadness.

He caught her even as Mac rushed into the room, saying, "The cavalry is here! We've got twelve MIBs bound up, and my posse is now six strong—whoa, what's wrong with Jenna?"

Jenna, do not do this, he cried into her head, panic filling him at the limpness that stole along her body. *Blip again. Go back in time. Go back before you met me. Save yourself, my love.*

A ghost of a smile curled her lips even as her head lolled back, and her eyes drifted closed. *I can't. But you can save me. Mac. Talk to Mac …*

A howl of sheer anguish rent the air. Keeley dropped to his knees, Jenna's face wet with his tears as he cradled her, his soul and every iota of his being unwilling to exist without her.

"Holy shitsnacks. She died? Her text said she thought she might, but I can't believe—no, Keeley, don't!"

Mac's voice penetrated his head even as he laid Jenna gently on a couch before turning his ravaged self toward Paris. The bloodlust roared over him, and for once, he gave it its head, pausing only when Mac, with her helots, grabbed his arm and stopped him.

He snarled at them, his gaze locked on Paris, who was even now being bound to a chair by the Dark Ones. He would kill them all for their part in the loss of his Beloved.

The act would destroy him, but that was a sweet solace to the thought of existing without her.

"Keeley!" Mac slapped him, catching his attention for a few seconds. She grabbed him by the ears and shoved her face in his. "Revenants, Keeley. Jenna texted me a little bit ago and said there were such things as revenants, and if things went pear-shaped, you were supposed to find someone who knows about them—"

Revenant. The word echoed in his head even as the bloodlust faded into nothing. He wasn't even surprised by the fact that he didn't have to struggle with it in order to keep it abated. Jenna had changed him in more than one way. Not only had she given him back his soul with her sacrifice; he now had something he had never thought to possess again.

He had hope.

"Revenants. That's what she meant," he said, his voice thick. "She wants me to save her."

Mac smiled, and released his ears. "She's a smart girl, our Jenna."

"What exactly is a revenant?" Tempest asked, moving over to stand next to him. "Is there anything we can do to help?"

"Jenna said revenants are basically people brought back to life by someone who can find their life essence. She said if we got someone here quickly to do it, there should be no problem. It's like a zombie, I guess, only minus the desire for brains." Mac patted Keeley on the shoulder as he knelt next to Jenna.

"Hey, I have another Thrall Baby vial left. Can I use it on him?" she asked, gesturing toward Paris, who had been screaming profanities until one of the Dark Ones gagged him with his own tie.

"Dibs I get him if you do," said the sour-faced tourist as she and the others pushed into the room.

Keeley had no time for any of them. Holding Jenna's body close to his, he used his free hand to pull up a search engine on his phone, and began the hunt for someone to return his heart to him.

EPILOGUE

"You'll tell us, won't you?"

I smiled, and patted Beth on the arm. "I will tell you, yes."

"Because we had a fabulous time," Lolly said, glancing behind me to where Keeley's hotel room was now at maximum capacity, what with all the vampires and helots stacked up everywhere. "Well, I could have done without being bound and gagged, but other than that—"

"We're so sorry about that, but the boys really did just want to keep you out of harm's way, not that I condone what they did, because tying someone up is not cool at all unless it's part of sexy time, and then only if explicit consent is given first, but still, they thought that just in case you weren't innocent, it would be a good thing to have you confined." Tempest stood next to me and smiled with a bright smile.

"That blond can tie me up any time he gets the urge. I'll even give him a tub of hog fat so we have fun after he does so," Mrs. Walsh said loudly, giving the vampire named Han a long, pointed look. He moved to hide behind the others, making me stifle a giggle.

"But you're sure you'll tell us," Beth said again, her face scrunched up as she held one of my hands in both of hers. "I'll happily spend all of next year's vacation with your tour company. Just let me know when you'll be running another tour, and I'll be there."

"So will I," Lolly said, nodding. "Assuming it's between semesters, of course."

"Of course." I squeezed Beth's hand, having already said good-bye to Madison and Tucson, who were even now filming themselves waiting at the elevator for the others. "Do you all have the handout with the name of the driver who will take you to the airport?"

All three ladies in front of me pulled out a neon green paper and waved it around.

"It's been a pleasure to have you all with us on Outta This World Tours," I said with another professional smile, and extricated my hand from Beth's.

"I didn't get me a Thrall Baby," Mrs. Walsh said, her nostrils flaring. "I'm gonna want one next time. Or that blond. Either will do."

"Next time?" Mac, who had been passing out beverages and snacks down the line of her helots, whom she'd parked sitting along one wall of the room to keep them out of the way, stopped next to me to say good-bye as well. "I thought you were closing down the company because we're moving to England to live in Keeley's house?"

"Keeley has a house in England?" Beth asked, a glint to her eye that warned me she was thinking of a trip there.

"He does, yes," I said slowly, not wanting to mention that he'd found that the company he used to take care of the house over the last century while he had been traveling had remained on the job during his time of incarceration.

"It's in London, and is worth a fortune now," Mac told the ladies. "Like, millions! We're going to be rich! I can't wait to see what sort of shed he has in his back garden."

I opened my mouth to tell her that it wasn't decided just what Keeley was going to do with his house, but stopped when a voice interrupted my thought.

You're going to insist she comes with us, aren't you?

She's my best friend, I answered, at the same time mouthing polite comments to the tourists as they finally left us. *You know as well as I do that she can't be left on her own. She's too eccentric. Does your expensive house in London have a back garden? Is it big enough to put a shed in it?*

His gaze strayed to the line of now six helots. *Not enough to house her herd, no. But given the worth of the property, it might be better to sell and buy something in the country. Would you like that?*

Yes, I answered swiftly, and wove my way through all the vampires to get to his side, snuggling into him. *I'd like it even if it was a tiny little cottage. One with a shed for Mac and her gang.* I looked down when my phone pinged, heaving a sigh at the message. "Mac, Britt has asked her mother to book her a plane ticket. Evidently her boyfriend dumped her when the Revelation office was closed down. Lucy is sending her husband out to pick her up and take her back home."

Do I want to know who Britt is? Keeley asked.

She's the reason I found you in the first place, but other than that, no. You'll like my friend Lucy, though. She doesn't take crap from anyone.

He laughed in my head, wrapping one arm around me and pulling me up closer, an action that melted everything inside me.

"That's great, not that I expect Britt to have learned anything from the trouble she's caused. But let's talk about more important things. You can't eat meat? Not at all?" Mac plopped down on the edge of Keeley's bed next to Tempest, her face scrunched up as she thought. "Like, not even a piece of really well-cooked steak?"

"No meat whatsoever," I answered, my soul filled with happiness. "From here on out, I'm strictly vegetarian. It's the one downside to being a revenant, but it's definitely worth it."

Keeley smiled, an act that warmed me down to my toes. He'd had so little to smile about in the last hundred years that it brought joy just to see him happy.

You make me happy, he said. *You also infuriate me, worry me, and drive me to near insanity with your idea of what is a reasonable plan of action, but I endeavor to cling to the love as the main emotion.*

"I'm just glad you could find a necromancer who brought you back, not that I entirely understand how that works, but you seem just the same as you were," Tempest said, her gaze running over me.

I straightened up from where I was melting into Keeley. "I'm not sure I understand the whole thing, either, since I was a bit wonky when the woman explained to me that she was empowered to bring me back if I agreed, but I honestly don't care how she did it. I'm grateful that Abbott took pity on me. On us."

Mac studied Keeley for a minute. "You don't look any different now that Jenna fetched your soul for you. How, exactly, does that happen?"

Keeley sighed into my mind.

I giggled.

"I'm not sure," he said finally, glancing at the other vampires in the room. "Perhaps one of them can explain."

"Not me," Merrick said when everyone looked at him. He was making googly eyes at Tempest, who was flashing him suggestive glances in return. Both stopped and turned to Keeley. "The wheres and hows of our origins are lost in the past, including the redemption by Beloveds. I assumed since you were a Thrall, you would know, but evidently not. Christian will no doubt question Paris to determine what he knows, since our history is a particular interest of his."

"Will you destroy Paris? He may have overseen the laboratory responsible for making the Thrall drugs, but there could well be others who have the formula. There could be other labs. Other chemists. What will happen to them?" Keeley asked Merrick.

"He's been taken into custody," he answered, the hard lines of his face giving me a little shiver. "Since he is a Dark One, he will answer for his crimes before the Moravian Council. They will either imprison him or banish him to the Akasha."

"That's a kind of limbo place," Tempest told me. "It's very bad juju. You don't ever want to be sent there."

"Then I hope they toss Paris's ass there pronto," I said, my mind returning to just how close Keeley had come to destruction.

"Merrick and the boys have been doing wonders capturing the members of the Revelation," Tempest said, giving her husband another look that had him squaring his shoulders, and giving her a speculative look in return.

To each his own, I said, but I can't for the life of me see what a nice person like Tempest sees in him. He's so … unmoving. Like granite.

She is his Beloved, he answered.

And that means she doesn't have a choice in the matter? I frowned a little, not liking that. I was very much all for autonomy.

No, it means they were meant for each other, but sometimes, or so my grandmother once said, fate gets its lines crossed. That's not the case with them, I suspect.

They do look almost, but not quite, as much in love as we are, I agreed.

"We will naturally speak to the Council about you," Han told Keeley. He'd been busy on his phone, but now tucked it away, his gaze not unfriendly, but not exactly warm. "Although I don't know how we are going to explain what you are."

Keeley said slowly, "I was born a Dark One. I thought I would never return to that once the madmen turned me into a Thrall. But the antidote that Jenna gave me instead of using it on herself, as she should have done"—he turned a look on me that warned we'd be having a discussion about that point in the very near future—"did not return me to being simply a Dark One."

"But you're not a Thrall anymore, either," I pointed out quickly.

"No," he agreed, still introspective. "I do not feel the bloodlust within me. I am neither fully a Dark One, nor fully a Thrall. I am …" He stopped, obviously unable to find a description that fit.

"Unique," I told him. "Wholly and completely unique. And this Moravian group better not think they're going to put you in prison, because if they do, they're going to have a very pissed-off zombie to deal with."

"Revenant," Mac and Tempest said at the same time.

"No, we can tell that the Old One—er—Keeley is no longer a Thrall," Andreas said, but I noted he didn't look very happy about that fact. I gave him a steely look that he completely missed. "He appears to us to be changed as well, although I agree that he is not a Dark One. Not completely."

Is this a bad thing? I asked, suddenly worried.

In what way would not being a Thrall be considered bad?

I gave a mental shrug, since it was my turn to have problems finding words. *These guys seem to be experts, and if they don't know what you are, too, it just makes me wonder.*

"Do you still need to feed from Jenna?" Mac asked Keeley, eyeing him in a familiar thoughtful manner.

"Yes," he answered.

"That sounds pretty vamp-like to me," she told the others.

They all looked at him.

"He does have a Beloved," Han admitted.

"But if he was to bite someone, would that make them a vamp, too, or a Thrall Baby? In other words, does bitey time with anyone but Jenna—since that nice necromancer woman said that revenants can't be helots—end up with Keeley exploding into a billion oozing, bloody pieces, or is it simply immortal time for the bitee?"

"First of all," I answered before Keeley could, turning to face Mac full on just so she could see the expression on my face, "he would not have exploded into a million oozing pieces."

Thank you, he said with great dignity.

"He would have turned into a deranged, unstoppable people-chomping monster," I finished, my hands on my hips. "Get your Thrall lore right. And second, you can stop angling for him to make you MacKenzie, Mistress of the Night, because he is not biting you and turning you into a she-vamp."

"Moravian," all five men said in unison.

Tempest snickered.

"Because only I get to be his bite-babe," I finished, shaking a finger at her. "Besides, you have a half dozen Thrall Babies. That should be enough for anyone."

The six helots, who had all been told to be quiet, looked adoringly at Mac.

"I have no intention of ever attempting to make another helot, but given that the bloodlust was an integral part of that, and the antidote appears to have eliminated that, then I gather that I would not be able to enthrall anyone even if I so desired. Which I do not," Keeley said, putting a lot of emphasis on the last few words.

"What is to be done with him, then?" Ciaran asked, looking at the others.

Keeley stiffened. "I will not be imprisoned again," he snapped, menace all but rolling off him.

"*Pax*," Merrick said, lifting a hand, a near smile on his face. "We have agreed that you are no longer a Thrall. I do not believe you pose any danger to Dark Ones. The opposite, I would say, is true, since you have been on the inside of the Revelation. We would welcome your aid in locating those who run it."

Oooh. Would we join their Horsemen club? Do we get to go around the world finding baddies and capturing them?

Is that something you would like? he asked, his eyes speculative.

Yes, I answered immediately. *So long as I was with you, yes.*

I admit that I would like to ensure no one else suffers for what the madmen have done, and what they may plan to do in the future. Although I would not like for you to be in any danger. After losing you twice, I am not going to risk you getting away from me again, he said.

Silly Victorian protective vampire, I answered, giving his ear a little nibble.

Instantly, heat swept through him, followed by a hunger that had nothing to do with sustenance, and everything to do with desire.

Keeley! I said, mildly scandalized. *You just ate! And we just had nooky time. You can't want to do it again!*

The others were speaking, suggesting that Keeley and I meet with the vampire council, which resided in Vienna, but we were too busy filling each other's heads with erotic images to do much but nod and make vague noises of agreement.

"I think it's time we leave," Tempest said, laughter rich in her voice as she gave my arm a squeeze. "I suspect Keeley and Jenna need time to reacquaint themselves after her resurrection. It's been a pleasure to meet you all. I have only met one other Beloved, so it's nice to have another in my circle of friends."

The vampires trooped out after giving Keeley information on how to contact them should he run into any more of the MIBs.

"I think we'll go check the baddie HQ one last time," Mac announced, herding her gang out the door.

"You said you did that twice while Keeley was tracking down the necromancer," I said, stopping at the door, and wishing like anything that she'd leave so I could pounce on Keeley as he deserved.

"Three times, actually. We did another sweep while you and Keeley were … er …"

"I was feeding him," I said, ignoring the lascivious thought he popped into my mind. He disappeared into the bathroom while I resisted the urge to shove Mac through the door and slam the door on her.

"Regardless, I want to make sure that there are no more stray MIBs lurking about. My gang says there were a couple we can't account for, and I don't want them getting away and spreading news about what happened." She saluted me. "Let me know when we're flying to London to move into Keeley's digs. I'll have to make sure my guys have their passports in order."

I closed the door, an almost overwhelming urge to laugh sweeping over me. I turned to face the room, but it was empty. Listening carefully, however, I could hear the sound of water running.

"Are you taking a shower … oooh!" I entered the bathroom and paused, admiring the sight of a naked, wet Keeley lounging in the tub, steam gently rising from the water. "Bath for two?"

"It's been on my mind ever since you bathed earlier," he commented, and held out a hand for me.

I shucked my clothes in record time, and before you could say "wet, hot vampire," I was sitting astride his knees, his hands full of my needy breasts. "You don't really mind taking Mac with us, do you? Oh, lord, yes! Your stubble is so … mmrowr!"

I don't mind, although if you insist on her staying with us, we will definitely get a house in the country. One with a separate building for her and her minions. Do you like this?

My eyes crossed when one of his fingers curled into me. It took me a few minutes to be able to get my mind working again. "Yes," I panted, enjoying the sensation for a moment before sliding backward enough to take his very aroused penis in my hand. "But two can play at the tormenting game, buster. What do you think of me being a Weaver?"

One glossy black eyebrow rose. "You wish to rejoin your guild? I assumed when you said the head of the order removed you from it, that you would be done with them."

"I was, but you have to admit, it would be very handy when it came to tracking down those Revelation dudes."

He froze, his gaze searching mine.

"Within the rules of the guild, of course," I said, leaning forward to kiss his delectable lips. "I've been reborn, Keeley. I'm not the same headstrong, act-before-thinking person I was before. Jenna version 2.0 is going to stick to the rules."

"I heard that," he said, his head lolling back against the edge of the tub when I stroked his long, silky length.

Heard what, my love? I asked, finding a rhythm that had him moaning in my head.

"Most of the time," he said on a gasp, then sat upright, and pulled me over him, thrusting upward even as I dug my fingers into his shoulders. "You ended that sentence with a 'most of the time.' Jenna, I will not have you endangering yourself on my behalf."

"Dammit. I'm going to have to practice my silent thinking," I said, laughing at the mental lecture he was queuing up.

His teeth pierced the so very sensitive flesh right behind my ear. I gave myself up to the pleasure of him both filling me with life even as he took it, my heart and soul and mind overwhelmed with joy.

"Don't worry," I told him eons later, when we were snuggled into bed just as the sun started to rise. "The present has everything I could ever want. There's no reason for me to blip into the past again."

Against me, his body relaxed. I smiled into his collarbone and added in a whisper, *Now, the future is another matter. I think it would be kind of fun to blip forward and see how things turn out …*

A NOTE FROM KATIE

My lovely one! I hope you enjoyed reading this book, which I handcrafted from the finest artisanal words just for you. If you are one of the folks who likes to review books, I'd love it if you posted a review for it on your favorite book spot. If you aren't a reviewing type, fear not, I will cherish you regardless.

I'd also like to encourage you to sign up for the exclusive readers' group newsletter wherein I share behind-the-scenes info about my books (and dogs, and love of dishy guys, and pretty much anything else that I think people would enjoy), sneak peeks of upcoming books, news of readers'-group-only contests, etc. You can join the fun by clicking on the SUBSCRIBE TO KATIE'S NEWSLETTER link on my website at

www.katiemacalister.com

ABOUT THE AUTHOR

For as long as she can remember, Katie MacAlister has loved reading. Growing up in a family where a weekly visit to the library was a given, Katie spent much of her time with her nose buried in a book.

Two years after she started writing novels, Katie sold her first romance, *Noble Intentions*. More than sixty books later, her novels have been translated into numerous languages, been recorded as audiobooks, received several awards, and have been regulars on the *New York Times*, *USA Today*, and *Publishers Weekly* bestseller lists. Katie lives in the Pacific Northwest with two dogs, and can often be found lurking around online.

You are welcome to join Katie's official discussion group on Facebook, as well as connect with her via Twitter, Goodreads, and Instagram. For more information, visit her website at www.katiemacalister.com

www.ingramcontent.com/pod-product-compliance
Lightning Source LLC
Chambersburg PA
CBHW021620030826
48979CB00034B/493

9781952737961